DONE GONE

Also by Marcia Talley

The Hannah Ives mysteries

SING IT TO HER BONES
UNBREATHED MEMORIES
OCCASION OF REVENGE
IN DEATH'S SHADOW
THIS ENEMY TOWN
THROUGH THE DARKNESS
DEAD MAN DANCING *
WITHOUT A GRAVE *
ALL THINGS UNDYING *
A QUIET DEATH *
THE LAST REFUGE *
DARK PASSAGE *
TOMORROW'S VENGEANCE *
DAUGHTER OF ASHES *
FOOTPRINTS TO MURDER *
MILE HIGH MURDER *
TANGLED ROOTS *

* available from Severn House

DONE GONE

Marcia Talley

SEVERN
HOUSE

First world edition published in Great Britain and the USA in 2021
by Severn House, an imprint of Canongate Books Ltd,
14 High Street, Edinburgh EH1 1TE.

Trade paperback edition first published in Great Britain and the USA in 2021
by Severn House, an imprint of Canongate Books Ltd.

severnhouse.com

British Library Cataloguing-in-Publication Data
A CIP catalogue record for this title is available from the British Library.

ISBN-13: 978-0-7278-9022-1 (cased)
ISBN-13: 978-1-78029-764-4 (trade paper)
ISBN-13: 978-1-4483-0502-5 (e-book)

All Severn House titles are printed on acid-free paper.

Typeset by Palimpsest Book Production Ltd.,
Falkirk, Stirlingshire, Scotland.
Printed and bound in Great Britain by
TJ Books Limited, Padstow, Cornwall.

For my husband, John Barry Talley – then, now and always.

ACKNOWLEDGMENTS

When I began writing this novel in the late summer of 2019, neither Hurricane Dorian nor the Covid-19 pandemic appeared anywhere on my bingo card. Thanks to all who helped me overcome these challenges, especially:

My husband, Barry Talley, who said to me one day, 'What if Hannah's neighbors disappeared? Poof! Just like that?'

The law firm of Tisi and Geyer, who guided me through the maze of federal law and jurisdiction.

Longtime friend, Ron Belanger, whose expertise on data encryption helped inform the plot.

Cocoa Village Marina in Cocoa, Florida, for a table tucked away in a quiet corner of the sailors' lounge where the first half of this novel was written.

Mr Pegman from Google Street View, who, unencumbered by 'stay-at-home' orders, was able to do a lot of the legwork for me.

My accountability partner, friend and colleague, Sujata Massey, who helped push me over the finish line.

Christine J. Thomas, winner of a character auction benefitting the Lyme Elementary School in Lyme, New Hampshire, where my grandchildren go to school. I hope Helen Lawrence and Irene Fogarty enjoy the roles they get to play in this book, and Dartmouth doesn't mind that, for plot purposes, I've transferred you temporarily to Cornell.

My Annapolis Writers' Group – Shaun Blevins, Mary Ellen Hughes, Becky Hutchison, Debbi Mack, Sherriel Mattingly and Cathy Wiley – who provided critical feedback during the pandemic via Zoom and Track Changes.

And, as always, to Vicky Bijur.

How do you know what your life will be like tomorrow? Your life is like the morning fog – it's here a little while, then it's gone.

James 4:14 (NLT)

ONE

Even before I felt his warm breath soft against my neck, I knew he'd been watching, his dark eyes focused on my back as I hovered over the baking pan. Now one arm snaked around my waist while the other made an end run for a meatball, but I was too quick for him. I rapped his hand with the wooden spoon I was using to stir an egg into a mixture of ricotta cheese and shredded mozzarella. 'Don't you dare!'

Paul withdrew his hand, winced unconvincingly and began to lick cheese off his knuckles. 'It's irresistible,' he said.

'There are only so many meatballs to go around,' I pointed out, waving the spoon for emphasis. 'Eight people, twenty-four meatballs. You do the math, professor.'

'*You're* irresistible,' he said, pulling me closer in a one-armed hug.

'I know, I know. Dab a bit of garlic behind my ears and you'll follow me anywhere.'

He laughed, then brushed my cheek with his lips. 'How can I help you, Hannah?'

'You can set the table. Use the red-and-white checked tablecloth and white napkins.'

'Like a bistro?'

'No, silly. Like a trattoria. Next month is French. This month we're eating Italian.'

'Right.' He tossed the word over his shoulder as he crossed the kitchen to the silverware drawer. 'The lasagna should have been a clue.'

'Italian night I can deal with,' I said as I spread tomato sauce evenly over the bottom of the pan. 'Bobbie's spanakopita last month was brilliant, of course, but if I ever volunteer to make dolmathakia again you'll know that aliens have landed and taken over my body.'

'Who knew stuffing grape leaves could be so labor-intensive?'

'Ugh,' I said. 'If there's ever a next time, I'll buy them in a can from Trader Joe's.'

Paul held an assortment of silverware with both hands, like a bridal bouquet. 'So, who's bringing what?'

'Bobbie and Ed volunteered to make an antipasto platter, Ruth and Hutch are in charge of salad and focaccia, and Trish is whipping up tiramisu for dessert.' I glanced up from layering lasagna sheets in neat rows over the sauce. 'Trish came over last night to pick up some Ghirardelli cocoa powder I promised to lend her.'

'Hershey's wouldn't do on Italian night, I suppose.'

'Trish aims for authenticity,' I said with a grin.

'How are they doing, anyway? You'd think living just across the street we'd see more of the Youngs, but I haven't laid eyes on either one of them since last month at Ed and Bobbie's.'

I shrugged. 'I see Trish a couple of times a week, but Peter's been busy at the store, I guess. Speaking of which, when are we going to replace this stove?'

'With a fancy-dancy one from Executive Appliance?'

'That's exactly what I mean,' I said as I twisted the dial on my elderly Hotpoint electric to 350 degrees. 'This stove came with the house, so who knows how old it is.'

'It works, doesn't it?'

'Of course, it works, Paul, but I'm lusting after one of those luxury gas ranges Peter carries in his shop. A Viking maybe, or a Wolf.'

'I like our stove, Hannah. It's so old, it's retro. You pay extra for that.'

Both hands were busy assembling lasagna or I would have tossed a dish towel at his head. 'Go away,' I said. 'Get busy on the table.'

'How about wine?' he called back from the dining room. 'Valpolicella with the lasagna, I presume?'

'That will do nicely. Prosecco with the appetizer, of course, and we'll pair the tiramisu with a nice Asti Spumante. I've got them chilling in the basement fridge.'

'I'm on it,' he said.

You could set a watch by my sister. The mantle clock had chimed only four of the required six when Ruth swished through the front door, calling out a cheerful, 'Yoo-hoo! Where do you want the salad?' Unsurprisingly, she was dressed like a well-to-do Central American peasant in a vibrant, ankle-length, woven skirt and a gauzy blouse, cinched in at the waist with a wide, tooled, leather belt.

'Where's Hutch?' I asked.

'Parking the car,' she explained as I relieved her of the salad.

Hutch, predictably attired in a polo shirt and khakis, followed almost immediately in his wife's considerable wake, carrying the foccacia in one hand and a chainsaw in the other.

'Whoa!' I said, taking a step back from the chainsaw. 'Expecting trouble? Or is that for slicing the bread?'

With a chuckle, Hutch handed over the bread. 'I'm lending it to Peter. Says he's got a poplar in the backyard that needs to go.'

Hutch propped the chainsaw up in a corner behind the coat tree, then turned to greet me with a hug.

'How's the lawyerly biz?' I asked, keeping one cautious eye on the chainsaw and the other on my recently refinished oak floors.

'Taxes, elder care planning strategies, a hotly contested divorce or two . . . it can get depressing.'

'Have some Prosecco,' I suggested. 'Things will start to look up.'

'I doubt it,' he said. 'My clients are fighting over custody of the damn Pomeranian.'

'Have a Scotch, then,' I said. 'Paul's in the kitchen.'

Seconds after I handed my brother-in-law off to Paul, the doorbell rang. I opened it to admit Ed and Bobbie Collins, old friends in both senses of the word. Ed had served in the Navy with my father; their duty stations often overlapped. And when retirement finally caught up with them, both officers had bought homes in the Providence Community on Mill Creek just outside Annapolis.

'How's your dad?' Bobbie asked as I followed her and the antipasto platter into the dining room. 'We miss him at happy hour. His mocktails were legend.'

My father, George Alexander, had embraced his hard-won sobriety by serious experimentation with non-alcoholic cocktail recipes. No Shirley Temples or cranberry spritzers in this captain's repertoire, no sir. Daddy's mocktails utilized exotic ingredients like Seedlip Grove 42, palo santo syrup, açai and chamomile. My favorite, the Mango Mule, would make even a Skid Row wino fall down on his knees and worship him.

'Neelie signed Dad up for a birdwatching trip to Madagascar,' I told Bobbie. 'Three weeks of birdwatching.'

'I didn't know George was interested in birds,' she said as she centered the platter on the dining table.

'He's not, in particular, but Neelie's passionate about her feathered friends. According to a brochure she showed me, there are five avian species unique to Madagascar. She's hoping to add the short-legged ground roller to her life list.'

'Who knew?'

'Well, exactly. They were supposed to take a trip to Cuba this fall, but when Scott died . . .'

Bobbie steered me away from the painful topic of my brother-in-law by laying a gentle hand on my arm. 'How's your sister doing?'

'The last time I talked to her, Georgina was toying with the idea of signing up with an Internet dating website.'

Bobbie frowned. 'Caveat emptor.'

'Georgina doesn't need advice from me,' I said with a grin. 'She's getting it in spades from her kids.'

'They don't approve?'

'You might say that,' I said. 'Dylan says parental controls ought to apply to parents as well as kids.' I shrugged. 'Not much *I* can do about it. Prosecco?'

Bobbie nodded, so I poured a glass of bubbly, shoved it into her hand and shooed her off to join the others in the living room. 'I'll be with you in a minute. Just need to take the lasagna out of the oven.'

While the lasagna sat on the counter to rest, I returned to my guests. Ruth was trying to interest Bobbie in a shipment that had just come into Mother Earth, the New Age shop she owns on Main Street, Annapolis. Bobbie listened politely, of course, nodding and sipping her Prosecco, but I knew that as my father had done not long after the death of my mother, she and Ed were downsizing from their waterfront home. Twig and mudcloth wall hangings from Guatemala, no matter how fair trade and fabulous, were going to be a hard sell.

Clutching a freshly opened bottle of Prosecco, Paul huddled in a corner by the fireplace with Ed and Hutch speaking together in fluent stock market. Ed had just bought IBM and it ran up three sticks, I gathered, while Hutch admitted to staring at the squiggly lines all day while something else was crunching through the price level. It made my head hurt.

'Where are Peter and Trish?' Ruth wondered aloud.

I glanced at the clock on the mantel. Fifteen minutes after six.

'They're running late, I guess.'

'Are you sure they got the day right?' Bobbie said.

'We've been meeting the first Thursday of every month for gourmet night for two years. How can they not get the day right?' Ruth said.

'Besides,' I added, 'Trish popped over last night to discuss dessert.'

'It's not like her to be late,' Bobbie said.

Silently, I agreed. I didn't want to admit that I was worried. I hovered nervously between the two groups, interjecting a comment from time to time but never stopped wondering what was keeping the normally punctual Youngs.

At twenty minutes after the hour, while Ruth nattered on about the virtues of woven yoga mats, I retreated to the dining room and made the call. After four rings, Trish's cell went straight to voicemail. 'Italian night!' I chirped after her cheerful message and the beep instructed me to go ahead. 'Don't tell me you've forgotten.'

With a 'see ya soon' and a sigh, I pocketed the phone. The Youngs hardly ever picked up on their landline, but I tried it, too. No dice.

'Hey, how long do we wait?' Ed appeared at my elbow, eyes straying hungrily to the antipasto platter. 'I put that platter together myself, my love. Bought everything from the Italian Market on Defense Highway, of course, but the arrangement is pure Collins.'

'It's a masterpiece,' I said, admiring the thinly sliced sopressata, salami and prosciutto fanned out on the platter. Ed had framed the platter with artichoke hearts and red peppers, dotted it with cubed pecorino, pepperoncini and peppadew peppers, and strewn mixed olives and miniature mozzarella balls on top.

'I'd been holding back, but . . .' Ed leaned over the table, stabbed a slice of prosciutto with a toothpick and raised it in the direction of the house across the street before popping it into his mouth. 'You snooze, you lose, Peter.'

'While you were setting up, I nipped across the street and knocked,' Paul informed us breathily from the archway. 'Definitely not home. How long do you want to give them?'

'Another ten minutes?' I suggested. 'The lasagna will be just fine, and it's not like the antipasto's getting cold.'

Paul nodded and turned on his heel. 'OK. More bubbly, anyone?' He made the rounds, topping off glasses, while more minutes ticked by.

I took a seat on the sofa between Bobbie and Ruth and feigned interest in beaded African spirit ornaments. When that discussion petered out, Ruth drained her glass and set it down on an end table. 'Well,' she said, checking her watch, 'I don't know what's keeping them, but I'd vote for getting this show on the road. I'm starving.'

I frowned. 'She didn't call. She didn't text. That's not like her.'

Paul extended a hand and helped me to my feet. 'I'm sure there's a reasonable explanation, Hannah.'

'Some emergency,' Ruth suggested. 'Trish will explain it all in the morning.'

'What do we do about dessert?' I said, feeling guilty about worrying over a stupid pan of tiramisu when our friends might be in trouble.

Bobbie stood and smoothed the hem of her gaily printed tunic over her navy blue slacks. 'I don't know about you, ladies, but I can certainly skip dessert!'

'Last time I looked,' Paul said, 'there was some rum raisin ice cream in the freezer.'

'Not very Italian,' I grumbled.

'Theme, schmeme,' my husband said as he escorted me to the dining table.

'Should I clear their places away?' Ruth wanted to know.

'No!' I snapped. 'They could show up at any minute.'

Ruth raised her hands in self-defense. 'Don't bite my head off.'

'Sorry,' I said, taking my seat.

And so dinner proceeded glumly with two empty chairs, reminding us of absent friends.

In the end, everybody got an extra meatball, not that I had any appetite for it.

TWO

Paul was making the rounds with a bottle of sweet, slightly chilled *passito*. I took a sip and melted into the upholstery of the Queen Anne chair set into the alcove by the fireplace. 'Thanks, I needed that.'

I turned, reached over to turn on a lamp and glanced through the living-room curtains. 'Paul!'

'Need a refill already?' he teased.

'No, not that, silly! Come here.'

As Paul leaned over my shoulder, I pulled the curtains aside. 'What do you see?'

'Where?'

'Across the street. At the Youngs'.'

'Their lights are on.'

'Exactly.'

'But what I didn't notice before is their car.' I leaned forward and tapped the window glass. 'Look, it's parked in a spot down by the Paca House.'

'Apparently they've come home.'

Earlier, I'd tucked my cell phone into my pocket. I eased it out, tapped 'recents' and redialed. I waited, but when Trish's voicemail kicked in again, I hung up without leaving a message. 'But apparently they're not,' I said.

'Unless . . .'

'Unless something's wrong.' I looked up. 'They could have been murdered in their beds, for all we know.'

'You've been reading too many crime novels, Hannah.'

I set my glass down on the end table and shot up from my chair. 'You all stay here,' I said, addressing my guests, two of whom were oblivious, fully engrossed in Thursday night football. 'Paul, you keep the boys happy while I run across the street to double-check on the Youngs.'

'I'm coming with you,' Bobbie said when I popped into the kitchen to inform the clean-up crew.

'No need,' I told her.

'I insist,' Bobbie said, laying down her dishtowel. 'Ruth can manage without me for a few minutes, can't you, Ruth?'

My sister glanced up from the baking pan she was attacking with a Brillo pad. 'Of course,' she said, 'but what if they don't answer the door?'

'Then I'm planning to go in,' I said, reaching behind the kitchen door to snag a key from the rack my grandson had made for me at Boy Scout camp one summer.

'You have a key?' Bobbie asked.

'Sometimes I look after their cat, Hobie. Trish gave it to me,' I said, dangling the key between my thumb and forefinger by its iconic Natty Boh fob.

A few minutes later, Bobbie and I stood on the Youngs' doorstep, shivering in the cool of the fall evening. I pressed the doorbell and we waited, listening to the chimes reverberate from inside the house. When nobody came to the door after a few minutes, I rang it again.

'Let me try,' Bobbie said, seizing the teardrop-shaped ultramodern door knocker and giving it three resounding whacks against the wood.

Still no response.

I leaned perilously over the stoop's wrought-iron railing and peered into the living-room window. Trish's taste in furniture was relentlessly Scandinavian, her décor monochromatic and uncluttered. A single lamp burned on the credenza behind the sofa. The room was empty.

I turned to Bobbie. Her hair, worn in a stylish bob, shone bright silver in the gas-style lamps that flanked the door. 'Shall we?' I asked.

Bobbie nodded.

I slotted Trish's key into the deadbolt, turned it, then opened the door. 'Trish? Peter?' I called out as I stepped into the entrance hall with Bobbie close behind. 'Anybody home?'

The silence, as they say, was deafening.

'Wait a minute!' Bobbie held up a hand. 'I hear voices.'

'Your ears are better than mine,' I said, straining to hear.

'It's coming from somewhere in the back,' she said, stepping past me and hustling down the hallway with me hard on her heels. At the kitchen door, we both paused, and I heard it, too – men's voices in low conversation. 'There *is* someone in the house,' she whispered.

'Peter?' I called out. 'Is that you? It's Hannah and Bobbie. We were worried when you didn't show up for dinner, so we let ourselves in.'

Taking the lead, I charged into the kitchen and through the butler's pantry, following the voices, heading for the back porch that the Youngs had glassed in, converting it into a sunroom. In stark contrast to the rest of the house, the sunroom was furnished with comfortable, overstuffed furniture, slip-covered in a cheerful, floral chintz.

Looking serious, Chris Hayes stared into the room from a fifty-two-inch, flat-screen television mounted on the wall. The bespectacled journalist, host of *All In*, was discussing the latest in a series of scandals in the nation's capital with a panel of legal and military experts. 'Damn,' I said. I reached for the remote and shut a former US Secretary of Defense off in mid-rant.

From his deeply padded, rainbow-colored cat cave in the corner, Hobie regarded us with disinterest. Then, recognizing me, perhaps realizing that a liver treat might be in his future, he extended one paw, then another, eased nonchalantly into the room and performed an elaborate yoga routine. He was a black-striped, gray-and-white ball of fluff the size of a bowling ball.

'Gorgeous animal,' Bobbie said, squatting to give Hobie an affectionate scratch between the ears. 'What kind of cat is he?'

'A lynx point Siamese,' I explained. 'A cross between a tabby and a Siamese. I'm not sure it's a recognized breed. Believe it or not, Hobie was a rescue.'

'What monster would mistreat a beauty like you?' Bobbie cooed.

Hobie responded by slinking out from under her hand and wandering in the direction of the kitchen.

Back in the kitchen, Bobbie and I glanced around in puzzlement. 'Is Trish usually this untidy?' Bobbie indicated the granite-topped kitchen bar where a knife, smeared with butter, lay across a lonely, cold-looking piece of toast on a plate next to an open jar of cherry jam. A covered saucepan sat on the stove. When I lifted the lid, a skimmed-over glob of cold oatmeal stared up at me unappetizingly. 'Breakfast,' I commented, stating the obvious. 'But there's no sign of them having lunch.'

I opened the refrigerator and peered inside. On an upper shelf, covered with plastic wrap, sat a rectangular pan. 'And here's our dessert. Ready to go.'

'And who leaves milk out on the counter to spoil?' Bobbie added as she handed the carton to me.

'An early morning medical emergency?' I suggested as I tucked the milk away in the door of the fridge.

Bobbie examined a balled-up paper napkin, then set it down next to the salt and pepper shaker where she had found it. 'Maybe, but that doesn't explain why they didn't call.'

'At least Hobie's dish is full,' I said, pointing to his bowl on the floor, overflowing with kibble.

'She wouldn't have left Hobie behind, surely?'

'Not in a million years,' I said.

'I'm going to check upstairs,' Bobbie said. 'If Trish and Peter planned to leave, they must have taken *something* with them.'

'Good idea. Hobie likes a little Fancy Feast mixed with his kibble. I'll just open a can, then check out the basement. Shout out if you find anything, and I'll do the same.'

'Will do.'

Paul and I had passed many a pleasant evening in Peter and Trish's basement, converted by Peter into a 'man cave', a sanctuary that oozed with testosterone and had once been featured in the Sunday edition of the Annapolis *Capital*. The basement was dark, so I flipped a light switch at the head of the stairs and made my way carefully down the customized staircase – Peter had replaced the banisters with antique baseball bats.

In the glare of a neon sign flashing OPEN, I could see that nobody was serving beer from a tap behind the bar made from the flatbed of a 1975 Ford F150 pickup. Nobody slouched on one of the whiskey barrel bar stools with 180-degree swivel. Nobody was playing the *Star Trek* pinball machine where I once scored 125,000 points in a single game. And nobody lay dead under the pool table or bleeding to death from a stab wound on the shuffleboard floor. I checked the bathroom, too, where Peter's pride and joy, a stainless-steel beer keg urinal, always made me smile.

Nothing to see here. Move on, Hannah.

I made my way back to the entrance hall where I stood at the foot of the stairs and called up to Bobbie. 'Anything to report?'

'Nothing in the bathrooms. Two bedrooms to go,' she yelled back, her voice slightly muffled.

While I waited, I pulled my cell phone out of my pocket, pressed redial and listened, feeling exasperated, as on the other end of the line Trish's phone rang once, twice . . .

'Nothing to report from upstairs,' Bobbie said, reappearing suddenly behind me. 'And it doesn't look like they've taken anything with them.'

'Why doesn't she answer her blasted phone, then, damn it?' I complained as I listened to it ring three times, then four.

'Maybe this is why,' Bobbie said. She held up Trish's iPhone, vibrating almost silently in its distinctive black-and-pink striped case. Bobbie turned the screen in my direction. 'Hannah Ives' the display read, and my own face smiled back at me.

'Did you find a phone for Peter?' I asked.

Wagging her head, Bobbie handed Trish's phone to me.

'Let's get out of here, then,' I said, and without thinking twice, pocketed Trish's phone.

THREE

The following morning I was up early. I brewed myself a cup of coffee, doctored it with half and half and a teaspoonful of demerara sugar, pulled out a chair and sat down. From the kitchen tabletop, Trish's cell phone stared back at me. Silent, solid and, without her passcode, about as useful as a brick.

A few minutes later, Paul stumbled into the kitchen wearing nothing but his cotton boxers and rubbing sleep out of his eyes.

'There's coffee,' I told him.

He planted a kiss on top of my head. 'You are a goddess.'

I smiled up at him. 'That's what all my boyfriends say.'

'What are you doing?' he asked as he inserted a K-cup into the Keurig and pushed the button to brew.

'Willing Trish's iPhone to talk to me,' I said. 'It's passcode protected, of course, and needless to say, I don't have her thumb print.' While the coffee machine gurgled and hissed, I said, 'It's so frustrating! I've watched Trish tap in her passcode lots of times, but I wasn't paying much attention, of course. It's six digits, I do remember that.'

Paul sat down across from me and sipped his coffee. 'Six digits. That's six to the sixth power.'

'What's that mean in plain English, professor?'

'With six digits, you can generate over a million possible combinations.'

I groaned.

Paul stared out the kitchen window, as if consulting the Japanese maple. 'If you eliminate zero and don't use any number more than once, the number of combinations drops to 60,840.'

'Swell,' I said, flexing my index finger. 'This little dude is gonna get a workout.'

'Not so fast, sweetheart. Last time I looked, Apple allows the use of zero, so that will up the number of possible combinations to 136,080.'

I laid my head on the table. 'I'm doomed.' After allowing myself a moment of quiet self-pity, I looked up. 'How do I know you aren't taking those numbers right off the top of your head?'

Paul laughed. 'Basic permutation theory. Any first year algebra student could work it out.'

I wagged a finger. 'Don't be a smarty pants.'

'That's my job,' he said with a grin.

'I can't know for sure how Trish has her phone set up,' I said after a moment, 'but if she opted for Apple's "Erase all data on this iPhone after ten failed passcode attempts" the phone will self-destruct and I'll be screwed. I'm two attempts down and eight to go.'

'You know Trish pretty well,' Paul said. 'Any educated guesses?'

'She once told me it was set to her birthday. That's December twenty-third, but I have no idea what year. She's in her early to mid-forties, I think, but looks can be deceiving. I tried one-two-two-three-seven-six and one-two-two-three-seven-seven but they didn't work. I only have eight chances left, so I'm treating each try like a nuclear access code.'

'You told me Trish left everything behind. If that's true, which, knowing women, I find extremely hard to believe, perhaps she left her handbag behind, too? It would have her wallet and drivers' license in it, which should help establish her birth year and maybe her social security number.'

I felt my face flush. 'I didn't notice any handbag, but then I wasn't really looking for it.'

'You still have Trish's house key.'

'I do, but that would be snooping,' I said.

Paul snorted. 'So exactly what do you call what you and Bobbie were doing last night?'

'Performing a welfare check,' I insisted.

'This from a woman who once broke into a doctor's office and rummaged through his medical files?'

'All in a good cause, if you recall,' I said. 'Look, I'm worried, too. If Peter and Trish are still not home, I'll go snoop, but let me finish my coffee.'

'I'm coming with you,' my husband said, unfolding his long legs and rising to his feet.

I smiled. 'I was just about to ask. But we'd better get dressed first.'

Paul tipped an imaginary hat. 'Partners in crime,' he said.

Carrying his coffee, Paul wandered upstairs to shower while I continued to stare at Trish's phone, willing it to cough up its secrets. I was concentrating so hard that when my own cell phone began to chime I started, jarring my coffee mug and slopping coffee all over the tablecloth.

'Hey, Julie.' My eighteen-year-old niece's face materialized on the FaceTime screen. Her glorious hair hung loose, curling around her face like a pre-Raphaelite angel, glowing like the setting sun in the light of the lamp at her right elbow.

I cringed thinking about the image of me that must be filling Julie's screen – a sleep-deprived bedhead still wearing pajamas. 'Sorry about the hair,' I apologized as I finger-combed my curls into desultory submission. 'It's my artfully messy look.'

'Aunt Hannah,' Julie said without preamble, 'you gotta talk some sense into Mom.'

I snorted. 'Since when has your mother ever listened to me?'

'Well, you can at least *try*,' she said. 'This time it's serious.'

I shifted in my chair, getting comfortable, settling in for the long haul.

'Dad's only been dead for three months and Mom's already going out on dates! Three months!'

I had to admit that even in this age of enlightenment, some people might consider three months an unacceptably truncated period of mourning, but I didn't want to take sides against my younger sister. 'Dylan told me about it,' I confessed.

'Well, he's appalled! Did he mention that?'

'The subject might have come up,' I said, thinking back to Dylan's three-minute rant. 'I'll tell you what I told your brother, Julie. Your mother deserves a little happiness. It's been a shitty year.'

In fact, 'shitty' didn't begin to describe Georgina's year. My brother-in-law, Scott Cardinale, had been bludgeoned to death to prevent him from reporting a serious case of embezzlement from the evangelical mega-church where he served as treasurer. Baltimore homicide detectives had tracked the suspect to a resort in Belize, but the government there, perhaps persuaded by the fruits of the crime – a duffle bagful of cash – had so far ignored all requests for extradition.

'But you don't get it, Aunt Hannah. She's meeting these dudes on the Internet.'

'And that upsets you?' I said.

'Darn right. I lost my dad, and I don't want to lose my mother, too.'

'That's not going to happen,' I said reassuringly, although I knew I couldn't guarantee any such thing.

'Women get murdered by maniacs they meet on the Internet all the time,' Julie pointed out.

'You're following the wrong Twitter feeds, Julie,' I shot back. 'I know some perfectly happy marriages that resulted from couples who met online.'

'Well, Dylan told me that the date she had last Saturday lied on his profile.'

'Imagine my surprise,' I said.

'*Really* lied,' she continued. 'Claimed he was an attorney at some big law firm.'

The way she said 'Big Law' I knew the words started with capital letters. 'And he turned out to be . . .?' I asked.

'A bank teller. She recognized him from the drive-through at Wells Fargo on Bay Ridge.'

'Embarrassing,' I said. After a moment, I continued, 'What website is she using?'

'How the hell should I know? She doesn't share that information with me, but Dylan said it was one of the biggies.'

I didn't know enough about online dating sites to comment, so I decided to change the subject. 'I like your wall hanging,' I said. I was referring to the Native American tapestry she'd recently acquired to brighten up the rather spartan room she shared with another AmeriCorp volunteer in the home of a host family on the Pine Ridge Reservation in South Dakota. 'How is the teaching going?'

Julie straightened from a languid slouch and seemed to bounce in her chair. 'It's good, really good. I'm helping the kids get ready for the annual buffalo harvest. It's going to be awesome.'

'Don't tell me they harvest actual buffalo?' I said.

'Just one,' she explained. 'It's part of the Lakota tradition and super spiritual. Everybody turns out to help and gets a share of the meat.'

'Will you be home for Christmas?' I asked.

'I think it's important that we're all there for Mom, particularly *this* Christmas, don't you? Between now and then, though, will you promise to at least *talk* to her? Make sure she's being super careful?'

'Maybe I should tag along on her dates, hang out in the corner, keep an eye on things?'

Her face brightened. 'Would you?'

'I was joking, Julie.'

My niece looked so distressed that I quickly added, 'OK, I promise to discuss it with her, but just like a mule, your mother can be stubborn and hard to turn.'

'Don't I know it! I'm still amazed that she agreed to let me take a gap year.'

'She's proud of you, Julie. She admires and supports your independent spirit. Your father was always a bit more conservative and by-the-book than your mom.'

'She's loosened up a bit since . . .' Tears welled in Julie's green eyes, glistening in the light reflecting from the laptop screen. She swiped at her cheeks with the back of her hand. 'Promise me you'll go up to Baltimore. Take her to lunch or something. Soon?'

'I'll call her today,' I promised.

Ten minutes later, fully dressed, Paul and I hesitated in the Youngs' front hallway. Somewhere from the back of the house Tammy Wynette, sounding miserable, was standing by her man. 'I turned the TV off last night,' I whispered. 'That sounds like country-and-western radio to me.'

I closed the front door behind us and followed the music down the hallway, calling out, 'Trish! Trish! Thank God!'

'Trish isn't here today. Just me,' a familiar voice sang out.

I froze in the kitchen doorway, forcing a smile. 'Glory! So sorry. I thought . . .'

'I don't know where she is, to tell the truth,' Glory said, turning away from the sink and patting her hands dry on her jeans. 'She said she wanted to help me plant bulbs, but I figure she changed her mind, so I just let myself in and got started.'

Glory Jeffers was Trish and Peter's gardener. Actually, 'gardener' didn't do the woman justice. Glory had a masters degree in landscape architecture from the University of Georgia, which had led to a paid internship at the Royal Botanic Gardens at Kew. Glory had come to the Youngs several years back on the recommendation of Historic Annapolis after Peter, while planting a Japanese maple in their back yard, dug up a natural spring and the foundations of an eighteenth-century colonial garden. She'd even lived with them during the early stages of the restoration project, supervising the preliminary archeological dig.

After the original garden had been surveyed, measured and studied, work had proceeded on recreating walls and the semi-circular brick paths that now curved, like parentheses, around a central sundial. The previous summer, Glory had laid out and mulched the kitchen garden, apothecary and flower beds, filling them with contemporaneous plants. The blackeyed Susans and pansies were now past their prime, but yellow winter jasmine, flowering cabbage, and frilly, purple kale lent spots of seasonal color to the garden.

As if reading my mind, Glory said, 'Those tulips, daffs and crocuses will sure be welcome color come spring.'

Using the back of her hand, Glory swiped a tendril of hair off her forehead. It had somehow escaped the confines of the wide, brightly colored headband that held her abundant black curls out of her eyes while she worked. The turquoise jacket and bright yellow tunic she wore popped against the deep bronze of her flawless and seemingly ageless skin. She was somewhere in her mid-forties, I suspected, because she once mentioned she'd watched the wedding of Prince Charles and Lady Diana on a television at school in her native Saint Kitts. She'd been eight years old at the time.

'I have a chainsaw over at the house that Peter wanted to borrow,' Paul said.

'Peter told me about that,' Glory replied. 'Next big blow, that old poplar's gonna crash right down on the house.' She smiled. 'As my nana used to say, "It be standin' on da promises of God."'

As I explained to Trish's twice-a-week gardener about the Youngs being a no-show for dinner the previous evening, her ready smile faded. She switched off the radio and gave us her full attention. 'It's not like Trish to forget something, especially a party!'

'She made dessert for the dinner, too, Glory, so I don't think she forgot.' I crossed to the fridge and opened the door. 'Look, the dessert's still here.'

'Something must have called them away,' Glory said. 'Something important.'

'I tried calling Trish's cell phone,' I said, 'but it just goes to voicemail.'

Paul shot me a glance, but I decided not to mention that I'd taken Trish's iPhone home with me.

Glory's brow furrowed. We watched as she hustled to the butler's pantry, stooped, and opened a cabinet next to the bar sink. When she looked up again, she said, 'I don't like this, Hannah. Her car keys are still here, hanging plumb on the hook where she always keeps 'em.'

'You roomed with the Youngs for a while, didn't you, Glory?' Paul inquired gently. 'You'd notice if anything is missing, wouldn't you? Clothing? Suitcases?'

Glory removed her jacket and draped it over a hook on the back of the pantry door. 'I haven't been upstairs in a while, but no harm in having a look.'

Paul and I trailed upstairs after her. Although I itched to pitch in, we stood politely to one side, observing as she paged through the hangers in the master bedroom closet, opened dresser drawers and examined books stacked on the bedside tables. She shrugged helplessly and shook her head.

At the linen closet in the hallway she paused to peek inside. 'Suitcases still here, too, Hannah. Trish always takes this spinner carryon.' She pointed out a flame red hardside Samsonite.

'How about the bathroom?' I asked.

Glory nodded and led the way to the master bath – a sophisticated, grown-up space decorated in warm neutrals, uncluttered and devoid of the usual bathtub toys and smelly soccer socks. Aromatic candles and a potted orchid decorated the windowsill over an antique claw foot tub that Trish and I had discovered in an antique store in Pennsylvania.

As we observed from the doorway, Glory opened the medicine cabinet, picked up a few of the prescription bottles and read the labels. After a moment, she held one of the bottles out to me, her face grave. 'These are Trish's thyroid pills. She wouldn't go anywhere without them, that's for sure. If she forgets to take a pill, she turns into a crazy lady by dinner time, and that's the truth.'

'Maybe we should call . . .' I began, turning to Paul, when Glory began to wail, reverting to her native Creole as she often did when upset.

'O me monkeys!'

I pushed Paul aside and rushed into the room. 'What . . .?'

Dangling from Glory's hand on a thin chain was a gold locket about the size of a quarter. The letter E was engraved on its face in a swirly, old-fashioned script. 'There's drug stores everywhere, so Trish could always get more pills, but . . .' A tear slid down her cheek. 'The only time she took this locket off was in the shower. Oh, oh, Hannah. She'd never leave it behind.'

'Where did you find it?' I asked.

'Back of the bathroom door. She must have hung it there in the morning when . . .'

'How is the locket special?' Paul asked as he squeezed past me through the doorway.

Glory handed the locket to me. 'Look inside.'

I pressed a tiny latch on the side of the locket and the lid sprang open. Tucked carefully inside, cut down to an oval to fit, was a photograph of a girl around four or five years old, smiling happily into the camera, her hair an unruly tumble of light brown curls. 'They had a daughter?' I asked.

'No, ma'am. They don't talk about it much, but I believe that's her baby sister. If the poor little lamb had lived, I reckon she'd be twenty-five years old about now.'

'My God. I had no idea.' I turned to consult Paul. 'Did Peter ever say . . .?'

Paul shook his head. 'Never.'

'What happened to her, Glory?'

Glory snatched a tissue out of a box on the marble countertop and dabbed at her eyes. After a moment, she said, 'Precious baby didn't have a chance. About a week after that picture was taken, Trish said, a drunk driver did her in. Killed the poor child's babysitter, too.'

Thinking of my own two sisters, as infuriating as they could sometimes be, I said, 'I can't even begin to imagine the grief.' I handed the locket back to Glory, saying, 'Let's put it back where you found it. When Trish comes home, she'll expect to find it there.'

As we went downstairs, headed for the kitchen, Glory said, 'I'm going home about four and don't come back till Tuesday. What are we gonna do about that cat?'

'Hobie?' I said.

'That cat's gonna be the death of me yet. Snaking round my feet. He's dead set on tripping me up.'

Hearing his name, Hobie gazed up lazily from his water dish, licked a paw and used it to dry his chin.

'He's just being affectionate,' I said, rising to Hobie's defense. After a quick, sideways glance at Paul, who read my mind and nodded almost imperceptibly, I said, 'Don't worry. We'll take Hobie home with us. We've been cat-less for a while. It'll be a pleasure.'

'Trish got some new-fangled litter box in the powder room. Best to take that, too.' After a moment's silence, Glory said, 'It's like they've been raptured up. Poof! Snatched straight up to heaven, leaving the rest of us sinners behind.'

I'd heard Peter Young take the Lord's name in vain on too many occasions to believe that God would give the man any priority, rapture-wise, but thought it best not to mention it.

'Yes, indeed,' Glory said with conviction. 'They simply done gone.'

FOUR

'**W**hat about you getting paid?' Paul asked Glory.

We lingered at the Youngs' – a disconsolate trio clustered around the kitchen island while Glory gathered up the 1850s' seed catalogs she'd strewn over Trish's ceramic cooktop and I worried about whether my friend would ever use the cooktop again.

Glory flapped a hand. 'Don't worry about that, Mister Ives. Peter always pays the first of the month, so I can make my rent, you know. They'll be home before next month rolls round, if the good Lord has anything to say about it.'

'I pray you're right,' I said, thinking that if anybody had a hotline to God, it would be Miss Glory. On Sundays, dressed head to toe in white, she sang in the Voices of Praise Choir at Open Door

Evangelical Church off Riva Road. I turned to Paul as another thought occurred to me. 'One of us should check with Executive Appliance to see if they know anything about Peter.'

'I'll stop by on my way into the academy,' he said. Friday was Paul's busy day at the Naval Academy, teaching back-to-back classes – Calculus, Differential Equations and Matrix Theory. It made my head throb just thinking about it.

'I'll come with you,' I said.

While Glory bustled about, I inched my way over to the alcove where Trish's laptop sat on a built-in desktop, surrounded by cookbooks and a jumble of file folders. Bits of paper – business cards, store coupons, recipes clipped from magazines or printed out from the *New York Times* – were pinned to a corkboard that hung over it.

Trish's laptop was closed. Password protected, I knew, like the cell phone, and dead to me.

'Do you think she'd mind if I looked through her papers?' I asked the gardener. 'I won't take anything, I promise.'

'I'm sure she won't mind,' Glory said with a sad smile. 'I'm worried about them, too.'

'Here,' I said, gathering the file folders into a pile and passing them to Paul. 'See what you can find in there.'

Meanwhile, I pawed through the top drawer.

I hit the jackpot almost immediately. Sandwiched between an outdated telephone directory and a recent catalog from Lands' End, I found an address book, the old-fashioned kind with a marbled cardboard cover and tabbed pages labeled A-Z. I riffled through the pages, noting that Trish had written little in the alphabetical section, rather using the pages as a notebook to record room dimensions, replacement part numbers for household appliances, and – in one instance – a poem she'd heard Garrison Keillor read on *Writers' Almanac*. But in the back, under NOTES, I discovered what I hoped was the Rosetta Stone – a list of Trish's passwords, all the way from Amazon to Zulily. It looked like I wouldn't have to sneak a peek at her Maryland driver's license after all.

I must have let out a small cry of success because Paul glanced up from the folder he was holding and said, 'You found something?'

'I hope so,' I said, pressing the book possessively to my chest. 'It's an address book.'

Glory, who had been paying close attention while I rummaged through her employer's private papers, said, 'You take that book home with you, Hannah. You call everybody in it.'

'Thank you,' I said, not correcting her erroneous assumption. I wouldn't be using the book to telephone Trish's relatives and friends. No. If we didn't get any reassuring news at Executive Appliance about the whereabouts of the Youngs, I'd be using the book to hack into her iPhone.

Neither Paul nor I was feeling energetic enough to walk the two-and-a-half miles from our Prince George Street home to Executive Appliance on Virginia Avenue, so we drove. The upscale appliance center was situated in an industrial park near the intersection of West Street and Chinquapin Round Road, strategically sandwiched between an interior design shop and a company that specialized in stone, granite and marble, with huge slabs of merchandise racked up like dominoes on their sprawling warehouse floor.

When we entered Peter's store, a distant bell dinged, but no one immediately appeared, so we headed straight for Peter's office at the back.

'Well, hello!' The store manager, Helen Lawrence, was chugging our way. By sheer coincidence, our paths converged at the five-burner Viking gas range – in San Marzano red – that I had been drooling over for the past several years.

Helen laid a beautifully manicured hand on the range – *my* range – and said, 'Hannah, Paul! So good to see you. Can we match you up with this beauty today?'

'Oh, Helen, I wish, but it's this guy you need to charm,' I said, giving my husband a playful punch on the arm.

'We've just popped in to see Peter,' my husband explained. 'Is he here?'

Helen's face clouded. 'I was about to ask you the same question. Peter hasn't been in for a couple of days. That's not unusual – he goes to the home and houseware shows in Chicago every year and takes vacations, too, of course, and we manage here just fine without him, but there's nothing marked on the calendar . . .' She paused to draw breath, then rushed on, 'And he usually calls to let us know when something comes up. Frankly, I'm a little worried, and I can see that you are, too, or you wouldn't be here.'

'Peter and Trish were supposed to come over for dinner last night, but they didn't show up,' Paul said. 'Looks like they haven't been home since sometime early yesterday,' he added, without explaining how we knew that.

'A family emergency?' Helen suggested.

'Must be,' I said, trying to sound hopeful.

'Another thing,' Paul said. 'I've been calling Peter's cell phone and it doesn't even give me the opportunity to leave a message.'

'Oh, that old thing!' Helen dismissed her boss's cell phone with an impatient wave of her hand. 'Peter doesn't own a smart phone. He's got a clam shell so ancient that the numbers are worn off the keypads. It's probably not even charged up. I always call Trish if I really need to reach him.'

'Thanks, Helen,' I said, thinking a lot of good calling Trish was going to do us. 'You'll let us know when Peter comes in, right?' I said instead. I rummaged in my handbag for a pen and wrote my cell phone number down for her on the back of a receipt from Safeway.

'I sure will,' she said. 'And try not to worry *too* much. As I said, it's not unusual for him to be gone for a day or two. He probably just had a senior moment, like we all do, right? Slipped his mind?'

I dredged up a smile. 'I'm sure you're right, Helen.'

'In the meantime,' she said brightly, 'I'd love to show you a range that's just come in. If you like the Viking,' Helen enthused, drawing us into the next aisle over, 'you will adore the Lacanche! *Si classique!*'

She was right. I did adore the Lacanche, a sophisticated classic in French blue and brass *avec quatre feux*, but at almost seven thousand dollars, it was way over budget, even if it had been designed by Burgundian artisans.

'Do you have a brochure?' Paul asked, with a sly, sideways wink at me.

'I can't remember the last time I saw a brochure for anything,' Helen said. 'Just go to their website. It's all there.'

'Think of all the paper we're saving,' I said with a smile.

'I'm calling Dennis,' I told Paul once we'd bid farewell to the store manager and returned to the privacy of our car. 'I don't care what Helen says. There is nothing remotely normal about Peter not letting his staff know he'll be away.'

As Paul eased our elderly Volvo – over 200,000 miles on the odometer and still ticking – up West Street toward Church Circle, I powered up my phone and instructed Siri to 'Call Dennis Rutherford'.

My brother-in-law was married to Paul's sister, Connie. Since retiring from the Chesapeake County Police Department, he tended to stick close to their south county farm, helping Connie manage a small herd of Dexter cows.

Connie answered the phone. While I waited for Dennis to come in from the barn where he was supervising the milk bottling, Connie and I chatted about the juried art show for which she was designing a series of gourd sculptures based on the Seven Deadly Sins. I was stuck on trying to envision my sister-in-law's concept of 'Lust' constructed out of crown of thorns, banana and bottle gourds when Dennis returned and Connie relinquished the phone.

'Dennis,' I said, cutting straight to the chase, 'how long does someone have to be missing before the police will start looking for them?'

'Depends,' Dennis said. 'If it's a kid or a vulnerable adult, a BOLO goes out almost right away.'

'I know about Amber and Silver alerts,' I said, 'but these are two adults. My across-the-street neighbors, in fact.' I explained about having been stood up for dinner and about Peter being AWOL from his store, and even confessed to snooping about the Youngs' home. 'It's like they've been beamed up by aliens,' I said. 'And if they took anything with them, I didn't notice and neither did Glory, their gardener.'

'You were in their house?' he asked.

'I sometimes feed the cat. Trish gave me a key.'

'Any sign of a disturbance?'

'No.'

'Blood?'

'No.'

'Early days, then,' my brother-in-law soothed.

'I have a really bad feeling about this, Dennis,' I said, refusing to be soothed. 'The Youngs have been our neighbors for almost ten years. This. Is. Definitely. Not. Normal.'

'We've heard it all before,' Dennis said. By 'we' I assumed he meant the cops. '"It's so unlike her",' he quoted. '"He was the nicest, kindest man!" Then we find out he's living off the proceeds of embezzled trust funds with a new wife, two adorable kids and a pit bull named Peaches in Albuquerque.'

'They're *both* missing,' I reminded him. 'And they're just ordinary people, not high-priced attorneys or Wall Street hedge fund managers. Trish volunteers twice a week at the hospital thrift shop and Peter owns an appliance store.'

'Ah, I remember them now,' Dennis said. 'Met them at your anniversary party. Peter tried to sell me an under-the-counter wine cooler.'

In spite of the seriousness of our conversation, I had to smile. 'That sounds like Peter.'

'Look, Hannah,' Dennis said, 'nine times out of ten, people who go missing turn up within forty-eight hours.'

'That means one time out of ten they don't.'

I blabbered on stubbornly, telling him about the car keys, the locket, the tiramisu and even the glistening globs of ice-cold oatmeal. I decided not to mention that Trish's cell phone was sitting on the desk in our basement office, stubbornly refusing to cough up its secrets.

'They've been missing since early Thursday morning, you said?'

'Sometime before seven would be my guess because it looks like they were in the middle of breakfast and the lights were still on. The sun rose at six fifty-six on Thursday. I checked.'

'Look, Hannah, if it will make you feel better, go to the police station on Taylor Avenue and file a missing persons report. But more than likely by the time you get back, the Youngs will have returned home with a perfectly reasonable explanation.'

'Can I just pick up a form and fill it out?'

'Sorry. In Anne Arundel County, the report has to be taken in person by a police officer, usually the detective in charge of missing persons.'

'What kind of questions do they ask? Other than the obvious ones, I mean.'

'You can probably find a copy of the form online,' Dennis said. 'It's called a SOMMPR – State of Maryland Missing Persons Report,' he added before I could ask for details. 'And you'll need a photograph, of course. You've got one, I assume?'

'From a trip we took to Longwood Gardens last spring.'

'Good. And Hannah?'

'What?'

'Keep me in the loop.'

'Thanks, Dennis. I appreciate that.'

FIVE

Paul squeezed the Volvo into a barely legal parking spot on the one-way street outside our home, gave me his stock warning about staying out of trouble, followed by a quick peck on the cheek, then left to walk the two short blocks to his office in Chauvenet Hall overlooking the Severn River.

While he was inspiring future naval officers with the joys of applied mathematics, I brewed myself a cup of coffee, tucked Trish's address book under my arm and carried them both down to our basement office.

I pulled my chair up to the computer. My hopes were high. Maybe I couldn't crack the code for Trish's iPhone, but armed with her account IDs and passwords I could check recent online activity for clues to her whereabouts.

Had she ordered any books, like *How to Disappear*? I started with Amazon, but the login failed. Had I made a typo? I typed it again, more carefully this time. Again, it failed.

Had she bought a plane ticket? Made a hotel reservation? This time I tried American Express. My login attempt failed.

Baltimore Gas and Electric. Failed.

Comcast. Failed

Gmail. Failed.

I worked my way doggedly down the list – Kohl's, Macy's, *New York Times* and PayPal – but site after site, login after login, every password failed.

'Damn, damn, damn!' I flopped back in my chair, thoroughly irritated. At some point, Trish had changed all her passwords. Clearly, I was using an outdated list.

But what if I . . .?

Freshly energized, I leaned over my keyboard, revisited the

American Express website, typed in Trish's account ID and clicked
on 'Forgot User ID or Password?' After a few seconds, Trish's cell
phone dinged – American Express was sending her an email with
instructions on how to change her password! I grabbed the phone
in short-lived triumph: without Trish's passcode, I couldn't open
the phone to read the message.

Thoroughly frustrated, I decided to switch gears. After spending
a few minutes online, I found the two-page SOMMPR Dennis
Rutherford had mentioned. I printed out two copies – one for Peter
and one for Trish – and leaned back in my chair to read them.

I was embarrassed to discover how little I knew about our
longtime friends.

The Youngs had moved to Annapolis from Santa Fe, New Mexico,
over a decade ago. Peter had been a tutor at St John's College Santa
Fe, the western campus of the famous 'Great Books' college in
Annapolis. He'd transferred to the Maryland campus for a year as
a kind of consolation prize, I gathered, when his application for
tenure didn't pan out. The next thing we knew, he'd traded in
Socrates, Hippocrates, Euclid, Galileo, Dante, Descartes and the
rest of the good old boys for a down-on-its-heels appliance store.
He'd poured thousands of dollars and hours of sweat equity into
the place, and made it a success. Or had he? What if Peter had
mortgaged the place to the hilt, cashed it in and run off with Trish
to some remote tropical isle?

I shook off the thought. Even crooks pack a change of clothing
before going on the lam, I reasoned, and how many would leave
critical medications behind?

Using a pencil, I began filling in what I knew about Trish and
Peter: name, race, sex, hair and eye color were a no brainer, and I
could make educated guesses about their height and weight. I only
had to look out my front window and a little ways down the street
to provide details about their Honda Acura, but since they'd left the
car behind, the police probably wouldn't find vehicle information
particularly helpful.

Blood type? Tattoos? Scars? Who knew? And when I got to the
question about whether Peter was circumcised, I screamed out loud.

The SOMMPR asked for a list of the Youngs' friends. Other than
Paul and me, and the four other members of our gourmet club, I
was clueless.

Parents? I leaned back in my chair and chewed thoughtfully on the eraser end of my pencil. Peter had once told an amusing one-that-got-away story about fly fishing with his father in Idaho, but even after mulling it over while carrying the papers upstairs to refill my coffee, I couldn't remember Trish ever mentioning her parents. Perhaps they had died.

Maybe Dennis was right. Peter and Trish had been missing only twenty-four hours. Give our friends another twenty-four hours, I thought as I set the forms on top of the microwave. Then I'll hit the panic button.

SIX

It was only one o'clock, but I felt I had lived a lifetime since chatting with Glory that morning. My stomach rumbled, reminding me that I'd forgotten to eat lunch, but the two-day-old mac and cheese I had set aside for myself didn't appeal. I decided to kill two birds with one stone – grab a bowl of pad thai at Noodles and Co. at the Annapolis Mall, then bop across Bestgate Road to visit Out of the Box, the consignment shop where Trish volunteered ten hours a week. Run by the Auxiliary of Anne Arundel Medical Center, the shop carried everything from lightly used clothing, jewelry and accessories to furniture and small appliances. I'd recently scored a Cuisinart toaster there, with slots big enough to handle the frozen waffles Paul liked to heat up for himself in the morning.

When I wandered into the shop an hour later, two smock-clad Blue Crew volunteers were busy assisting other customers, so I killed some time browsing through a merry-go-round rack of blouses. A red KikiSol tunic with white anchors caught my eye, so I slipped it over my arm. Several minutes and a pair of white drawstring trousers later, the last customer left, so I carried my purchases over to the cashier.

'Hi,' I said, as a volunteer whose ID badge read *Molly* removed the consignment tags and began to ring up the sale. 'Is Trish Young working today?'

'Not today,' Molly said. 'Trish is Tuesday and Thursday, right, Jan?'

Jan was bending over, returning some jewelry to a locked case. Without looking up, she said, 'Who's asking?'

'Trish is a good friend,' I explained. 'She and her husband live across the street from me.'

Jan turned a key, straightened and studied me over the tops of her reading glasses. 'Maybe you can tell me why she didn't show up for work yesterday. She helped out on Tuesday as usual, but yesterday she was a no-show.'

'I know,' I agreed. 'She skipped out on a dinner party at our place last night, too.'

Jan and Molly exchanged glances.

'Do you know something I don't know?' I asked.

Jan shrugged. 'Trish is one of our most reliable volunteers. It's very unlike her not to call. One can't help being a little concerned.'

I helped Molly fold my purchases and tuck them into the ecologically responsible string tote I keep in the console of our car for shopping emergencies. 'When she was working on Tuesday, did she seem worried about anything?' I asked. 'Distracted?'

Jan made a thoughtful moue. 'Not that I recall, but we're closing in on the end of our winter consignment period, so we were super busy that day.'

I looked up from signing the credit card receipt and managed a lackluster smile. 'I'm sure there's a perfectly reasonable explanation.'

Jan didn't smile back. 'There almost always is. Although we once had a volunteer call in sick because she was having a bad hair day.'

'But at least she *called*,' Molly added.

That made me chuckle.

I was tucking my VISA card back in my wallet when my cell phone began to chime. 'Sorry!' I told the two women as I rooted in my handbag for the phone. 'I'll just take this outside.'

I pushed through the glass doors, turned right, and leaned against the wall next to a free-standing, gently flapping red, white and blue OPEN flag.

I squinted at the iPhone display, not recognizing the number from a 315 area code. But my RoboKiller app hadn't tagged the call as spam, I wasn't in any particular hurry, so I decided to take the call.

'Hello?'

'Hannah? It's Trish.'

I gasped, stumbled and nearly toppled off the yellow-painted curb. 'Trish! Thank God! What happened? Where the *hell* are you?'

Her words tumbled out. 'Not now, Hannah. But I need to see you.'

'Of course. Anywhere. Anytime.'

She sighed with apparent relief. 'Meet me in the parking lot in front of Trader Joe's. This coming Monday. Around eleven.'

'I'll be there. Trish! Everyone's so worried!'

'I know. I'm sorry. But I gotta go. I'll explain when I see you.'

'Wait!' I said, thinking about the Honda she left behind. 'What will you be driving?'

'Don't worry, I'll find you.'

'Trish—'

'Really, I gotta go. Promise me you'll be there.'

'Trish! What the hell is going on?'

'I just can't do this any more, Hannah.' And the line connecting me with my missing neighbor went dead.

I stared at the screen in stunned silence for several seconds before I came to my senses. God bless Apple! I tapped *Recents*, found the 315 number and hit redial.

On the other end, the phone rang and rang and rang. I was about to abandon the call when someone picked up. 'Hello?'

'Trish?'

'Not Trish, lady. My name's Trevor. Just walking by and the pay phone started ringing, so I answered it, you know, like you do.'

'Where are you, Trevor?' I asked.

'Drivers Village. Where are you?'

'Annapolis,' I said.

'I went to Indianapolis once,' he said, 'when A J Foyt was still driving. Totally awesome.'

I decided not to correct his geography. 'Where's Driver's Village?' I asked.

'Cicero.'

'Illinois?'

'Naw.' He laughed. 'Up near Syracuse. In the old Penn-Can Mall.'

'Can you do me a favor, Trevor? Do you see a middle-aged woman, about five-eleven, thin, shoulder-length dark hair, anywhere around?'

Trevor was silent for a moment, then said, 'Sorry.'

'That's OK. She just called me from this number, so I hoped . . .'

'She a runaway or something?'

'You might say that.'

'Damn. Well, I hope you find her.'

'I do, too, Trevor. I do too.'

I thanked the guy and broke the connection.

I stared at my phone until the screen saver kicked in, feeling helpless. I'd just arranged to meet Trish in the parking lot at Trader Joe's in the Annapolis Mall, but at that very moment, Trish was in Cicero, in the middle of New York state, most likely in the parking lot of a mall I'd never heard of.

I tapped up Google. In early 2000, the bankrupt Penn-Can Mall had been purchased by a local area car dealer and turned into showrooms and service centers for sixteen auto brands. Swell. Even if I could pinpoint Trish's exact location within the automotive sprawl, there'd be no point in going there. My friend was a moving target, presumably leaving Cicero soon for a drive back to Annapolis.

I can't do this any more, she'd said.

Do what?

And where was her husband, Peter?

Today was Friday. It would be a long, long weekend.

SEVEN

I had promised Julie that I'd check in with her mother, but in my growing panic over our missing neighbors, I'd shamelessly put a visit to Baltimore on the back burner.

Now that Trish had checked in, alive if not entirely well, I reordered my priorities. I texted Dennis first, informing him of Trish's call, then let the other members of our gourmet club in on the news. 'No details yet,' I explained, 'and very mysterious. Stay tuned.'

That's why I found myself early Saturday morning – more of a distraction than out of any sense of sisterly duty – sitting across from Georgina at Common Ground on the Avenue in Hampden, a friendly neighborhood Cheers kind of place. A coconut muffin that had been calling my name sat in front of me, half-eaten.

I swallowed a tasty mouthful and asked, 'Will you be playing the organ for Sunday Services at All Hallows tomorrow?'

Georgina nodded. 'My music is what's keeping me sane.'

'Meet any eligible bachelors at church?' I asked, plunging a spoon almost reluctantly into the tulip-shaped design the barista had made in the foam on top of my cappuccino.

'Ha ha, you can't be serious,' Georgina said, waving a forkful of kale and quinoa salad. 'The last guy who tried to sweet talk me after the service looked like Jabba the Hutt stuffed into a business suit.'

'Maybe he's rich?'

'I don't need the money, Hannah. I just need adult companionship.'

That was certainly true. At his untimely death, Scott, a successful CPA, had left his wife and children comfortably provided for.

Fortunately, I didn't have to rat out Georgina's children for spilling the beans about their mother's online dating because a few moments into our meal she brought the subject up herself.

'I've started dating again, Hannah.'

I feigned surprise. 'Don't you think it's a bit too early for that, Georgina?'

She scowled. 'Don't judge.'

While Georgina toyed with her quiche du jour, giving me the silent treatment, I pretended indifference, admiring an exhibit of watercolors by local artists that hung on the popular coffee shop's bare brick walls.

'With the twins out of the house for good, and Julie in South Dakota, it's just me and Colin,' she complained. 'There's only so much scintillating conversation one can have with a ten-year-old.'

Julie was well launched on her gap year, the twins had enrolled in graduate programs at Johns Hopkins University and sometimes came home on weekends, but other than hearing about his enthusiasm for soccer, I had been a less than diligent auntie with Colin. 'What's Colin up to?' I asked. 'Other than soccer.'

'Since you last saw him, he's moved on from Minecraft and is getting hooked on Dungeons and Dragons.' She shivered. 'Ruth tells me the game's harmless, but one hears stories.'

'Unless Colin gets sucked into forty-eight-hour fantasy sessions without eating or sleeping, you probably don't have anything to worry about,' I said. 'Emily was addicted to the game in high school, and look how she turned out.'

'Eventually,' Georgina said cattily.

'All's well that ends well,' I quoted, thinking about the posh spa my once nomadic daughter and her husband now owned on prime Chesapeake Bay waterfront. After Spa Paradiso was featured in *SpaLife Magazine*, business had been booming. My son-in-law, Dante Shemansky, was even exploring franchising.

Georgina laid down her fork, rested her elbows on the table and leaned toward me. 'Anyway, I took the plunge and signed up with Date♥Line.'

'Isn't that a TV news show?' I asked.

'That's *Dateline*, silly, one word. This is date line, two words, with a heart in the middle.'

'Cute,' I said, 'But I've never heard of it.'

'You won't *believe* how many dating apps are out there, Hannah. I considered all the usual suspects, but some of those sites have thirty or forty million members.'

'That many? You're kidding? I'll bet some of the profiles are fake.'

'Yeah, and what do you do if your perfect match lives way out in Seattle?'

I watched my sister stir a straw around in her chai peanut butter banana smoothie, a local favorite that made my taste buds recoil in horror.

'What made you decide on Date♥Line?' I asked.

'It's local, for one thing. You have to live in the DC metro area. Baltimore, Washington, Annapolis, Delaware, too, I suppose. So I don't have far to drive.'

When she didn't elaborate, I asked, 'And for another?'

'When you join, you upload a picture and a ten to fifteen second video clip. When you get a match you can check out the video, like a preview of coming attractions. Or not!' She grinned. 'Anyway, if you like what you see, you can follow up on FaceTime.' She took a long pull on her smoothie, swallowed, then added, 'That would have saved me from wasting time on the guy from You&Me.com who offered me ten thousand dollars to marry him.' She laughed.

'He was cute, too. Norwegian, although why anybody from Norway would want to marry an American for a green card, I have no idea. I decided he must be insane.'

I laughed out loud.

'I've had a couple of other dates.' She raised a cautionary hand. 'And before you say, "I told you so", they were pretty disastrous, too.'

'How so?' I asked.

'Men lie on their profiles for one thing.'

'I'm shocked.'

Georgina sighed. 'Some guys should come with a warning label on their foreheads. I'd been on two dates with this one guy before he confessed to being a practicing nudist.'

'Dodged that bullet,' I said.

'He was serious about it, too,' she said. 'Insisted I join him at a clothing optional resort where he'd help me work through my self-concept problem. I blocked him on Messenger before he could start sending illustrations. Besides,' she added with a sly grin, 'think of all the extra sunscreen I'd have to pack.'

'Are you having better luck with Date♥Line?' I asked.

Georgina shrugged. 'Early days yet.'

'What picture are you using?' I asked, genuinely curious.

Georgina fumbled in her handbag, pulled out her iPhone, tapped the icon for the Date♥Line app and handed the phone across the table.

I recognized the picture. It had been cropped from a family portrait, taken for the member directory of Church of the Falls where, up until September, Scott and his family had attended. Georgina's hair was the color of buttered sweet potatoes, and with her green eyes and fair, Irish skin, she was a knockout.

'I'll bet you got a lot of clicks with that,' I said, laying the phone down on the tabletop.

Georgina flushed. 'Maybe I should have used that picture of me all pudgy and splotchy from when I was pregnant with Colin. Might have narrowed the field down to guys who were more interested in reading my profile than drooling over my picture.'

I remembered that photo, too, but differently. In pregnancy, Georgina had looked especially radiant. 'Wouldn't have worked,' I said. 'Haven't you heard? Body shaming is out. Rubenesque is in.'

'Date♥Line is better than most at sorting the wheat from the chaff,' Georgina said. She tapped the screen again and scooted it toward me. 'This guy and I have been texting for a couple of weeks. His name's Zachary Curtis. Goes by Zack.'

Zack looked pleasant enough. A grey-eyed, ruggedly handsome fellow with abundant salt and pepper hair combed straight back. Mid to late fifties, I guessed. 'What does he do?' I asked.

'You'll laugh,' she said.

'No, I won't!'

'He's an airplane repo man.'

I laughed. 'You're kidding!'

'I knew you'd laugh,' she said. 'But seriously, that's what he does. He's a pilot. When an airline goes bankrupt or a deadbeat tycoon defaults, the bank hires Zack to get the airplane back.'

'Wasn't there a show about that on the Discovery Channel a few years back?'

She nodded. 'Zack says those guys are cowboys. The real job isn't all that glamorous.'

'How do you . . .?' I began, but she interrupted, anticipating my question.

'He's totally legit, Hannah. I had Scott's former partner check him out. There's only a handful of companies that do that kind of work, and he runs one of them, ZCI, out of Martin State Airport in Middle River,' she said, referring to a suburb in Baltimore County, just east of the city.

'So, where are you and Repo Man meeting up?'

'At the Walters Art Museum café. We'll check out the exhibits, then if all goes well, stick around for a concert in the Sculpture Court.'

'Ah, a man of culture and erudition.'

Georgina shrugged. 'At least he wants me to think so. Once burned, twice shy, as they say.'

'I hope you tell someone where you're going,' I cautioned.

'I just told you.'

'That's not what I meant, Georgina.'

'Colin's babysitter knows.'

I made a production of mopping my brow. 'Well, that's a huge relief!'

Georgina leaned across the table and squeezed my hand. 'Don't worry, Hannah. I'll be safe. There'll be hundreds of people around.'

I seized her hand gently and held on. 'It'd be safer not to date people you meet on the Internet at all.'

Georgina pushed her plate away, her kale and quinoa salad barely touched. 'If you were in my shoes, you'd understand.'

EIGHT

Trader Joe's, the South Seas tiki-styled grocery store chain with a cult following, was located in Annapolis Plaza, adjacent to the sprawling Annapolis Mall. Monday morning, I arrived early and parked close to the entrance, not far from the cart return where I was certain Trish could not miss me.

The weatherman had predicted an unseasonably low fifty degrees, so I kept the engine running, the windows rolled up and both the heater and the radio on while I waited, nerves thoroughly frazzled, for my friend.

Eleven o'clock came and went with no sign of Trish.

By eleven fifteen, she still hadn't shown up, but anybody can get stuck in traffic, I reasoned. She'd have to be driving south on I-95, and it always seemed to me that there was no part of that aging interstate – running nearly two thousand miles along the east coast from Miami, Florida to Brunswick, Canada – that wasn't under construction.

At eleven thirty-five, Gustav Holst launched into 'Jupiter, the Bringer of Jollity' on the radio, none of which I was feeling.

At eleven forty-five I decided that I'd been stood up – again! I gathered up my handbag, thinking I might as well not waste the trip. Trader Joe's carried a brand of spicy chicken sausages that Paul adored, and their chocolate lava gnocchi was to die for. A friend had raved about their Everything But the Bagel Sesame Seasoning Blend, so I'd put that on my list, too, along with several bags of ready-to-bake pizza dough.

I was reaching for the ignition key when someone rapped on the passenger side window – a blond wearing oversized sunglasses and a zip-up white hoodie. I mashed on the switch to power down the window, leaned across the seat and said, 'What can I . . .?' before I recognized the woman's face. Trish.

'Trish! Thank God. Get in, get in!' I said, pressing the lever to unlock the car doors.

'Sorry I'm so late,' she said as she slid into the seat next to me. 'There was a fender-bender in the Harbor Tunnel.'

I leaned across the console and embraced her. 'Never mind about that. You're here, that's all that counts.' I held her tight for a few seconds, then pulled away. 'What on earth have you done to your hair?'

'You don't like it.' It was a statement, not a question.

I squinted at my friend's new do. Trish's shoulder-length hair had been gracelessly cropped just short of her ears, and instead of being the dark chestnut I'd known for years, was now a high-voltage blond. 'It's certainly different,' I said, without elaborating on what was clearly a do-it-yourself job.

'My gawd, it's like a greenhouse in here, Hannah!' Trish struggled out of her hoodie and draped it carelessly across her knees.

'Sorry.' I switched off the ignition, killing both the engine and the heater. 'It's cold out, in case you hadn't noticed.' I smiled to let her know I was teasing. 'It would be a lot more comfortable meeting at your house, or even mine. And there'd be hot coffee.'

Trish's gaze was steady and unblinking. 'I won't be going back to Prince George Street again, Hannah. Maybe not ever.'

For a moment, I couldn't speak. 'I don't understand,' I said at last. 'You left all your stuff behind! Don't you need it?'

'It's not safe. That's why I asked you to meet me here where it's more public. Lots of people around.'

'Stop it! You're scaring me.'

'I'm scaring *you*?' She extended a hand, palm down. It trembled like a leaf in the wind. 'Look at me. I'm a basket case.'

'What the hell is going on?'

'Before I explain, I need to give you something.' She fumbled in the pocket of her hoodie and pulled out a bright blue flash drive. She cradled the drive in her hand, staring at it for a long moment, as if absorbing its digital contents using some sort of Jedi mind trick. 'I need you to keep this for me,' she explained, holding it out. 'Someplace safe. And for God's sake, don't tell anybody you have it, not even Paul.'

I had reached out, but jerked my hand away. 'I can't promise . . .'
I began.

The corner of her mouth quirked up. 'Right. I know you tell Paul
everything, so I won't make you promise to keep him in the dark.'
She thrust the drive in my direction. 'Here, take it.'

'Not till you tell me what's on it,' I said, still holding back.

'I can't.'

'Jesus, Mary and Joseph, Trish! Are you selling government
secrets to the Russians or something?'

'Of course not. You know me better than that.'

'I'm beginning to think I don't know you at all,' I snapped. 'What
kind of person simply walks away from a house, a job, her friends
and all her possessions without saying a single word to anybody?
Even a text message would do. We've all been worried sick.'

Her head drooped. 'I know, and I'm sorrier than I can say. What
I'm about to tell you, you can't tell anybody. Promise?'

'Except Paul.'

'Yes, except Paul.'

'Thank you,' she breathed, seeming to melt into the upholstery.
Without looking at me, she said, 'First of all, you need to know
this. My real name is Elizabeth Stefano.'

I felt like I'd been sucker-punched. 'What?'

'It's a long story, which I'll get to in a minute. What's important
now is this flash drive,' she said, thrusting it in my direction.

Elizabeth Stefano. Elizabeth Stefano. Should I have recognized
the name? Was my friend a notorious fugitive? My fingers itched
to find my iPhone and consult Google, but instead, I took the drive
from her, curled my fingers around it and folded it protectively into
my palm.

'Gosh, Trish . . . or should I call you Elizabeth? Lizzie? Liz?'

'Trish will do just fine, Hannah. I haven't been Liz for over
twenty years.'

'I don't know what to say,' I said.

'Just listen, then,' Trish said. 'Two weeks from today, a case is
supposed to be filed in the Southern District Court in New York.'

'And this drive . . .?'

She held up a hand, cutting me off. 'The case will be big news,
and involve the Lynx Media Corporation.'

I was familiar with Lynx, a sprawling American media company headquartered in nearby Alexandria, Virginia, with operations world-wide: Lynx Broadcasting, Lynx News and Lynx Productions. Several years before, I'd been strong-armed by a former Lynx News associate into stepping in as a last-minute substitute for a cast member on *Patriot House: 1774*, a television reality show filmed over the course of three months in Annapolis's historic William Paca House. I still had the costume and the DVDs to prove it.

'Listen to the news,' Trish continued. 'Listen carefully, and if you don't hear anything about the case by the following day, I want you to get that flash drive to the *New York Times*. Pronto. Promise me you'll do that.'

'Why? What's on it?'

'Documents,' she said. 'An insurance policy, of sorts. The Feds have the originals.'

'Why me, though, Trish? Can't you turn it over yourself?'

She shook her head. 'Impossible. I'll explain in a moment.'

'But who do I give it to?' I asked, accepting her explanation at face value, but feeling totally unqualified for the job.

'David Reingold at the *Times*. Remember him? The guy who won a Pulitzer for exposing that worldwide Internet adoption scam?'

I nodded. The story had been national news for months – child trafficking in black market babies.

Trish's flash drive seemed to grow hotter in my hand. 'But, why wouldn't this case, whatever it is, go forward?'

Trish stared thoughtfully out the windshield for a moment. 'If you're rich and powerful and well-connected, you can make inconvenient things disappear.'

'"Things"?' I repeated. 'You're acting like you actually mean "people".'

Trish nodded silently.

'It sounds like you don't trust the federal prosecutors to do their job,' I said.

Trish snorted. 'In this administration with a stooge of an attorney general calling the shots, would *you*?'

'I see your point,' I said, tucking the flash drive securely into my bra. 'But I think you owe me an explanation.'

'It all started when I ran away from home. I was fourteen,' Trish confessed, settling deeper into the passenger seat as she began her tale. 'Some silly fight with my mother about a slumber party she

wouldn't let me go to because she figured there'd be boys there.'
She turned to me and grinned sheepishly. 'There would have been
boys there, of course.'

'Where did you run to?' I asked.

'New York City. Where else?' She shrugged. 'Crashed at a YWCA
on Lower Broadway and got a job bussing tables in a deli.'

'They hired a fourteen-year-old?' I asked, incredulous.

'Totally legit, as long as I wasn't serving booze,' she explained.
'And with some creative paperwork, fashion models can be as young
as thirteen.' Trish swiveled in her seat to face me. 'Can you imagine
how easily you could exploit . . .'

Trish started, her eyes grew wide and a poppy blossomed on her
forehead. As she toppled across the console, I heard a second *pop*,
and the passenger side window dissolved into a spider web.

Instinctively, I ducked. In the eerie quiet that followed, all I could
hear was the blood pulsing in my ears, followed by Trish's raspy
breathing. My friend was slumped against my shoulder, her blood
flowing profusely, soaking into my sweater.

'Trish? Can you hear me?' I shouted, using my right hand to
cradle her head, holding her upright. Blood flowed wet and warm
over my fingers, gushing out of a wound at the back of her head.
'Trish! Stay with me. You've been shot.' With my left hand, I
fumbled around, searching for something, anything to bind up her
wound and staunch the blood. So much blood!

Trish's hoodie had slipped to the floor, but I managed to grab it
by a sleeve and pull it into my lap. I rolled the body of the hoodie
up like a sausage, leaving the sleeves free, then used
the sleeves to tie the makeshift bandage around Trish's head and
draw it tight. 'Help will be here, soon,' I babbled, hoping she
heard me. 'The hospital's right around the corner. Stay with me,
Trish. Please, stay with me.'

No time to locate my cell phone and dial nine-one-one. I fumbled
for the steering wheel, mashed my palm firmly down on the hub
until the horn began to blare.

NINE

'You will not die on my watch,' I murmured. 'You will not.' I'd passed a first-aid course given by the Red Cross. I could handle burns, choking, heart attacks and strokes. I could save someone from drowning, splint broken bones and knew you should never try to suck the venom out of a snake bite, but nothing had prepared me for what to do in case of a gunshot wound.

I reached for Trish's neck and found a pulse, faint but steady, so there was no need for CPR.

The voice of the Red Cross instructor echoed in my head: *Stop the bleeding! Remember, a victim can bleed to death in five to eight minutes.* I checked to make sure the bandage was secure, hoping I've done the right thing.

Trish moaned. Was she in pain? Maybe I'd tied the bandage too tight, but I hesitated to adjust it now.

Gradually, I became aware of bystanders closing in around the car, a blur of colorful shapes, drawn there by my Volvo's strident, unrelenting horn. Someone rapped on the driver's side window. 'Is everybody all right in there?'

I took my hand off the horn. 'She's been shot!' I shouted into the welcome silence. 'Call nine-one-one!'

My door creaked opened. Cool air rushed over me, feeling like a blessing.

A twenty-something woman wearing a bright red beret over a shoulder-length tumble of blue-black curls leaned in. I flinched instinctively, twisting my body to form a makeshift barrier between the woman and my friend. Was she a good Samaritan, or the assassin, checking on her handiwork, perhaps aiming to finish the job? If so, she should be satisfied. A bullet had torn a path through Trish's brain. What were the survival rates for a wound as grievous as that?

'I called the minute I heard the gunshots,' the young woman told me. 'They're on the way.' She placed a hand lightly, but reassuringly, on my shoulder. 'You can hear the sirens now.' The West

Annapolis hospital was less than a mile away, I knew, adjacent to the county jail on Jennifer Road. It wouldn't take the ambulance long to reach us.

I turned to Trish, choking back a sob. 'Help is coming,' I soothed as the wail of sirens grew louder.

Trish stared at me with wide eyes. 'Buh, buh, buh,' she said. 'Buh, buh . . .'

'They're coming,' I repeated. 'Hang in there, sweetie.'

Blood was beginning to seep through my makeshift bandage. 'Hurry, hurry,' I whispered as I counted her breaths – in and out, in and out, shallow but steady. Trish was breathing on her own – that was a good sign, surely?

I found myself synchronizing my breathing to hers – in and out, in and out – like a coach, encouraging her on.

The sirens died.

The next face I saw was too young, surely, to belong to an EMT, yet he wore the uniform of one. 'L. James, FF/Paramedic' was embroidered in white on his blue polo shirt, and a handheld radio was strapped across the opposite side of his chest. The emergency lights of the ambulance strobed crimson across his lightly stubbled cheeks. As he wrenched the passenger side door open, the muscles of a bodybuilder rippled reassuringly beneath his shirt. 'Ma'am. What happened here?'

'Somebody shot her! Somebody shot Trish through the window!' Hot tears sluiced down my cheeks.

The paramedic rested a knee on the upholstery and leaned further into the car. 'Trish,' he said in a voice as soft and soothing as a late-night radio host, 'you'll be OK. I've got you.'

'What's your name?' he asked. I'd been so involved in the important job of keeping Trish alive that it took me a moment to realize that he meant me. 'I'm Hannah Ives, Trish's friend.'

'You can relax now, Hannah. I'll take it from here.' Behind him, two other paramedics were rolling a gurney piled with equipment closer to the passenger side of my car.

'She's been shot in the head!' I sobbed. 'The bullet came out her forehead!'

'My name's Lou,' the paramedic said, as if he hadn't heard. He pried my arm gently away from around Trish's back. 'Did you notice anything suspicious, Hannah?'

'I don't know!' I wailed. 'Lots of people were going back and forth in the parking lot. It could have been anybody. One minute Trish and I are talking, and the next . . .' I gulped air. 'Oh, God, I need to tell Peter, but I don't know where he is!'

'She has a pulse,' Lou said after a moment. 'That's good. That's very good. Did you bandage her head, Hannah?'

What a stupid question, I thought. Who else could have done it?

Lou's face was serious, but his green eyes were kind. 'You did exactly the right thing.'

He eased Trish out of her slump and into a sitting position. As I watched, feeling lightheaded, another paramedic, a woman, crawled into the back seat and took a position directly behind Trish. She placed a hand on each side of her head, holding it straight and steady against the headrest while Lou carefully fitted Trish with a cervical collar.

'Are you injured, Hannah?' A new voice, deep and gravely. I wrenched my attention away from the paramedics who were helping Trish. The speaker was one of the two who had been pushing the gurney, but now he was leaning through the open driver's side door.

'What?' The question took me by surprise. I took a quick inventory, examining my hands, turning them over and over, curiously, as if they belonged to somebody else. My fingertips felt numb. I glanced down at my clothing – the pale pink fleece and blue jeans I'd chosen to put on that morning. All were drenched with blood. 'I-I don't know.'

He made a come hither gesture, but when I didn't budge, he extended his hand. I took it gratefully and climbed out of the car. As he led me toward the ambulance, he said, 'You'll need to be checked out.'

'Here? Now?' I began to shiver uncontrollably.

The paramedic reached into the ambulance and grabbed a gray polyester blanket. He shook out the folds and wrapped it around my shoulders like a shawl.

'I'm getting blood all over it,' I whimpered, drawing it closer around my neck. 'It'll be ruined.'

'They're disposable,' he told me as he helped me climb into the cab of the ambulance. When I made no move to do it myself, he pulled out the seatbelt, leaned across me and strapped me in. Sometime during all the confusion he'd retrieved my handbag from the car. He laid it on my lap and gave it a gentle pat. 'Thought you might need this.'

This brought a flood of fresh tears. 'I need to ride in the back with her.'

'I'm sorry, but you'll just be in the way. And if, God forbid, we have an accident on the way to the hospital, you'll need to be strapped in.' He stepped back, fixed me with the stern gaze of a high school principal. 'Promise me you'll stay put. We're doing everything we can for your friend.'

Still shivering in spite of the blanket, I nodded.

After he left, I slumped in my seat and pressed my forehead against the window glass. Police cars were beginning to arrive – the black and gold Ford cruisers driven by the Annapolis Police, as well as the two-toned blue squad cars of the Anne Arundel County police. Uniformed officers had herded spectators and potential witnesses to one side of the parking lot, lining them up on the sidewalk in front of the Bike Doctor. Other officers began to cordon off the area around my car with yellow crime scene tape. I found myself wondering where Trish had parked, or if someone had simply dropped her off.

As I watched through the window, Lou eased a stiff-looking dark green, butterfly-shaped brace between Trish's body and the seat cushion, wrapped its wings around her head and torso and secured it top to bottom with a series of straps. Additional rolls of padding protected her injured head, held in place on each side by crisscrosses of wide, white tape. After Trish was wrapped up tighter than an egg roll, the paramedics eased a backboard under her legs and in one deft movement that left me gasping, swiveled her onto it and from there, onto the gurney where they straightened her legs and secured her to it with Velcro straps.

In less than a minute, Trish was loaded into the back of the ambulance and, siren blaring, we sped out of the mall, careening left through the traffic light onto Jennifer Road.

'Where are you taking her?' I shouted over the racket.

'To the ER,' the driver said.

'God, no!' I cried. 'Why aren't you calling a helicopter! She needs to be medivacked to the trauma center in Baltimore!'

'We don't make that decision, ma'am. It's usually up to the doctors in the ER.'

As he slowed for the traffic light at the intersection of Jennifer Road and Medical Drive, he shot a glance my way. 'We've got IV fluids started and administered TXA for the bleeding. Once she's stabilized, she'll probably be airlifted up to Shock Trauma.'

'How long will that take?' I asked.

He steered the ambulance under the hospital's ER portico and set the brake. 'I've already called the helicopter. They'll be waiting on the hospital helipad.'

'Thank you,' I breathed as I unbuckled my seatbelt.

'If you'll wait . . .' he began, but I'd already wrenched open my door and hopped down from the cab. I stepped to one side, keeping out of the way, until the back doors of the ambulance yawned open and the gurney bearing my friend had been rolled out. At that point I fixed the paramedics with my best don't-mess-with-me gaze and announced, 'I'm going with her.'

As the gurney passed by, I reached for Trish's hand and trotted alongside as she was taken through the automatic doors and into the welcoming arms of ER professionals.

TEN

'Hannah, Hannah.'

A familiar voice penetrated the fog, drifting through a back door into the sanctuary where my troubled mind had taken refuge.

I struggled to open my eyes. 'Paul.'

My husband leaned over, brushed an errant strand of hair aside and kissed my forehead. 'You're awake.'

I seemed to be in a glassed-in cubicle, lying on a cot, warmly cocooned in a soft blanket. 'Where's Trish?'

Paul stroked my arm where it lay under the blanket. 'They airlifted her to Shock Trauma. It doesn't look good, Hannah.'

A tear leaked out of the corner of my eye and dripped into my ear. 'I know. How did you get here?' I asked after a moment. 'The Volvo . . .'

He cut me off in mid-sentence. 'Is a crime scene. I know.'

'I remember calling you when we got to the hospital,' I said, 'but nothing much after that. After they wheeled Trish away, I, uh . . .' I paused, eyes squeezed tight, trying to assemble the fragmented pieces. 'They asked me all kinds of questions I didn't know the answers to.'

'The nurse told me you fainted.'

I turned my head on the pillow until I could see his face. 'I don't believe it. Alexander women are made of hardy Puritan stock. We don't faint.'

He stroked my cheek with his fingertips. 'Well, this one apparently did.'

Gradually it came back to me. The light-headedness, the sweating, my pounding heart and a mouth so dry . . . 'I thought I was having a heart attack,' I said.

'Hyperventilation,' Paul said. 'They gave you something to calm you down.'

'It must have put me to sleep,' I said, suddenly aware that my bloody clothes had disappeared and I was dressed in a hospital gown. I eased an arm from under the covers and examined my hand. Traces of dried blood still rimmed my fingernails, but someone – a nurse's aide perhaps – had washed most of it away.

As if reading my mind, Paul said, 'I brought you some clean clothes. Rick loaned me his car,' he said, referring to one of his math department colleagues.

Although I felt like closing my eyes and sleeping whatever remained of the day away, I managed a wan smile, threw off the blanket and struggled to sit up. 'Thanks.'

Paul held out a hand and steadied me as I swung my legs around. My head swam dangerously as I perched on the edge of the cot, legs dangling several inches from the tile floor.

'The police are waiting to talk to you,' Paul said.

'Not while I'm dressed like this,' I said, indicating the hospital gown. 'Help me down, OK?'

Paul positioned the blue vinyl chair he'd been sitting in next to the cot and held my hand until I got comfortable in it. 'You might want to avoid mirrors for a while,' he said cryptically.

'Why?'

'You had two minor scalp wounds, probably from flying glass, but one of them required four stitches.' He pointed.

I patted my head and immediately came into contact with a bandage taped over my left temple. 'Right. It's coming back to me now. The doctor was a jolly sort. Whistled "Sitting On the Dock of the Bay" while he worked. Give me your iPhone,' I said after a moment. When he handed it over, I tapped the camera icon and flipped it to selfie mode.

'Swell,' I said as I examined my image on the screen. My left eyebrow had become bruised and puffy, and a patch of bangs it had taken me over a year to grow out had been shaved away.

'Never hire a doctor to style your hair,' Paul advised.

'This is nothing compared to . . .' I choked on the words.

Paul squeezed my shoulder. 'Hannah . . .' he began, then apparently at a loss, abruptly switched gears. 'There's a homicide detective waiting to talk to you. Feel like getting it over with?'

'Homicide? But Trish isn't . . .' I flapped a hand in front of my face, waving away fresh tears. 'OK,' I said when I regained control. 'Tell him I need a minute to collect myself.'

'It's a her,' Paul said.

'How long have you known the Youngs?' Detective Irene Fogarty stood barely five feet tall, but every inch screamed 'I'm in charge here'. Her thick black hair was cut in a no-nonsense bob. Even her eyeglasses, tortoiseshell and professorial, exuded authority.

'They've lived across the street from us for about ten years,' I said.

'Where can I find Mr Young?' she asked, consulting her notebook. 'Peter.'

'Honestly, I don't know, and after what happened to Trish, I'm really worried.' I described the mysterious circumstances surrounding the Youngs' sudden departure from their Prince George Street home and told her about my fruitless visit to Executive Appliance. 'I was about to file a missing persons report when Trish called and asked me to meet her at the Annapolis Mall today.'

'What did she want to talk to you about?'

'She told me her real name was Elizabeth Stefano and that she had run away from home when she was fourteen.'

From his spot in the corner, I heard Paul mutter, 'I'll be damned.'

'As you can imagine,' I continued, 'that news pretty much knocked my socks off. We had just started to discuss some of the jobs she had worked when . . . well, you know.'

'Where did she run away to?' the detective asked.

'New York City.'

'Did she happen to mention where her husband might be?'

I shook my head. 'She didn't get the chance. All I know for sure is that she called me from a mall in Cicero, New York. From a pay phone. I can get the number for you, if that will help.'

'Yes, thanks,' she said. Then continued in a gentler voice, 'Can you think of anyone who might benefit from Mrs Young's death?'

While I remained silent, considering how much to tell the detective in light of the promise I had made to Trish, Fogarty's bright blue gaze never wandered from my face. 'I think you need to ask the Feds about that,' I said at last. 'Trish told me that there was to be a case filed in New York District Court in a couple of weeks, and that she was somehow involved.'

'She was a witness?'

I shrugged. 'Maybe.'

Involuntarily, my hand wandered to my breast, feeling for the flash drive Trish had entrusted to me, the one I'd tucked into my bra for safekeeping. Too late, I remembered that the clothing I'd been wearing that morning had been removed.

'Sounds like she was in witness protection,' Paul commented from across the room.

'She was hiding from somebody, that's for sure,' I said, clamping down hard on my rising panic over the missing flash drive. 'She worried that it wasn't safe for her to go home.'

'What did she mean by "home"?' Fogarty asked.

'Prince George Street, I assume,' I said. 'I had asked her why we were meeting at Trader Joe's instead of her house.' I snatched a tissue from a box on the rolling bedside stand and gave my nose a good, honking blow. 'Turns out she wasn't safe anywhere.'

'I know this will be difficult,' Fogarty continued, 'but I need you to walk me through everything that happened this morning, starting from when Mrs Young first entered your vehicle.'

Detective Fogarty took careful notes as I talked, glancing up from time to time to prompt me whenever I seemed to stumble. At one point, I opened my mouth to tell her about the flash drive, but

decided against it. Trish was still alive. Only her death could release
me from that solemn promise.

'Something just occurred to me, Detective Fogarty,' I said. 'Trish
simply appeared at my car window. She had to have gotten to the
mall somehow. I assumed she drove down in a rental car from
Cicero, but she could just as easily have taken the train, or flown
into BWI and taken a cab. Or an Uber.'

'We're checking into that.' Fogarty stood and dug into the back
of her notebook, producing a business card. She handed it to
me. 'If you think of anything else that might be helpful, please
give me a call.'

I dutifully studied her card. 'Of course,' I said, 'But please, *please*,
find Peter. Trish needs him, now more than ever.'

'We're doing our best, Mrs Ives. And what you've just told us
should certainly help.'

I shuffled to the doorway and held on to the jamb, keeping my eyes
on Detective Fogarty's back until it safely disappeared around a
corner at the end of the corridor. 'Paul! Where are my bloody
things?'

He stood, shaking a kink out of his leg. 'They handed them to
me in a plastic bag.'

'Yes, but where are they *now*?'

'In the trunk of Rick's car. In parking garage A, to be exact.'

I laid the flat of my hand on Paul's back and gave him a gentle
shove in the direction of the doorway. 'Let's go.'

He refused to budge. 'Hannah?'

'What's wrong? I'm free to go, right? You signed me out?'

'Yes, but . . .' He cocked his head, narrowed his eyes. 'That
hospital gown looks charming on you, but . . .'

'What? Oh.' I smiled sheepishly.

After negotiating a succession of elevators and stairways that
reminded us in colorful signage that 'taking the stairs/is free/conven-
ient/burns seven calories a minute' we closed in on Rick's silver
Azera, parked on the seventh level. Paul had the ignition keys ready,
aimed and popped the trunk just as I got there. I leaned in, grabbed
the patient belongings bag by its drawstring and began pawing
through it. My handbag, bra and panties, shoes, jeans and pullover,

darkly encrusted with dried blood – all accounted for, but no sign of the flash drive.

Paul, who up until then had been standing to one side, arms folded, observing silently, said, 'What are you looking for, and how can I help?'

'Trish gave me a flash drive. I tucked it into my bra.' I lifted the leather flap on my handbag and upended it over the floor of the trunk. My cell phone, wallet and lip balm dropped out, as well as a small packet of tissues and a cellophane-wrapped caramel. No flash drive. Growing increasingly frantic, I pushed them aside, reached for my shoes and shook each of them out. Nothing.

I turned to Paul, tears glistening in my eyes. 'It's not here.'

Paul's long arm swept up and closed the trunk; there was a simultaneous peep of the remote locking the doors. As we retraced our steps, hustling back to the ER, he said, 'You forgot to give it to Detective Fogarty, right?'

I punched the down button on the elevator. 'I didn't forget.'

The elevator doors yawned open and we stepped inside. On the way down, I explained about the promise I had made. 'Trish told me that the flash drive contained copies of documents she'd already turned over to the Feds. She gave it to me as some sort of insurance policy, just in case . . .'

The doors opened on the third floor and a woman carrying one small child and holding the hand of another stepped in. I shot Paul a hold-that-thought look.

As we waited our turn at the nautical-themed emergency room reception desk a few minutes later, Paul leaned close and whispered, 'Just in case what?'

'In case the Feds don't do their duty,' I whispered back.

'Did Trish think that was a serious possibility?' Paul asked, still keeping his voice low.

'So serious, that she gave me explicit instructions on where and who to send it to.'

'This is sounding spookily Deep State, Hannah.'

'I know. Particularly with Trish . . .' I swallowed hard. 'If Trish dies, her voice will be silenced forever. Whoever did this . . . that was their intention: to shut her up.' I seized his forearm and squeezed hard. 'That's why I've *got* to find that flash drive!'

When it was my turn, I smiled at the receptionist, pointed to my bandage as a kind of passport and said, 'I was just treated back there, and when I got to the car, I noticed that something I'd come in with didn't make it into my property bag. It's a little blue USB flash drive.' I illustrated using my thumb and index fingers, holding them about two inches apart. 'It's so small, I thought maybe it'd slipped behind something or fallen on the floor.'

'Lost and Found is at Security. Extension 1430,' the receptionist informed me.

'I'm sorry,' I said, 'but I was just back there, like five minutes ago, so there won't have been time for anybody to have found it and turned it over to Security. Can't I simply go back and look?' I leaned across the desk and hoped I looked as pitiful as I felt.

'Well . . .' she hesitated.

'It's really, really important,' I said. 'I'm writing a novel and it's my only copy.'

Paul stifled a gasp, turning it into a polite cough.

'What did you say your name was?' she asked. When I told her, she tapped away on her keyboard, then squinted at the screen through a pair of pink-framed reading glasses. 'Nobody's using the room right now, Mrs Ives, so I guess it will be OK. Let me find a volunteer to go with you.'

Five minutes later, Paul and I and a pink-shirted volunteer named Ellie were searching the cubicle where I'd been treated. It didn't take long. The room was so small, spare and clean that I couldn't imagine where something, even as small as a flash drive, could hide. Except for a used tissue, even the flip-top trash can was empty.

'Only one other place it could be,' Ellie said, eyeing the medical waste bin. She extracted a pair of blue rubber gloves from a dispenser, snapped them on and dived in.

'Is this what you're looking for?' Ellie asked, straightening from a position bent over the bin of contaminated gauze, gloves and other medical waste discarded there after my treatment. Trish's flash drive, stained with her blood, lay in the palm of Ellie's gloved hand.

'Yes!' I cried. 'How can I ever thank you?'

Ellie handed me the flash drive. 'No need. All in a day's work around here.'

ELEVEN

Thankfully, I was spared the doleful responsibility of notifying my family and circle of friends about Trish's attempted murder. By six o'clock that evening, the shooting at Annapolis Mall was 'Breaking News' on every metropolitan area television station. It was trending on Facebook and Twitter, setting WhatsApp ablaze and glaring at me in living color from the front page of the Annapolis *Capital*.

From WBAL-TV at six o'clock, the entire state learned that following a shooting at the Annapolis Mall, forty-two-year-old Patricia Young of Annapolis had been hospitalized in a critical condition at the R. Adams Cowly Shock Trauma Center at the University of Maryland Medical Center in Baltimore. Surgeons had removed a portion of her skull to allow for the swelling of her brain. She was in a medically induced coma, breathing with the assistance of a ventilator. Her assailant was still at large.

Apparently Stan Stovall, the news anchor, had inside sources who were unencumbered by the same HIPAA Privacy Rules I'd run into when I telephoned the hospital for information late that afternoon.

I'm sorry, ma'am, but patient information is confidential.

Did the patient have a family spokesperson?

Not according to our records, but please check back later.

Stovall compared Trish's injury to the one sustained by Congresswoman Gabby Giffords in a 2011 assassination attempt outside a Safeway store near Tucson. He replayed ancient footage of Ronald Reagan's press secretary, Jim Brady, taking a similar bullet intended for the president back in 1981. Quoting sources from an article in *The Atlantic*, he even opined that had Abraham Lincoln been shot today, he would have survived because, like the current president and recent others before him, it is the shock trauma unit at the University of Maryland Medical Center that is alerted and remains on standby whenever the president travels in the area.

That Trish was being cared for by the same medical

professionals deemed competent enough to treat the President of
the United States, and that both Giffords and Brady had survived
similar brain injuries was semi-encouraging news. But I'd seen
Trish's wound, and so I worried. If Trish likewise survived, I feared
her recovery would be a journey along a long, rocky road.

The news had moved on to the important business of college
basketball scores when Paul returned home from a trip around
the corner to Galway Bay bearing takeaway boxes of their signature corned beef and cabbage. I switched off the television and
followed him into the kitchen.

'Thank God you're back. I'm starving,' I said as I laid silverware
and paper napkins rather haphazardly on the table. 'I carelessly
missed lunch.'

'Sit,' Paul instructed, shooing me toward the table with a one-
handed wave of salt and pepper shakers. 'I'll take care of that.'

Gratefully, I sat.

Paul rummaged in the pantry, eventually producing a jar of strong
Irish mustard and a bottle of gourmet vinegar I'd bought at the farmers'
market on Riva Road. As we tucked into our meals, I relayed what
I had learned from the television news about Trish's condition.

Paul chewed thoughtfully, swallowed and said, 'Somebody must
have given the hospital permission to talk to reporters.'

'Do you suppose the police have located Peter?'

'That's a possibility,' he said.

I waved a fork. 'I'm all for protecting people's privacy, but I
was in the car with her. She is my friend. They owe me *some*
information, don't you think?'

'Rules are rules,' Paul reminded me.

'It's lucky I wasn't shot, too,' I said, feeling suddenly cold.

Paul looked up. 'You weren't the target, Hannah.'

'Are you suggesting that this was a professional hit?'

'That's exactly what I'm suggesting.'

'You can't imagine how reassuring it is to think that nobody
wants *me* dead,' I muttered over a forkful of boiled potato.

'Which brings us back to Trish, and to that flash drive you are
hiding from authorities. If whoever shot Trish knows that you
have it . . .' His voice trailed off.

I leaned toward him across my dinner. 'But nobody knows I have
it except Trish and you.'

'And that volunteer, Ellie, at the hospital.'

I snorted. 'She thinks it's a novel. I promised to send her an autographed copy.'

Paul gazed at me with such tenderness that my heart nearly burst. 'Hannah, I need you to be serious. Just this once? Please?'

I laid down my fork, abandoned my dinner and walked around the table. I wrapped both arms around my husband from behind and rested my chin on the top of his head. 'I think we need to find out what's on that flash drive, don't you?'

'That's my girl.'

'But first,' I said, 'finish your dinner.'

TWELVE

Silently, almost reverently, Paul slipped Trish's bloodstained flash drive out of my fingers. 'Why don't you pour a couple of glasses of wine. I'll be right back.'

By the time he returned to the kitchen, I had filled two glasses to the brim with Sauvignon Blanc. Paul eyed them critically.

'It may be a long evening,' I said.

'Here,' he said as he returned Trish's flash drive. 'I went over it with an alcohol wipe.'

I suppressed a shiver as I curled my fingers protectively around the freshly cleaned data storage device.

Carrying the wine for both of us, Paul led the way down to our basement office where we settled in, side by side, in front of our desktop computer's twenty-seven-inch screen.

I plugged the flash drive into a vacant USB port in the back, and when its icon appeared on the desktop, moused over it. 'Here goes!' I said, double clicking.

A list of files populated the screen. We leaned in.

'Oh, oh,' Paul said.

'What?'

Paul moused over one of the files: Page1.gpg. 'See that extension? These files have been encrypted.'

The flash drive held forty-three such files, labeled Page1.gpg to

Page43.gpg, as well as several files with .exe extensions, indicating that they might be files used to execute other programs.

'What does that mean?' I asked, although I feared I knew the answer.

'It means that your friend Trish is more clever than I ever gave her credit for. She encrypted these files using an open source encryption tool called PGP, which you'll be amused to learn stands for "Pretty Good Privacy".'

'So it means we can't read the files without this Pretty Good Privacy program.'

'Right.'

'Can we get the program? Buy it? Download it from the Internet?'

'We could, but it's more complicated than that. Even if we had the program, even if we downloaded and installed it right now, unless we have Trish's private key . . .'

'We're screwed.'

'Exactly.'

'You're the mathematician in the family,' I said. 'Can't you crack the code?'

'Let's look.' Using the Text.edit program, Paul clicked on Page1. gpg and opened the file:

```
Ö
õWƒis
}˘~®¨y-'æÙèHRU9@#O°"∂Æ-ʃvıy(ÛlıUÃ~ÃÌa¡å°—
⁄çvo÷ß°ö4r˘ ≥›—6fi-:6íÇæ]V"~¨i)p,†g80iKò80Ωıõsó,†Ã◊ʃ"
£63yü óMÜ∞Œau˛\ƒëæu»XGñF"aÃŒÜáYÔBuKI&ÙÃŸ
ÕéQmòâÊ'∂w?ó Æ◊1¶ûKæÒ»Äk^p8Ápõ~„áÃy®Ø@ë∑rà/
î80„Ye"ª õ·,œ_pi√›WπLy‡§æ-fiÙH¨ı.ùπ‹∞QJÅ≤:®¨UU˘∞œ
ùÑXeÔÏ'. . .‹î5µK≥˘å™g}DìÙ!hR˝/oj~ Õ^ŒÜ`sïëØÒ'˛0Õ
Ó["í,VÒ6‹†Ú˛üÚ‹¶om‰Å(P˛80-˜ÃÂ≈Ñ™s∂;‰ó80à†%y
„k‹)Bfl80„ÉE˛‚ÀÓiÌoYƒØ†2˛úK^
```

'It's gibberish,' I said.

'You noticed?' He laughed. 'Not even NSA could crack this file without having the key.'

'Can you tell what kind of files they are by looking?' I asked. 'Documents? Photos? Emails?'

Paul shook his head. 'Maybe the spooks over at NSA could, but I can't.'

'But Trish wanted me to give the files to a reporter at the *New York Times*. How the heck will he read it, without the key, I mean.'

'Was she specific about that, Hannah? That you give it to the *Times*? Not the *Washington Post* or the Baltimore *Sun*?'

I nodded. 'Very.'

'Two possibilities. Either she made arrangements in advance and provided the reporter with her private key, or more than likely she encrypted the files using the *New York Times*'s own public key, knowing that's where she was intending to send it.' He hunched over the keyboard and tapped away. 'Look, here's the tips page from the *Times*. Anyone can download their public key from here. They give complete instructions on how to process and submit files. It's designed to protect the identify of whistle-blowers.'

'Well, damn.' I reached over Paul to seize control of the mouse. I made a backup copy of the flash drive and saved it to my computer under a file folder named 'Trip to Grand Canyon', then ejected the flash drive icon and jiggled the device out of the USB port. 'Maybe I won't have to. There's still two weeks to go before whatever it is that Trish said is supposed to happen happens. Or, it doesn't.'

'The only person who seems to be left out of this equation is our good friend Peter. Where the blazes is he?' Paul said.

'All indications are that Trish and Peter left their house together early on Thursday morning. But, when Trish called me on Friday, she said she just couldn't do it anymore. I don't know what "it" is, but if it was something Peter was involved in, maybe she's left him to sort it out on his own.'

Paul frowned thoughtfully. 'Peter's a college professor who sells home appliances, he's not an inside trader or running some sort of Ponzi scheme.'

'That we know of,' I hastened to add. 'But I tend to agree with you. Trish told me that the case had something to do with the Lynx Media Corporation. I can't think of any way Peter could be involved with Lynx, can you?'

Paul parked his reading glasses on top of his head. 'Maybe in a past life.'

'Which brings us back to Elizabeth Stefano,' I said. 'Clearly, it's *Trish* who had a past life.' I opened the top right-hand desk drawer where I keep paperclips, staples and Post-it notes and tucked the flash drive for safekeeping into a slot underneath my checkbook.

'While you were fetching dinner, I Googled "Elizabeth Stefano" and came up with over four thousand hits. There are even more Liz Stefanos in this world. I narrowed it down some by eliminating the third grader on the honor roll at St Timothy's Catholic School and the gal who sells real estate in Fresno . . .'

I was about to close the drawer, when my eyes landed on Trish's cell phone. I picked it up and waved it in my husband's face. 'This! This! If there was some way I could hack into this, maybe we could figure out what the hell is going on, but none of her passwords worked. Here,' I said, handing the phone over to him, 'maybe you'll have better luck. I've tried every trick in my rather limited repertoire.'

Paul powered on the phone and stared at Trish's screensaver until it faded to black. He tapped the home button again and the photograph reappeared, one that I already knew by heart: a carnival fairground taken at twilight, its midway ablaze with color and light. 'You tried all her passwords?'

'Amazon to Zulily,' I said.

'Do you still have that address book?'

'Of course. Shall I go get it?'

'Please.'

When I returned with the book, Paul said, 'Think about your own accounts, Hannah. Which one would be the biggest pain in the ass to reset?'

'My bank,' I said. 'Everything I buy online is linked to BB&T. Remember when my credit card was stolen? I thought I'd lose my mind.'

'So, what bank does Trish use?'

'Wells Fargo. There at the bottom.' I waggled a finger over the entry. 'But that password was bogus, too. Wait a minute!' I snatched the address book out of his hand so quickly that he flinched. 'Another one I'd hate to change is my Apple iCloud account. All my Apple devices are synched to it.'

'And Trish uses a Mac.'

'Indeed she does. A MacBook Pro. I imagine the police have taken custody of it by now,' I said, 'but until this afternoon, it was sitting on that little desk in her kitchen.' I scanned Trish's list again.

'I can't believe I didn't notice this before, but she didn't write down her iCloud password.'

'Maybe not any place obvious,' Paul said, reaching out for the book. 'Let me have a look.'

While Paul leafed through the pages, I trotted upstairs to top up our wine glasses. When I returned, he was wearing a look of triumph. 'She's a clever girl, your friend Trish.'

'You found it?'

'In the Cs. Imbedded in a recipe for cloud bread, disguised as a website URL.' He smiled. 'You do the honors.'

I commandeered the keyboard. At the Apple website, while Paul read out Trish's login and the lengthy combination of letters, numbers and symbols that she had chosen for her password, I typed. 'Moment of truth,' I said, and hit return.

'Good news, bad news,' I grumbled. I was in, but Trish had taken the precaution of protecting her iCloud account with two-factor identification. 'If I were Queen of the World,' I said, 'there would be no such thing as two-factor identification.'

From its face-up position on the desk, I could see that Trish's phone was receiving messages from Apple containing the authentication code I needed, but I couldn't unlock the phone to actually *see* the code. 'Talk to me!' I yelled, shaking the obstinate phone, demanding it cough up its secrets.

The corner of Paul's lip turned up in a sly smile. 'What do you do when you upgrade your iPhone, Hannah?'

I stopped threatening Trish's phone. After a moment's thought, I said, 'You take the SIM out of the old one and put it in the new one?'

'Bingo!' Paul said, tipping an imaginary hat.

'What are you getting at . . .' I started to say before the penny dropped.

I aimed my finger at him, like a gun. 'Hand over your cell phone, mister.'

Paul raised up on one hip and eased his iPhone out of a back pocket in his chinos. 'Yes, ma'am.'

I scrabbled in the desk drawer for one of the paper clips, straightened it and jammed the tip into a tiny hole on the side of Trish's phone, ejecting the tray where her SIM card lived. Once I had the tiny SIM in hand, I repeated the process with Paul's phone, carefully replacing his SIM card with Trish's.

When Paul rebooted his phone, it now had Trish's telephone number.

Back on the desktop computer, I revisited Trish's iCloud account. This time, I clicked the link that said I hadn't received the two-factor passcode it sent earlier, requesting another one. Almost instantly, Paul's phone buzzed with the code. When I entered the code into the site, *voila!* I could see her Apple Mail, her notes, her bookmarks, her photos, her tunes . . . everything that she'd synched to and stored in the Cloud.

With Paul looking over my shoulder, sipping wine, I spent the next half hour impersonating Trish. At every website, I said I'd forgotten her password. The website would obligingly confirm her identify by texting a code to Trish's registered phone number which went, of course, straight to Paul's phone. Once I was logged in using that code, I could change both the password and the trusted phone number associated with that particular account.

It took the rest of the evening, but by the time Paul had showered and padded back downstairs in his bathrobe to check on me, I'd gained control of Trish's Amazon account, and her bank and credit card accounts. 'I've just started on the retail accounts,' I said, preening a bit.

Paul frowned. 'Aren't you overdoing it a bit, Hannah?'

'Discovering that Trish bought a pair of hiking boots from LL Bean could be an important clue,' I insisted. 'At least we'd know she wasn't planning a getaway to the Bahamas.' I removed my reading glasses and looked him straight in the eyes. 'Trish and I trust each other. If I were the one lying in a hospital bed and fighting for my life, I'd expect her to do exactly the same for me.'

'What are you going to do when Trish asks for her phone back?'

'I pray she *does*,' I said. 'In which case, I'll give her the new password list. At least she'll know I cared enough about her to stick my nose into her business. It's not like I'm going to order a bunch of antique jewelry on eBay and charge it to her credit card.'

'I didn't imagine for a moment that you would,' he said.

'Privacy schmivacy. All bets are off. We need to find out who shot her, and why, in case they try to do it again.'

Paul stretched an arm behind the computer and the screen went blank. 'This can wait, Hannah. I order you to get some rest.' He nudged me up the stairs.

When we reached the landing, he turned me around by my shoulders, wrapped me in a bear hug then kissed me, good and proper. When we finally came up for air, he said, 'I have a question for you, though.'

'Yes?' I said a bit dreamily.

'What the heck is cloud bread?'

THIRTEEN

Tuesday morning found me back at the computer, trawling Trish's iCloud drive. If she'd been plotting a getaway, no hint of it appeared in her emails.

Her last had been on Wednesday evening, confirming a cut and blow dry with Karen James for Saturday. Nobody skips out on a hair appointment with Karen James. Even long-standing customers need to book months in advance.

Otherwise, she OK'd her shifts on the Out of the Box calendar – she *had* been scheduled to work on Thursday – and was busily coordinating a tea for the Women's Democratic League of Anne Arundel County. There were group emails about our ill-fated Italian night dinner, and a message to Glory asking her to pick up some paper towels on her way to work. I jotted down Glory's email address for future reference.

Did Trish have another, perhaps secret email account? I was searching for evidence of one, when my cell phone rang.

'Hannah, it's Helen at the store.'

'Hi, Helen,' I said. 'Why are you whispering?'

'Peter's back!' she said. 'He's in his office right now, and . . .' She paused, pitching her voice even lower. 'And there's somebody with him.'

'Somebody who?'

'I think it's the police.'

'Uniformed?'

'No, wearing a business suit. He just looks like a cop, you know, like on TV.' I heard a sharp intake of breath, and then: 'No, wait a minute. There are two guys! One is lurking outside the front door. What the blazes is going on?'

'They must be investigating Trish's shooting,' I said.

'I got to hug Peter and tell him how sorry I am to hear about Trish, and he said . . . Wait a minute, they're coming out now. I'll call you back.'

And the line went dead.

Fifteen long minutes later, Helen kept her promise. 'Oh, Hannah, it's so awful. Peter's been crying, I could tell. His eyelids are nearly swollen shut.'

I swallowed hard, fearing the worst. 'Oh, please don't tell me Trish has died.'

'No, she's hanging on by a thread, Peter says.'

'Is Peter still there? I'd like to—'

'He left in a car with the two guys,' she explained, cutting me off. 'Said he was going up to the hospital.'

'I'd hoped—'

'I told him you and Paul stopped by,' she barreled on. 'Then Peter told me that you were in the car with Trish when it happened! Is that true?'

'Yes, I'm afraid it is.'

This news shocked her into a silence so long I thought I'd lost the connection until she quietly breathed into the phone, 'Geeze Laweeze.'

'Did Peter say anything else?' I asked, probing for answers that might explain the couple's unexpected disappearance.

'No! So frustrating. He gave me the key to the safe and a folder with instructions. Also a list of account names and passwords. Basically, he's handed the store over to me. I hope I don't screw it up.'

'You'll do just fine,' I said truthfully. 'You could sell Obamacare to a Republican.'

That made her laugh. 'I asked when he'd be back, and he said he didn't know, which isn't surprising. If Trish is in Shock Trauma, I imagine he'll want to sit at her bedside twenty-four-seven. But why would anyone want to shoot her? Trish of all people?'

'If we can figure out why, we'll probably find out who,' I said, channeling Jessica Fletcher, or maybe Miss Marple.

Somewhere in the background, a familiar bell dinged. Helen must have covered the phone with her hand because I heard a muffled, 'I'll be right with you.' To me, she said, 'Gotta go, but keep me in the loop, OK?'

I promised I would, even though nobody seemed to be telling me anything.

Instead of coming home, Paul spent his lunch hour haggling with the insurance company and arranging for a rental car while our Volvo was being 'processed'. Meanwhile, I threw together a peanut butter sandwich for myself and washed it down with a cup of microwave tomato soup, before turning my attention to the plastic bag of clothing retrieved from the hospital. While I ate, it stared back at me accusingly from a sad heap next to the basement door.

I'd considered discarding the clothing I'd been wearing that day, but my Puritan genes recoiled. The jeans fit me perfectly and I'd worn the pink, cowl-neck fleece only once, so both seemed worth salvaging.

Down in the basement, I filled the utility sink with cold water and began adding garments from the bag one at a time – bra, under-pants, fleece, jeans – and my heart turned a somersault. They'd given me Trish's hoodie.

Trish won't want it, I reasoned, and I certainly didn't need a graphic memento of that horrible day. I scrunched the hoodie into an untidy ball and aimed for the trash can. Halfway between my hand and a rim shot into the canister, something slipped out of the hoodie's pocket and floated to the floor. Curious, I bent to pick it up.

It resembled an oversized cash register receipt printed on slick, flimsy paper, folded into quarters. Dried blood flaked off the paper as I separated the layers, unfolding it to reveal a rental car receipt. Midday on Friday, someone named Mary Goodrich had rented a Kia Forte from Budget rentals on East Circle Drive in Cicero, New York.

Wait a minute!

Trish had told me her real name was Elizabeth Stefano. So, who the hell was Mary Goodrich?

I closed my eyes and leaned back against the washing machine. If Trish wasn't Trish, or even Elizabeth . . .? I stashed the receipt in a desk drawer for safekeeping, then fished the hoodie out of the trash can in order to check the pockets. Both were empty. Eager to distance myself from the loathsome garment, I stuffed the hoodie back into the canister, shoving it well to the bottom and weighing it down with an empty laundry detergent bottle.

But nothing could distance me from the cold, iron smell – sharp and metallic – of the water in the sink where my clothes lay soaking. I'd rinsed blood out of clothing before – Emily's nose-bleeds, my rambunctious grandsons' scraped knees – but this was Trish's blood sloshing around in the sink, turning the water a dusty rose. I agitated, squeezed, wrung and rinsed. It wasn't until I watched my friend's blood spiraling down the drain that I lost it, breaking into sobs.

'Meow!'

I was so busy refilling the sink for a second soak and feeling sorry for myself that I didn't notice the cat until he leapt up on the washing machine. I turned, swiping away tears with the top of my wrist.

Hobie considered me, his blue eyes disconcertingly bright. He mewled again, even more plaintively. I patted my hands on my jeans before reaching out to give Trish's cat an affectionate scratch behind the ears. 'Oh, Hobie, I miss her, too.'

I returned to the task at hand while Hobie supervised silently, curled up on the washer, head resting on his paws. I welcomed his company. 'Thanks for cheering me up, young man,' I told him. 'Just for that, there's a tasty tuna treat in your future.'

'Did somebody mention tuna?' my husband said.

I nearly jumped out of my Crocs. 'Paul! You scared me to death. First the cat, now you sneaking up on me.'

Paul's gaze wandered from me, to Hobie, to the sink and back to me again. What little composure I had mustered instantly evaporated.

'Come here.' He folded me into his arms and rested his chin on the top of my head. 'Don't do this to yourself, sweetheart.'

'They're my favorite pants,' I sobbed into his shoulder, my wet hands dangling limply at my sides. 'And the fleece cost me sixty-nine dollars at J. Jill. Plus tax.'

'Leave it,' he said.

'But . . .' I started to pull away. 'And I found a rental car receipt . . .'

His grip on me tightened. 'Leave it. It can wait until tomorrow.' Paul extended his arm and switched off the light, ending the discussion. In the semi-darkness, he turned me around and urged me out the laundry room door ahead of him. 'Don't you want to see what we'll be driving until we can get the Volvo back?'

'I'm not sure I want it back,' I sniffed.

At the head of the stairs he grabbed my hand and dragged me down the hallway and out the front door like an uncooperative two-year-old. Half a block down Prince George Street he paused next to a sleek black Mercedes Benz CLA, long, lean and low. Only then did he release the death grip on my hand. He swept his arm wide, gesturing at the car as if it were a game show prize. 'Tah dah!'

'Are you sure we can afford—?'

'It's all they had left, so they rented it to me for the cost of a Hyundai.'

'I'm speechless,' I said.

'Car karma, my dear. You've either got it or you haven't.'

FOURTEEN

While Paul watched, smiling like a proud father, I circled the car, admiring it from all angles. 'Sweet,' I said. 'You do good work, Paul.'

Paul didn't reply, turning and waving instead to a familiar figure strolling up Prince George Street from the direction of City Dock, toting a leaf green padded cooler bag from Whole Foods.

'Yoo-hoo!' she called out, waving back.

'Emily! What brings you here?' I asked, offering my daughter my cheek for a kiss.

'You, silly,' she said with a smile. She handed the bag off to her father before enveloping me in a hug.

'What's in the bag?' Paul wanted to know.

'Sliced ham and a mac and cheese casserole with buttered bread-crumbs on the top just the way Dad likes it,' she explained. 'Cut-up fruit, too. I thought Mom could use a break from the kitchen.'

'You're right,' I agreed.

Emily grew quiet, staring at the Youngs' house whose windows stared back from across the street like empty eyes. 'How's Trish?'

'Fighting for her life,' I said. 'Can you stay a while?'

Emily checked her watch, a rose gold Swatch that had been a gift from her father on her last birthday. 'Gotta pick Timmy up from soccer practice at four, but I can carve out a few minutes.'

As we wandered back to the house, I filled Emily in on what little I knew about Trish's prognosis. 'But we should know more soon. Peter is up at the hospital as we speak. I hope to be able to check in with him later today.'

'Thank God they didn't mention you on the news, Mom. Chloe could handle it, but the other kids . . .' She shrugged.

Chloe was Emily's eldest, eighteen, the same age as her first cousin, Julie Cardinale. While Julie opted for a gap year in South Dakota, Chloe enrolled as a freshman at St Mary's College in southern Maryland where she planned to major in Anthropology. 'Have you told Chloe?' I asked.

'Me? God, no! I can't even get *my* head around it. You could have been killed!'

'Coffee?' I inquired, feeling cold and eager to change the subject. 'Iced tea?'

'Coke if you have it,' Emily requested, trailing after me into the kitchen where we found Paul transferring the contents of her cooler bag into the refrigerator. He rustled up a soda for each of us, then joined Emily and me at the kitchen table. As succinctly as I knew how, I brought Emily up to date on what Paul and I had been doing to solve the mystery of the vanishing Youngs. I even confessed to the 'requisitioning' of Trish's cell phone.

Emily's eyebrows disappeared under her bangs. 'You hacked Trish's iPhone?'

I nodded.

Emily beamed. 'Awesome!'

'Your mother also—' Paul began before I silenced him with a death ray, just in case he was about to bring up the one piece of the puzzle I had intentionally avoided mentioning: Trish's flash drive.

But I worried for nothing. Emily's mind seemed to be elsewhere. 'Cicero, New York?' she mused, her voice flat. When I nodded, she continued, 'I'm sorry, Mom, but if you're going to totally disappear and need to hide out somewhere, you go to New York City, San Francisco, or Chicago, some cosmopolitan place like that, not Cicero, New York.'

'Paris,' Paul offered, waving a soda can. 'Or London.'

'Nah,' Emily said. 'You need a passport to go abroad.' She took a sip of her Coke then set the can down carefully on the tabletop. 'My point is, if you're going to Cicero, New York, it's for a reason. You don't pick a place like Cicero by throwing darts at a map.'

'So, what's in Cicero?' Paul wondered.

I shrugged. 'Penn-Cann Mall. That's where Trish called me from. I'm pretty sure that's where she rented a car.'

'So Penn-Cann. What else?'

I had to confess that other than the Penn-Cann Mall, I hadn't done my homework on Cicero.

'Family.' Emily stated firmly. 'You'd go there for family. Or friends.'

'Other than Peter, I don't think Trish has much family,' Paul said.

'That you know of.'

'That we know of,' I agreed, recalling with a sharp pang the locket Glory had found hanging on the back of Trish's bathroom door.

'And what's with the switcheroo of names?' Paul mused. 'Trish told your mother her real name is Elizabeth Stefano, but she's been using Patricia Young as an alias for as long as we've known her. And now she's renting a car under a *third* name?'

'I have a theory,' Emily said. 'What if Elizabeth Stefano *is* her real name, but she had to go into the witness protection program for some reason. So as Patricia Young she's chugging along for . . .' She paused to consult me. 'How many years have you known Peter and Trish?'

'Around ten,' I said.

'OK. So, for ten years she's living happily as Trish, and then, let's say her cover got blown. Maybe the Feds showed up in the middle of the night and whisked her away again.'

'And gave her a new identity,' Paul said, following Emily's line of reasoning to its logical conclusion. 'This Mary Goodrich who rented the car.'

Paul and I exchanged glances. He gave me a slight nod – tacit permission to go ahead.

'Emily, I think you hit the nail on the head. Sitting in the car, just before she was shot, Trish told me that a case would soon be filed in federal court, and that she'd provided evidence for it.'

Once again, I didn't mention the flash drive.

Emily slapped the table with the flat of her hand. 'There you go. So, she's a witness, and somebody wanted to shut her up. Permanently.'

'So it would seem,' I whispered.

Emily leaned toward me. 'Mom! This is serious. Promise me you won't get involved. It's obviously not safe. Leave it to the professionals.'

I reached out and covered Emily's hand with my own. 'Honey, all I want right now is for my friend, whatever her real name is, to fully recover. I'd also like whoever shot her to be wearing an orange jumpsuit for life, but . . .'

'Hannah?' Paul spoke so quietly that I almost missed his question. 'If Trish Young is an alias, isn't it likely that "Peter Young" is an alias, too?'

'I know one way to find out,' I said. 'Back Peter into a corner and ask.'

FIFTEEN

As much as I wanted to lay eyes on Trish, to reassure myself that she was still alive, still breathing, it was Peter I needed to talk to.

He hadn't returned home, I knew, because his Honda hadn't budged from its parking spot down the street. According to Helen Lawrence, he wasn't at the store either, so that left only one place my errant neighbor could be.

According to their webpage, visiting hours at Baltimore's shock trauma center were noon to six-thirty and eight to ten. I had no idea whether Trish would be allowed visitors, but if I needed to bluff my way in, I figured it would be easier to accomplish during, rather than outside, regular visiting hours.

Mid-morning on Wednesday, Paul headed off to the academy on foot, as usual. I filled a travel mug with coffee, snagged the keys to the Mercedes-Benz and took it on my maiden voyage. I cruised north past Baltimore's football stadium and Orioles Park at Camden Yards and continued straight up Paca to Fayette, deftly navigating

Baltimore's familiar pattern of one-way streets. After a left on Fayette and a left again on Greene, I arrived opposite the main entrance of the University of Maryland Medical Center complex at the corner of Baltimore and Greene.

On previous visits to the hospital, back when my mother had been a patient, I'd parked in nearby parking garages where the rates were somewhat cheaper, but today – hey, dude, I'm driving a Mercedes Benz! – I made a tight, one-hundred-eighty-degree turn and pulled in under the hospital portico. At the outer traffic island, I eased up to the curb near a kiosk where a uniformed attendant stood under a navy and green umbrella next to a sign that read: Valet Parking.

'Nice wheels,' the attendant said as I slid out of the driver's seat.

'Thanks,' I said, forking over twelve dollars (cash only) and surrendering the car keys. 'It's new, so treat it gently.'

He tipped an imaginary hat and flashed me a crooked grin that telegraphed, 'Just as soon as you're out of sight I'm going to reset all the radio stations to heavy metal and turn the stereo up full blast.' So, I fished another five out of my handbag, smiled sweetly and added, 'Thank you so much.'

The main reception desk was where I remembered it – just inside the entrance, adjacent to the gift shop. When it was my turn, I leaned across the desk and told the bald-headed, apple-cheeked volunteer that I had come to visit Patricia Young. 'She's in Shock Trauma,' I explained unnecessarily as that information was probably displayed on the computer screen in front of him.

'Your name again?' he inquired, eyeing me somewhat suspiciously over the tops of his reading glasses.

'Hannah Ives,' I repeated.

'I'm sorry,' the volunteer explained gently, 'but your name doesn't appear on her visitors list. We'll need permission from the designated family spokesperson to add you to the list.'

'Oh, dear,' I whimpered. 'I got here as soon as I possibly could after my brother-in-law called with the terrible news. I've driven all the way down here from, uh, Cicero, New York,' I added, hoping I looked as pitiful as I felt. 'Trish is my *sister*! Please, isn't there something you can do?'

'Why don't you telephone your brother-in-law right now?' he suggested gently.

'Well, I tried, but he doesn't pick up. Peter *never* picks up,' I whined with genuine exasperation. 'Besides, he's probably with Trish right now. Can't I go—?'

The volunteer raised a beefy, blue-veined hand, cutting me off. 'Ah, in that case, let me make a call.'

Five minutes later, wearing an official neon pink visitor's wristband, I followed the volunteer's directions along the scenic route to the shock trauma waiting area where Peter had told the volunteer he'd meet me. I strolled past Au Bon Pain and an M&T mini-bank heading toward the Gudelsky Building where I took a hard right past the elevators. When I emerged from the rotunda into the airy, wide open space of the Weinberg Building's seven-story, glass-covered atrium, I caught my breath. Hospital staff, visitors and patients bustled past me on the concourse while I stood gap-mouthed, rooted to the polished marble. Clearly the architects had been sipping Chianti and dreaming of town squares in Italy while designing this hospital's *piazza*. On the main level, visitors lounged comfortably in seating areas delineated by flowering plants, Algerian ivy and black olive trees. Floating staircases drew my eyes upward to similar terraced gardens on the third and fifth levels.

But it was the fountain that sucked me in: a slightly-domed black disk, large enough to accommodate all the Knights of King Arthur's Round Table. I perched on a slatted wooden bench for a few moments, listening to the fountain burble in a zen-like way, breathing slowly and evenly to calm my jitters. What waited for me up on the fourth floor was uncharted territory. I prayed I'd be prepared.

Shock Trauma had its own waiting area. I was nearly there, just passing the doors that led to the Medical Records department when Peter emerged from the bank of elevators near the end of the hallway.

'Peter!' I cried, quickening my step.

He wore rumpled chinos and a white polo shirt that looked like he'd slept in them, which he probably had. His mop of tight sandy curls was squashed flat on one side and frizzed out on the other, giving him a lopsided look. He moved toward me slowly, zombie-like, but his arms were outstretched and he folded me into them. 'Hannah, my God. I'm so glad you're here.'

After a moment, he stepped back without releasing my upper

arms. His eyes, bloodshot and weary, locked on mine, and he managed a wan smile. 'So, you're my sister-in-law, I hear.'

I touched his cheek, stubbly under my fingertips. 'It seemed like a good idea at the time.'

'Thank you,' he said, squeezing my arms gently. 'Thank you.'

'For what?'

'They tell me you were with Trish when it happened. That you—'

I flapped a hand, waving his unspoken words away. 'Let's talk about that later, OK?'

He surprised me then by asking, 'Have you eaten?'

'Not since breakfast,' I said. 'But—'

'They only escort visitors up every thirty minutes,' he said, checking his watch. 'We've just missed it. There's nothing we can do upstairs at this point, anyway.'

'Peter, I'm—'

'Look, I haven't had anything to eat since last night. The cafeteria's right here. I can bring you up to date while we eat.'

As we wandered through the maze of food stations in the Courtyard Café, Peter rested a hand on my shoulder and said, 'The nurses tell me the sushi's pretty good, but recommend giving the hot food a pass and heading straight for the sandwiches.' He steered me toward an overhead sign that read DELI. Behind the deli counter two women busily assembled sandwiches to order, serving cheerful chatter to the doctor in line ahead of us along with his smoked turkey and provolone on rye. 'Meet Minnie and Synell,' Peter informed me, 'better known as the Sandwich Ladies.'

'You first,' I said, as I considered the options listed on a free-standing menu board. While I waited for Minnie to 'masterpiece' my tuna salad on honey wheat with tomato and lettuce, I turned to Peter and asked, 'Tell me, how is Trish doing?'

'She's in a critical condition, as you probably heard. Fortunately, they got her off the helicopter and into surgery almost right away. The famous Golden Hour, you know. It was invented here. By the guy the place is named after.' Peter paused to collect the sandwich that Synell held out over the counter. 'The good news is that Shock Trauma has a ninety-six percent survival rate.'

'That sounds hopeful,' I said, all the while worrying about the four percent who didn't survive. 'But what can you tell me about her surgery, Peter? All I heard on the news was that they'd removed a portion of Trish's skull to allow for swelling.'

'Yes, a decompressive hemicraniotomy.' He tossed the ten-dollar words over his shoulder as he moved away.

I collected my sandwich and caught up with Peter again at the drinks station. 'The good news, if you can call it that,' he continued as Diet Coke foamed up over the ice in his cup, 'is that her injury was "through and through".' He set his Coke down on the counter. Using an index finger to illustrate the bullet's trajectory, he said, 'It went in from the back, ricocheted around the side of her skull, just over her left ear, then exited out her forehead.'

I stuck my cup under the iced tea spigot and tried to hold my hand steady as the cup filled and Peter went on to describe Trish's surgery in more detail. 'The surgeons removed fragments of bone and cleared out as much dead brain tissue along the bullet's trajectory as possible. Thankfully, it looks like the bleeding is under control.'

'And the prognosis?' I inquired gently.

'Too soon to tell,' Peter said. 'But the doctors warned that Trish's recovery could be measured not in days or weeks, but in years. Let me get this,' Peter said, reaching for his wallet as the cashier began to ring up my meal.

Too depressed, I didn't argue.

A few minutes later, seated across from my neighbor at a table in a quiet corner, Peter said, 'By some miracle, the bullet didn't cross the midline into the other hemisphere, so it's only the left side of Trish's brain that's damaged. If it had . . . well, I'd rather not think about that.'

A sudden flashback made me shudder. Trish, sitting next to me, staring straight through the windshield. Trish saying, 'Fashion models can be as young as thirteen,' then swiveling in her seat to face me. 'Can you imagine how easily you could exploit . . .' Just as the bullet plowed through the passenger side window.

That sudden sideways swivel could have saved Trish's life.

Peter picked up his sandwich with both hands, took a bite and chewed appreciatively. 'God, that's good.'

To calm my roiling stomach, I nibbled on a few potato chips, then took a sip of iced tea before starting in on my sandwich which, like Peter's, turned out to be delicious.

'I have to ask,' I said after several bites.

Peter glanced up from the banana he was peeling, one eyebrow raised.

'Where the hell did you vanish to last Thursday? When you didn't show up for the dinner party, we were worried half to death. And why didn't you call?'

His face flushed. 'It's a long story.'

'I'm sure it is, old friend, but there's nowhere I have to be right now.'

'Before I go into that, Hannah, can you answer a question for me?'

I laid my tuna sandwich down on the plate, stared back at him and nodded.

'What were you and Trish doing in the parking lot in front of Trader Joe's?'

SIXTEEN

'Trish called me on Friday afternoon,' I explained. 'She set up the meeting.'

Peter frowned. 'What did she want to talk to you about?'

'She shared two things with me, Peter. One, that she was involved in a legal case that might soon be filed in federal court, and two, that her real name is Elizabeth Stefano.'

'That's all?'

'We were interrupted,' I said.

My mind churned as I watched Peter toy with the empty banana skin, arranging it on his plate as if the banana were still in it. This man had been our friend for more than a decade, but how well did I know him, really? I had assumed Peter and Trish had vanished together. But now, as he studied me coolly from across the table, I began to wonder. What if I had been completely wrong? What if *Peter* was the person in trouble with the Feds? What if Trish held incriminating evidence against Peter? What if Trish had fled to Cicero, New York to escape from her own husband? What if *he* . . .?

Play it cool, Hannah. Don't jump to any conclusions, but until you have more information, play it cool.

I picked up my napkin and dabbed mayonnaise off the corners of my mouth. 'Honestly, Peter, when Trish told me her real name wasn't Patricia Young you could have knocked me over with a feather. What the hell is that all about?'

Peter grimaced. 'It was a shock to me, too, Hannah. I'd never known Trish by any other name.'

'The police told you, then?'

He nodded.

'What else did they have to say?'

'They interviewed me for a couple of hours, but they really didn't tell me much.' He closed his eyes for a moment and massaged his temples. 'It's clear to me that they think I know more about what Trish was up to than I do,' he said, without looking up. 'Where Trish is concerned, I'm flying blind.'

'When did you two meet?' I asked, keeping the conversation casual.

'Back in 2000,' he said wistfully. 'She wasn't Patricia Young back then, of course. Her maiden name was Tucker . . . or so I thought.' Peter began to twist his wedding ring – round and round and round – looking so forlorn that I felt my apprehensions begin to slip away. The man badly needed a hug.

'We were both twenty-three,' he continued after a moment. 'I was going through the masters program at St John's College in Santa Fe and she was working at the Sudsy Dawg.'

'As a waitress?'

Peter snorted. 'It sounds like a beer and hot dog joint, doesn't it? But no. Sudsy Dawg was a salon for pampered pets, where the elite and their canines meet. I inherited this big, sloppy, hairy mess of a dog from a student heading off on a Fulbright. I took the beast to the Sudsy Dawg for a makeover and, well, it was love at first sight. For Trish and Snowshoes, that is.' He lifted his cup, chug-a-lugged what remained of his soda, rattled the ice and said, 'I need a refill. Can I get you one?'

I handed him my cup. 'Please.'

While he was gone, I polished off my sandwich, smiling as I tried to picture Trish as a dog groomer. When Peter returned, I asked, 'And you married?'

'In Vegas. 2001. Neither of us had family, so . . .' He shrugged.

I smiled. 'Emily and Dante married in Vegas, too. I hope you and Trish passed on the Elvis impersonator.'

'Little Church of the West,' Peter said with a quiet chuckle. 'Near Mandalay Bay. It was featured in the movie *Viva Las Vegas*, where Elvis marries Ann-Margaret. Does that count?'

I held up three fingers and grinned. 'Three points out of a possible five.'

Peter didn't notice. He seemed miles away, staring past me, his eyes unblinking and unfocused. Leaving him alone with his thoughts, I peeled the plastic wrap off my chocolate chip cookie. I had nibbled around the entire circumference and begun another lap when Peter said, 'Trish will be forty-three on her next birthday.'

'Ah. I remember the day, but not the year,' I said.

'Trish and I always wanted children, but it wasn't in the cards.' His eyes suddenly brimmed. 'Theoretically, it's possible, I suppose. Trish's biological clock is still ticking, but now . . .'

I covered his hand with mine, gave it a reassuring squeeze. 'We had just the one child, Emily, but it wasn't for lack of trying.'

'You know the gold locket Trish always wears?' Peter asked.

I nodded.

'Have you ever seen inside?'

'Yes,' I said, truthfully. I didn't mention that it had been on the occasion of snooping about their master bath. 'A beautiful child.'

'That's Trish as a little girl.' He smiled wistfully. 'Our children might have looked like that.'

I simply stared, too surprised to speak. What had Glory said? The girl in the photo had been Trish's sister. Killed in a car crash, along with her babysitter. Had Glory been mistaken? Was Peter in denial? Or was this one more thing Trish had lied to Peter about?

'You'll need to know how to get a hold of me,' he said at last. He rose slightly on one hip, eased a cell phone out of his back pocket and centered it on the tabletop between us.

'Praise God, it's a miracle!' I said when I recognized it as an iPhone. 'Peter Young dragged kicking and screaming into the twenty-first century.'

He smiled sheepishly. 'The old one was about as useful as an ashtray on a motorcycle. And under the circumstances . . .' His voice trailed off.

'Call me on it,' I instructed, 'then I'll have your number stored in my memory.'

That task accomplished and Peter officially added to my contacts, I asked, 'I'd really love to see Trish. When do you think I'll be able to visit?'

'Give it a few days, Hannah. See if the swelling goes down. That's super critical.'

'Of course.' I set my half-eaten cookie aside, skewered him with my eyes and said, 'I've answered your question about Trader Joe's – now it's your turn, Peter. What the hell happened on Thursday?'

'It all started with a phone call,' he began.

As if hearing Peter calling its name, his cell phone began to vibrate, startling us both. Peter held up an index finger. 'They're paging me,' he said, checking the screen. He squinted. 'Just some insurance form, thank God.' He slipped the phone back into his pocket. 'Gotta go. Call me any time and don't worry if I don't pick up. Cell phones aren't allowed in the inpatient rooms.'

'I expected that. Now, shoo!' I said, flapping my hand. 'You can fill me in later.'

Peter stared at me without speaking for so long that I worried I had mayonnaise on my chin.

'Peter? You OK?'

He sighed. 'I love that woman to the moon and back, no matter what she calls herself.'

'Me, too, Peter. Me, too.' I dredged up a smile from somewhere and pasted it on my face. 'Come stay with us, Peter,' I said after a moment.

'I don't—'

'Don't argue,' I said. 'It's fruitless. We have your cat.'

SEVENTEEN

That evening, over generous portions of Emily's macaroni and cheese, I filled Paul in on my conversation with Peter.

'I've invited him to stay with us,' I said. 'I knew you wouldn't mind. While I was throwing the salad together he texted that he's taking us up on it, starting tomorrow after he gets back from the hospital.'

'Peter? Texting? Are you sure you've got the right Peter?'

I grinned. 'Indeed. He's got an iPhone now. I've sent you his contact card.'

'So, what was Peter's explanation for their sudden departure?'

'That question topped my list, too, but when I first asked him about it, he put me off. He seemed more interested in learning why Trish was meeting *me*, treating it almost like a kind of betrayal.' I speared a tomato wedge and used it to mop up the cheese sauce remaining on my plate. 'But you know what?' I said, waving the tomato for emphasis. 'I have a feeling Peter genuinely doesn't know what it's all about. By the time lunch was over, I came to believe him when he said he'd never known Trish by any other name. It sounds like Trish's life began, for Peter at least, when he walked into that Sudsy Dawg in Santa Fe.'

'Well, she must have come from somewhere,' Paul said, stating the obvious. 'People don't rise up out of cabbage patches as fully-formed twenty-three-year-olds.'

'Thank you, Dr Einstein,' I said. 'But, seriously. After dinner I'm going to do a deep dive into Miss Elizabeth Stefano. If she even existed.'

Paul stood, shoving his chair back. He picked up his empty plate and reached for mine. 'Go on now. I'll do the dishes.'

'Thank you.' I gathered up the dirty silverware, carried it over and dumped it in the sink.

Paul glanced up from slotting plates in the dishwasher. 'If you need to consult, I'll be in the living room grading papers.'

'And binge-watching *Bosch*?'

'That, too,' he said with a grin.

My earlier, fruitless search for Elizabeth Stefano had encompassed the world at large. Armed with more information, including a possible date range, I could limit my queries to places I thought she might have lived: Santa Fe, New Mexico for sure and, remembering what Emily had suggested about the magnet of family and friends, Cicero in Onondaga County, New York.

I discovered Elizabeth Stefanos in Santa Fe – a recent homecoming queen, a firefighter, and somebody's great-grandmother, lovingly memorialized by a photograph of her elaborately carved pink granite headstone. Cicero produced a Cindy, Kathleen, Victoria and even a Salvatore, none of whom fit my criteria, so I expanded my search to all of New York state.

And hit the jackpot.

In August of 1997, according to the Syracuse *Post-Standard*, after an exhaustive search, a woman named Elizabeth Stefano of South Collingwood Avenue, whose body had yet to be recovered, was the presumed victim of a suicide leap off the Hiawatha Bridge over Onondaga Creek.

No details were given, leading me to suspect that locals had been following the case so closely that the reporter didn't feel any need to elaborate.

Using the newspaper's database, I typed in the search terms 'suicide', 'Hiawatha Bridge' and 'Onondaga Creek'.

Elizabeth's suicide had occurred on August tenth, two weeks earlier.

> Syracuse, NY – Syracuse police are searching for a possible suicide victim in Onondaga Creek off the Hiawatha Boulevard bridge near Carousel Center mall.
>
> Police received a call from a woman around one p.m. who reported seeing someone standing alone in the middle of the bridge, according to Sergeant John Knowland.
>
> Police called to the scene found sunglasses, a pair of shoes and a handbag at the bridge. They are searching the water for a body. No one actually witnessed anyone jump off the bridge.
>
> A helicopter flew over the area. The fire department had a boat in the water.
>
> 'This is all precautionary,' Knowland told reporters.
>
> An Onondaga County sheriff's office dive team was getting set to go into the creek and search, Knowland said.

Subsequent updates in the days ahead reported that the victim's car had been found nearby, and that divers had been dispatched to search the creek, but again, no body had been found.

I paged forward, scanning the newspaper for any further mention of the case. By the time I reached early September 1997, there had been such extensive coverage of the death of Diana, Princess of Wales that I nearly missed it – an ad buried in the Personal pages, placed there by Elizabeth's family:

HAVE YOU SEEN ME?
Elizabeth Lorraine Stefano
Born December 23, 1977
'Partings come and hearts are broken,
Loved ones go with words unspoken . . .'
Greatly missed by her loving family:
Father Gregory, Mother Nora and Sister Dicey

There was a photograph, too. A girl on the cusp of womanhood, her ethereal face framed by dark hair cut in a choppy, flipped-out bob with highlighted ends, no doubt inspired by Jennifer Aniston in an early episode of *Friends*. A much younger version of the woman I knew as Trish.

Ponying up via credit card the $2.95 that the paper's online archives required for access to its articles, I printed out a copy of each story, logged off and trotted upstairs to show Paul.

As expected, I found him sitting on the living-room sofa with his feet propped up on the coffee table, student papers piled in his lap and scattered across the sofa next to him.

'You'll never guess.' I shoved his papers gently aside and settled in next to him.

'Then you'll have to tell me.' Paul aimed the remote at the television, shutting Harry and Jed off in mid-high-speed pursuit.

I took a deep breath, let it out slowly. 'Elizabeth Stefano committed suicide in Syracuse, New York on August tenth, 1997. She jumped off a bridge, but as far as I can tell, her body was never found.'

I handed the printouts over and waited silently as Paul read. 'Well, I'll be damned.'

'You must have gotten to the picture,' I said.

He tapped the photo with his index finger. 'That's either Trish or her identical twin.'

'My thoughts exactly. And apparently she has a sister, too. Dicey.'

'An unusual name, Dicey,' Paul mused. 'I wonder what it's short for?'

I shrugged. 'Dunno.'

Paul flipped through the pages a second time, then turned to me and said, 'Well, if Trish is actually the not-so-late Elizabeth Stefano, it appears that somebody finally tracked her down. Somebody wants her to *stay* dead.'

I eased the printouts gently from his hand. 'And we're going to make sure that they don't get their wish.'

EIGHTEEN

Over breakfast the following day, Paul and I agreed on a game plan for Peter's stay. 'Not one word about Elizabeth Stefano's so-called suicide,' I insisted. 'Not until we solve the Mystery of the Vanishing Neighbors.'

Just after ten o'clock, Peter texted that Trish's condition had stabilized: *Swelling gone down!* He'd even mastered the art of using emoticons – the message was punctuated by a big thumbs up.

Peter telephoned at lunchtime to report that doctors had cut back on the drugs in order to test his wife's responses. Even though her eyes weren't tracking and she couldn't speak, Trish responded to commands by wiggling her toes and squeezing a nurse's hand. 'She's able to communicate!' If he had won the Mega-Million Lottery, Peter couldn't have sounded more excited.

'The police delivered me here on Tuesday, so I'm carless,' Peter explained. 'I sure would appreciate a pickup.'

Paul, who had been listening in on speakerphone, volunteered. 'Tell you what. I'll grab your car keys and fetch you in the Honda. It's been sitting in front of Paca House for a week. It could probably use the exercise.'

'Thanks, buddy. Text me when you get here, and I'll come down to meet you.' He sighed slowly, deeply, in apparent relief. 'I've been cat-napping in the chair in Trish's room for two days. I can't tell you how much I'm looking forward to horizontal sleeping.'

'Is there any news from the police?' I asked. 'Do they have any idea who shot her?'

'If they do, they're not sharing it with me,' Peter said, sounding bitter.

'The detective who interviewed me in the ER, Fogarty? She gave me her card. Maybe it's time I gave her a call.'

'I'd appreciate that, Hannah. None of this makes a damn bit of sense.'

Paul nudged my arm. It was time to wrap up.

'Well, plenty of time to talk about that later,' I told Peter. 'See you soon.'

I'd promised Peter a home cooked meal, so I dug one of my famous turkey tetrazzini casseroles out of the freezer and left it on the counter to thaw while I drove down Route 2 to Fresh Market to pick up some broccoli. I visited the dessert bar, too. Who could resist?

When Paul straggled in with Peter around six, they both looked like they'd slept in their clothes. 'Rush hour,' Paul explained when I greeted them in the entrance hall. 'I'd forgotten what it was like.'

Me? I remembered it well. There were things I missed about my job as records manager at Whitworth and Sullivan, but the one-hour commute to Washington, DC – each way – wasn't one of them.

I gave my husband a peck on the cheek. 'A miracle you survived.' Then I turned my attention to our guest. 'Let me show you to your room.'

Peter's pale face suddenly pinked. 'Hannah, are you *sure*? I can always—'

'Of course! I wouldn't have invited you otherwise.' I made a shooing motion in the direction of the staircase. 'You shouldn't have to worry about anything right now except getting up and going to bed. First left at the top of the stairs,' I added, as Peter trudged up the steps ahead of me carrying nothing but a rolled up, hanging toiletry bag. 'You'll have your own bathroom. You can bring the rest of your stuff over later.'

I grabbed some fresh towels from the linen closet and caught up with him.

'This is Emily's old room,' I explained as I delivered the towels. 'We redecorated after she graduated from Bryn Mawr and moved away.'

I'd aimed for a light, airy, beach house vibe, inspired by years of subscribing to *Coastal Living*. With the exception of an antique brass bed, the furniture was no-frills. A quilt in the Honeycomb pattern, hand-pieced in the early 1930s by my grandmother, Lois Mary Smith, added pops of color to the simple blue and white décor.

'This is soothing,' Peter said. 'Don't let me lie down or I may never get up.'

I grinned. 'I'll give you some time to settle in, then we'll see you downstairs where the beer is cold, and the wine comes in both flavors.'

'Thank you, Hannah.'

'Dinner's at seven thirty, so don't be late.'

It seemed odd that we knew so little about Trish's life before she married Peter. I was eager to find out more about Peter's background that evening.

Promptly at seven, Peter appeared, requesting an ice-cold Dogfish Head IPA. He'd tamed his unruly curls by slicking them back with water, but by the time we sat down to eat, a tendril had escaped, trembling adorably over his forehead as he talked, filling us in on his early life.

The son of an unknown father by an alcoholic mother who died when Peter was eight, Peter had been shuffled from one foster home to another before earning a place at Berea College, a tuition-free liberal arts college in eastern Kentucky where he'd majored in history. In lieu of tuition, Berea students work at least ten hours a week. Peter's stint in the college ceramics shop led to a full-time job managing the warehouse of a high-end ceramic art gallery in Santa Fe after graduation.

For the rest of dinner, we'd kept the conversation light, if you call deconstructing the Oriole's dismal 54-108 win-loss record 'light'. I attempted to steer the conversation away from sports – the scientific instrument has yet to be invented that can measure how little I care about football – but, when those dudes got together, it inevitably wandered back in the sports direction. Eventually Peter began waxing eloquent about the pros and cons of playing with juiced balls, so I decided to excuse myself.

'Just going for dessert,' I said as I circled the table, gathering and stacking the dinner plates. 'Hold on to your forks.'

Less than three minutes later, I was back carrying a key lime cheesecake in one hand, three dessert plates in the other and a can of aerosol whipped cream tucked under my arm.

'I like the way your Honda performs,' Paul commented to Peter as I began to cut the pie. 'We may have to replace our Volvo. It's old, and . . . well, Hannah's not sure she wants it back, even after the police are finished with it.'

'I think we should keep the Mercedes,' I said, easing a wedge of pie from the server onto a plate.

'How ya gonna keep 'em down on the farm after they've seen Pay-ree?' Peter quipped.

I stuck my tongue out at him, then grinned. 'Whipped cream?' After he nodded, I decorated his serving with a generous, high-topped squirt, then prepared identical slices for Paul and me.

Paul looked up from his plate and caught my eye.

I nodded.

'So, Peter . . .' Paul began. 'This is what really threw us off. Both you and Trish disappeared, yet your car was still parked on the street.'

'Glory thought you'd been raptured up,' I cut in.

That made Peter laugh. 'Oh, I wish. Better than what actually happened, as it turns out.'

'Tell us about it,' I urged.

'I guess I should start at the beginning, or at least what's the beginning for me.' Peter plucked the wine bottle out of the ice bucket. 'I think this is a two-glasses-of-wine story. May I?'

'Of course,' I said, holding up my glass.

After topping off our glasses, Peter continued. 'Wednesday night, late, Trish gets a call on the landline. I don't know who it's from, but she's upset. Her best friend from high school is dying, she says. Only a few days left to live, she says. She has to go see her right away. So, I say, sure, of course you have to go. Take the car. And Trish says, no, she's too upset to drive. So, I say I'll drive, but she says, no, she's going to take the train.'

'Where was she going?' I asked, although I thought I already knew the answer.

'Syracuse, New York,' Peter said. 'Amtrak actually goes there. Can you believe it?'

'So you drove her to BWI train station?' Paul asked.

Peter nodded. 'At three thirty-six Thursday morning. I thought she was crazy.

'Anyway, around two o'clock that afternoon she calls and says she got in OK and plans to stay for three or four days. I ask about her friend and Trish says she's in a home hospice, weak but not suffering. Trish is staying in the friend's guest room and they're having a nice, quiet visit. Reminiscing.'

'What's the friend's name?' I asked.

Peter screwed up his face. 'Mary something? I'm not sure. Trish had never mentioned her before.' He frowned. 'But then, there seem to be a lot of things Trish never mentioned to me before.'

'Goodrich?' I supplied. 'Mary Goodrich?'

'Yes, that's the name. How the hell did you know?'

I confessed to finding a rental car receipt in the pocket of Trish's hoodie.

'That's odd,' Peter said. 'Trish could certainly rent her own car. Maybe it was an old receipt, something Trish picked up at Mary's during her visit.'

'Maybe,' I said without conviction. 'But why did Trish rent a car in the first place, Peter? Why not come back the way she'd gone up, on the train?'

'We talked about booking a round-trip ticket, but she didn't know how long she'd be staying, so she bought a one-way just to keep flexible.'

'All that last-minute rushing around. I think I understand why your kitchen was such a mess,' Paul mused. 'Not Trish's usual MO, is it?'

'Busted!' Peter said good-naturedly. 'But with Trish out of town, who would be around to complain?'

'Hobie, for one,' I said. 'With you gone, who'd feed him?'

'I topped up his bowl,' Peter said, 'and besides, Glory'd be there.' His face flushed.

'There's one other thing that puzzled me,' I said, rising from my chair. 'I'll be right back.' When I returned to the table, I was carrying Trish's iPhone. I set it on the table next to Peter's placemat. 'Why did Trish leave home without her cell phone?'

'She didn't,' Peter explained. 'That's her old one.' He raised up on one hip, dug into a back pocket and produced his own iPhone, the one he'd showed me at the hospital. 'Earlier this week, we decided to switch carriers. When we went to buy a phone for me, Verizon was having a two-for-the-price-of-one special, too good to pass up, so we upgraded Trish's phone at the same time.'

'But this phone still works,' I said. 'I must have called it a million times. Didn't she want to keep her old number?'

Peter shrugged. 'The salesman said it might take up to twenty-four hours to activate, so she decided to think about it. Frankly, I kinda liked the idea that our phone numbers are just one digit apart. Makes it easier for me to remember.' He picked up Trish's old phone, sandwiched it against his own and slipped them into his hip pocket together. 'She didn't have time to transfer her data before catching the train, either. Now that will have to wait until . . .' He swallowed the words.

'How about her thyroid pills, Peter? Glory found the prescription bottle in the bathroom.'

Peter quirked an eyebrow. 'She's got this little silver pill box, enameled top with flowers? I'm pretty sure she wouldn't leave home without it.'

I was an idiot. Of course.

Paul stabbed the last morsel of cheesecake with his fork, popped it in his mouth, then asked cheerfully, 'So, tell us. How come you didn't show up for the Italian dinner?'

Peter squirmed; even the tips of his ears flushed. 'I forgot.'

As I sat there, slack-jawed, he raised a defensive hand. 'I know, I know. And the last thing Trish said before stepping on the train was "be sure to call Hannah." I can't believe I forgot to let you know.'

'I can't believe it either,' I said. 'You've got a pan of tiramisu big enough to feed the Green Bay Packers taking up half of the refrigerator, and you *forgot*? Where were you, and what the hell were you doing that was so important that you simply forgot?'

Paul gave me the evil eye. 'Hannah!'

'Leave it, Paul,' Peter said. 'Hannah's got every right to be annoyed.'

'Sorry I lost my cool,' I said, smiling sweetly. 'More pie?'

Looking contrite, Peter held out his plate. 'I'll tell you why it slipped my mind. No excuse, just an explanation. Shortly after Trish called from Syracuse, I got an email from a dealer I know in West Virginia. I'd put out word that I was looking for a vintage stove for a client in Epping Forest, and he'd come across a 1930s' Windsor gas range in perfect working condition, no chips in the porcelain, a real beaut. With Trish out of town . . .' He shrugged. 'I decided to drive to West Virginia and take a look.'

'But the car—?'

'Oh, I didn't take the car, Hannah. I took the company van.'

I felt seven kinds of stupid for not remembering the company van, a white, late-model Ford Transit with the appliance store logo painted on the side.

'Did you buy it?' Paul wanted to know.

'What? The stove? You bet. As they say, it'd been previously owned by a little old lady who only drove it to church on Sundays.' He chuckled at his own joke. 'Then I spent most of the weekend poking around Old Central City. Ever been there?'

I shook my head.

'It's part of Huntington now but retains a lot of its old, turn-of-the-last-century charm. A dozen antique stores, give or take. Trish's taste runs more to ultra-modern, so I don't go antiquing as much as I used to. Trish was away, so . . .'

'The mouse decided to play?' Paul quipped.

'Coffee, anyone?' I asked, standing up. 'Regular, decaf, mocha, hazelnut, vanilla – we've got all kinds.'

While I put the Keurig through its paces, Paul and Peter migrated to the living room where gas logs blazed cheerfully in the fireplace.

I decided to wait until Peter finished his Green Mountain Southern Pecan before ruining his evening.

Earlier, I'd slipped the printouts about Elizabeth Stefano's unsolved 'suicide' into a manila folder. Now, I fetched it from the bookshelf where I'd stashed it before dinner. 'I've got something important to show you,' I said, handing it over.

I watched Peter's face as he flipped open the folder and read, his expression changing from curiosity, to surprise and then to disbelief. 'But how do we know it's the same Elizabeth Stefano?'

'Check out the next article,' I said.

Slowly, almost reluctantly, Peter flipped to the following page. He stared at the memorial notice and at Liz's picture for what seemed like an eternity, exploring the image thoughtfully with his finger. 'My God, it *is* Trish. Younger, of course, and oh my God the hairdo, but it's definitely Trish.'

He looked up, his gray eyes wide. 'Twenty years we've been

together. Twenty years. And it turns out I don't know this woman at all.' He blinked rapidly, fighting off tears. 'What the hell do I do now?'

NINETEEN

Every once in a while, you attain perfection. Water the correct temperature, lavender-scented bubbles gently brushing your chin, inflatable pillow tucked behind your neck at precisely the correct angle, sea salt and orchid candle flickering aromatically on top of the vanity. I adjusted the hot water tap to drizzle directly on the mosquito bite blossoming on my ankle – wondering what any self-respecting mosquito would be doing out in mid-November, anyway – ooched down a bit more and closed my eyes.

Someone tapped lightly on the bathroom door.

Keeping my eyes shut, I called out, 'You better be Paul.'

The doorknob rattled. A breath of cool air brushed my cheek as my husband eased into the room and closed the door behind him. 'So, do we believe Peter or not?' Paul asked from his seat on top of the toilet lid.

'Shhhh,' I said. 'Turn on the bathroom fan.'

'Peter's not going to hear you,' Paul said as he reached out and did as he was told. 'Passed his door just now. He's snoring like a freight train.'

Nevertheless, I waited while the vintage exhaust fan revved up to jet plane decibel level before answering. 'Peter certainly has an answer for everything. So either it's the most carefully constructed alibi in the history of the world, or he's telling the truth.'

'Or a mixture of the two,' Paul said. 'We always assumed both Peter and Trish's parents were dead. That neither of them had any living relatives. I can see why they bonded, but I'm finding it hard to believe that Peter knows so little about Trish's life before they met in Santa Fe.

'I know where you went to first grade, how you once got sick eating watermelon, and even about the time your dad took away the car keys when he caught you smoking Marlboros in the bathroom.'

'Yeah,' I said with a grin. 'I still can't believe I thought he couldn't smell the smoke if I stood in the bathtub and blew it out the window. But I had a fairly happy childhood. Nothing to run away from. Nothing that I'm struggling to forget.' I eased the half-drawn shower curtain aside, peeked around it and smiled up at my husband. 'Besides, I'm a chatterbox.'

'There is that,' he said. After a moment's thought, he added, 'You know Trish better than I do, but she always seemed to keep herself to herself.'

'I do,' I agreed, glancing at him sideways from my semi-submerged position. 'And if she's keeping secrets from Peter, too, it must be because she's afraid that knowing about them would put his life in danger, as well as hers.' I paused to turn off the tap with my foot. 'She'd been hiding out for years, so the stress must have been unbearable. Remember what she said to me on the phone?'

'"I just can't do this any more."'

I nodded. 'And until you so rudely interrupted, I was lying here racking my brain, trying to remember something – anything – she might have mentioned about her early life. Until last Monday in the car, there was practically nothing, except a casual mention of having attended a Fleetwood Mac concert at the Hollywood Bowl when' – I drew wet quote marks in the air – 'Stevie still had her voice.'

'But now we know' – Paul ticked them off on his fingers – 'that up until at least August of 1997 Trish had a father, mother and sister and that they lived in the Syracuse, New York area. That six years earlier, when she was fourteen, she quarreled with her mother and ran away to New York City where she worked for a time. And we can also assume she must have gone back home at some point, if only long enough to fake a jump off a bridge into Onondaga Creek.'

'Hmmmm,' I said, dreamily. 'New York City has no lack of bridges for jumping-off purposes. I'll bet she was living at home then.'

'Or visiting, maybe,' Paul said.

'I wish I could talk to her,' I said.

'Everyone does, sweetheart. Especially the police, I imagine.'

'Peter told me Trish was wriggling her toes, responding to commands. Maybe there's *some* way we can communicate,' I said, trying to sound more upbeat than I felt.

'Early days yet, Hannah. Early days. Injured brains can't be rushed.'

'If only she hadn't encrypted the files on that damn flash drive.' I smacked my hand against the surface of the water, causing a mini tidal wave.

'Whatever it is – and it has to be serious if the Feds are involved – it'll all come out eventually,' Paul said reasonably. 'Either when the case is filed in federal court, like Trish expected, or after you turn the flash drive over to that *New York Times* reporter.' He paused to brush water droplets off his chinos. 'You *are* going to do that, aren't you, Hannah?'

'Hey! I've done my homework, buster. I have David Reingold's work address, home address, phone number, email address and Twitter handle all written down. His shoe size, too. If the Feds don't come through, I'm ready to rock and roll. I keep my promises.' I made a shooing motion with my hand, smiling up at him so he'd know I wasn't just being bitchy. 'Now go away and let me think.'

Paul got to his feet. 'Are you going to need the car tomorrow?'

I nodded. 'If you don't mind. I'm planning to visit Trish in the hospital. Peter made sure I got added to her visitors' list.'

'No problem.' He leaned over to caress my shoulder. 'I'm going to bed. Are you coming?'

'As soon as I work a couple of things out,' I said dreamily. 'Ruth believes that hot baths increase the flow of dopamine to your brain, helping you relax and make insightful connections.'

'Your sister is sometimes full of bologna,' he said with a grin.

I studied my fingertips, waggled them in his direction. 'They're not even pruney yet. See?'

Paul twisted the doorknob and stepped halfway out into the hallway. 'I shall leave you to your insightful connections, then. But don't take too long.'

'Why Professor Ives,' I drawled, eyelashes fluttering. 'Someone might assume you have ulterior motives.'

He waggled his eyebrows. 'You might very well think that. I couldn't possibly comment.'

TWENTY

I hadn't needed an alarm clock for years, not since my grueling commuting-to-Washington-during-rush-hour days at Whitworth and Sullivan. Friday morning was no exception. The sun slanting through the branches of the sycamore tree outside the window set shadows dancing across the bedroom walls, informing me more gently than any alarm clock that it was well past seven o'clock.

Coffee beckoned – Paul was already up, his side of the bed vacant but still warm – yet still I lingered, snuggled under the duvet, my mind drifting lazily.

Visiting hours at Shock Trauma didn't begin until noon, so I had the whole morning ahead of me. Coffee first, of course. A boiled egg and toast. Maybe a banana. A little poking around on the Internet, for sure – exactly when did Fleetwood Mac perform at the Hollywood Bowl?

Paul had tuned the kitchen radio to WBAL morning news – the low rumble of voices drifted up from downstairs – and I was moments from crawling out of bed when Paul appeared in the doorway, carrying a mug in each hand. 'Get up, get up, you sleepyhead. Get up, you lazy sinner. We use the sheets for tablecloths, and it's almost time for dinner.'

I had to laugh. 'If you weren't worshiping at my feet, bearing coffee as tribute . . . well, let's just say I'm letting you off easy. Where'd you dredge that up?'

Paul sat on the foot of the bed, handed me a mug. 'Dunno, exactly. Something my mother used to say. An old nursery rhyme, I suppose. Mom was full of 'em.'

'Meanwhile,' I said, 'the queen is in her parlor eating bread and honey.' I took a deep, savory swig of the dark roast brew. 'She's drinking coffee, anyway.'

My mug was half empty before I asked, 'Anything on the news about Trish?'

Paul shook his head. 'No. All they're talking about this morning is former mayor Pugh being indicted for fraud over that children's book scandal.'

'Serves her right,' I grumbled, feeling annoyed that 'Healthy Holly' and her dancing vegetables were receiving more media attention than the attempted murder of my friend, Trish. How was the investigation going? Even Peter didn't seem to know.

'That policewoman who interviewed me at the hospital? Fogarty?' I said after a moment.

Paul straightened. 'What about her?'

'She gave me a card, didn't she? I wonder what I did with it.'

'You gave it to me. After we got home, I pinned it up on the bulletin board in the kitchen.'

'You are a prince.' I smiled at him over the rim of my mug. 'Thank you.'

'You were suffering from a lack of pockets at the time, remember?'

'A lot of what happened that day is a blur,' I confessed, reaching up with my free hand to gingerly finger the sutures on my forehead. 'Which is not necessarily a bad thing.'

'Fogarty gave you her card for a reason, Hannah. Why don't you call her? Ask for a progress report.'

'Top of my to-do list,' I assured him, 'although I don't expect she'll be particularly forthcoming about the investigation. Cops rarely are. Even Dennis is hard to pump for information, and we're related to him.'

'But this time, maybe you have something to bargain with,' Paul suggested, grinning slyly.

'What? The faked suicide?'

'Exactly.'

I snorted. 'Fogarty's probably way ahead of me on that. And if she's not, she ought to turn in her badge.'

Paul patted my duvet-shrouded leg affectionately. 'Aren't we grumpy this morning?'

I touched my wounded forehead again. 'The stitches are driving me nuts. I feel like clawing them out with my fingernails.'

'Itching? That's a good thing. It means you're healing.'

'Thank you, Dr Ives.'

'The doctor also prescribes breakfast,' Paul said, standing up. 'Peter took off early and I've already had mine, but we left you some cut-up strawberries.' At the bedroom door he paused and turned. 'I've got a few things to finish up in the office before I head off to class. You can kick me off the computer any time.'

I set the mug down on the bedside table, threw the covers aside and slid out of bed. 'You must be reading my mind.'

'Ha!' Paul clicked his heels together and saluted. 'I learned a long time ago never to stand between Hannah Ives on a mission and Professor Google.'

According to her business card, Lieutenant Irene Fogarty was assigned to the Major Crimes Unit of the Anne Arundel County Police Department's Criminal Investigation Division, working out of county police headquarters in Millersville. The telephone number on her card connected me with a switchboard. Detective Fogarty wasn't in, the youthful-sounding operator informed me, so I left my name and number and asked for a call back.

Meanwhile, I added a cut-up banana to the strawberries Paul had left out for me and topped them with a quarter cup of muesli and a glob of vanilla yoghurt. I listened to the radio while I ate, but Paul had been right – impeachment hearings, congressional budget impasses, Democratic presidential candidate debates – all the usual suspects. I finished my breakfast, ran another cup of coffee through the Keurig and headed for the basement.

Fleetwood Mac first performed at the Hollywood Bowl on September 1, 1980 on the final lap of their famous worldwide Tusk Tour. In 1980, Trish would have been three years old. The band appeared at the Bowl again on October 24, 1997 and after that, not until May 2013, long after Trish and Peter's move to Annapolis.

October 1997. So, two months after her faked suicide in Syracuse, New York, a woman calling herself Patricia Tucker showed up at a rock concert in Los Angeles, California. But, aside from offering a leisurely stroll through the intense on-and-off-stage relationship between Lindsey Buckingham and Stevie Nicks, the search didn't leave me much smarter than when I logged on fifteen minutes before.

Some people have way too much time on their hands, I mused as I cruised idly through the Hollywood Bowl links. Not only was that evening's complete playlist posted online – with audio links to the individual songs and an option to download the playlist to Spotify – but I learned that 'Don't Stop', the tune that went viral after Bill

Clinton adopted it as his 1992 presidential campaign's theme song, had been the band's first encore.

Too bad Professor Google had no idea what 'Patricia Tucker' had been doing out in California while the band was performing.

Professor Google also failed to enlighten me on what connection a teenage girl like Trish might have had to Lynx, a small potatoes New York City television station some two decades before it became a global media empire. Their Wikipedia entry – fact, date, fact, date – might have been written by a high school student as a term paper assignment. It was times like these that I missed Whitworth and Sullivan and the ready access my job gave me to expensive, subscription-only databases like ProQuest and Factiva.

A few minutes before noon, just as I was emptying the dishwasher and thinking about telephoning her again, Detective Fogarty returned my call.

'Sorry it's taken me so long,' she said, 'but I was waiting for the ballistics report to come in.'

Although I had been alternately pacing the floor and losing consecutive games of Words with Friends to Bobbie on my iPhone, I said breezily, 'That's OK, Detective. What are you able to tell me about that?'

'Ms Young was shot with a Glock 19. We dug two nine-milimeter cartridges out of your Volvo. One was imbedded in the roof and the other lodged in the driver's side door.' She paused. 'You were very lucky, Mrs Ives. It looks like the first bullet struck your friend. The second probably missed you by inches.'

I caught my breath. 'I think I need to sit down.' Knees trembling, I pulled out one of the kitchen chairs and collapsed gratefully into it. When I could speak again, I said, 'What's a Glock 19 exactly?'

'It's a semi-automatic pistol. Used by police, but also popular with gun enthusiasts. Around sixty-five percent of the handguns in the United States are Glocks.'

'Swell,' I said. 'That really narrows down the field.' When Fogarty didn't respond, I said, 'Sorry. I'm feeling a bit edgy today.'

'How's *your* injury?' she inquired, sounding as if she actually cared.

'I get the stitches out on Monday,' I told her. 'And not a minute too soon. They itch like a son-of-a-gun.'

'Means you're healing.'

'So they say.'

'Any word on Mrs Young? I'll be checking with the hospital later today, but maybe you could give me a heads-up?'

'I haven't been able to visit Trish yet, but her husband, Peter Young, is staying with us and, according to Peter, her doctors are cautiously optimistic.'

'Shock Trauma has an awesome track record,' Fogarty said.

'That's what I hear. I'm planning on visiting Trish this afternoon. I haven't seen her since . . .' I paused, struggling to talk around the lump that had suddenly formed in my throat. 'Do you have *any* idea who did this to her?'

'The investigation is moving forward,' Fogarty said. 'That's all I'm prepared to tell you at this time.'

I resisted the urge to hang up on her. Maybe if I kept Fogarty talking, she'd let something slip. 'You asked me to call if I thought of anything that might be helpful,' I said.

'I did. Go on.'

'I'm a little fuzzy about what I told you that day in the ER, Detective, so you'll have to excuse me if I repeat myself.'

'I think I can handle that,' she said.

I took a deep breath. 'Trish said her real name is Elizabeth Stefano and that she ran away to New York City when she was fourteen. I figure that would have been around 1991. She also indicated that she was involved in a case to be filed in New York District Court, as a victim or as a witness, I don't know, but whatever, she was definitely afraid of something,' I rattled on, 'because between the time she left Annapolis on Thursday and when she met me at Trader Joe's on Monday, she'd cut and bleached her hair and rented a car under another name.'

'We found the rental car parked in front of Joanne Fabrics,' Fogarty said, being uncharacteristically candid. 'Tell me how you know about it.'

'Peter told us she rode Amtrak up to Syracuse, but she didn't come back on the train, I know, because I found a rental car receipt in the pocket of the hoodie she was wearing the day she got shot. The ER returned the hoodie to me by mistake.'

'I'll send someone over to pick up the receipt and the hoodie, if that's OK,' she said.

I figured 'no' wasn't the correct answer, so I agreed. But before

I handed the receipt over, I'd be taking a picture of it with my cell phone, that was for sure. As far as I knew, the hoodie was still in the trash can. I wouldn't be sorry to see it go.

'If you found the car,' I said, 'you probably know that it was rented from Budget by someone named Mary Goodrich. We asked Peter about that last night, and he has no idea who this Mary is or why Trish didn't use her own credit card for the rental.'

'We're looking into that,' Fogarty said.

'And you also must know about a woman named Elizabeth Stefano who was missing, presumed drowned after jumping off a bridge in Syracuse, New York.'

'We do. Once you gave us the name, she popped up in NamUs.'

'Name us?' I asked.

'The National Missing and Unidentified Persons System maintained by the Justice Department at the University of North Texas,' she explained. 'Capital N, lowercase AM, capital U little s. NamUs. It's kind of a one-stop shop for missing, unidentified and unclaimed persons cases in the US. Fortunately, New York is one of the states that actually requires NamUs listings.'

I'd never heard of NamUs and told her so. 'Can anyone use the database?'

'That's the whole point,' she said. 'It has private areas exclusively for the use of law enforcement, medical examiners, coroners, forensic professionals et cetera, et cetera, where they can store information like fingerprints, ballistics, DNA data and so on. But the public can use it, too. You can enter information about a missing loved one, or search the database for one. A couple of months ago, a woman in Ohio identified a body we found along the bike trail ten years ago by his tattoos. They'd been described in the database.'

'Wow,' I said. 'I don't always approve of where my tax dollars go, but from what you tell me, I'm all in favor of NamUs.'

'Now, if we could only get our crime labs more generously funded . . .' Fogarty muttered, before hurrying on. 'Sorry, the DNA testing backlog is a sore spot with me. It's improved a bit, but a hundred-and-fifty-day turnaround is still unacceptable.'

'Can you tell me one thing, at least?' I asked, not bothering to keep the pleading out of my voice. 'Do you believe, as I do, that *that* Elizabeth Stefano is *our* Elizabeth Stefano?'

'I'm sorry, Mrs Ives, but this is all part of an ongoing federal investigation. Even if I knew what the task force was up to, I couldn't tell you.'

That figures, but I kept that thought to myself. Nothing to be gained by alienating the police. 'Task force, you said. Does that mean the state and local police are working closely with the Feds?' I asked.

'We are,' she said. 'But I still can't tell you anything.'

I heaved an exaggerated sigh and said, 'Maybe Trish will miraculously open her eyes and tell me the whole story. But until then, one thing I can tell you for sure. Ever since Trish pretended to jump off that bridge in Syracuse, she's been running away from something. It appears that past has caught up with her.'

TWENTY-ONE

S hortly after one-thirty, I pulled up to the curb in front of the hospital and handed the Mercedes over to the same cocky young parking attendant from my previous visit. 'Welcome back,' he said, grinning.

'Wish it were under better circumstances,' I said as I relinquished the car keys.

'Sucks,' he said.

'Yeah,' I said. 'Big time.'

Ten minutes later, I'd checked in, donned my visitor's wristband, snagged a cappuccino from Au Bon Pain and sat down with three other visitors to wait for the next escort up to the shock trauma ward.

'Husband?' The speaker was a frowsy blond dressed in a pink tracksuit, swigging Dr Pepper out of a sixteen-ounce bottle.

'Best friend,' I told her.

'My Terry's an asshole,' she said. 'Got into a tussle with some buddies after the ball game. Tripped over the third rail. Electrocuted hisself.'

I turned sideways to face her. 'Yikes.'

She snorted. 'Drunk, ya know?'

I didn't know, but I nodded sympathetically. 'Is he going to be OK?'

She shrugged. 'If he pulls through, he'll have a bunch of skin grafts to remind him what happens when you can't lay off the vodka.'

I shivered at the thought.

'No insurance neither,' she grumped.

'Gosh,' I said. 'What are you going to do?'

'Not my problem,' she said as she twisted the cap back onto her bottle. 'We're divorced. I'm just here to bring his mom.' She bobbed her head, indicating the older woman dozing in the chair beside her, then proceeded to unleash a litany of her ex-husband's marital transgressions. I was spared from learning more than I ever needed to know about the bleach-blond bitch tending bar at The End Zone by the arrival of our escort, a trim young man – Tony, his nametag said – dressed as neatly as a Mormon missionary.

Five minutes later, the elevator disgorged us on the fourth floor where patients were treated in a series of glassed-in private rooms separated by individual charting alcoves. Nurses and aides, wearing pink scrubs, moved in quiet choreography among them. Because of the glass, patients would never be out of their sight.

The wronged wife and her former mother-in-law trundled down the hallway without further instruction, while Tony turned to me and pointed to a nearby room. 'Mrs Young is in there.'

'Thanks, I see,' I said, having already caught a glimpse of my friend through the window.

Trish slept on a bed of pale green sheets, cool as icebergs, with the head slightly elevated. Peter sat at her bedside in an upholstered chair, reading something on his Kindle.

'Hey, you,' I said as I eased into the room.

Peter set the Kindle aside, ran a hand through his hair and stood, shaking the kinks out of his legs.

'My bionic wife,' he commented, waving an arm that took in the ventilator and a baffling array of computerized monitors. A tangled web of intravenous lines, feeding tubes, nasogastric tubes, drains, and catheters snaked over, under and around her bed, in and out of her body. Nearby, IV bags dangled from a multi-tiered stainless-steel pole, feeding directly into a syringe pump. Extending from the ceiling on mechanical arms, fastened to the walls, affixed to rolling carts, here was the plethora of space-age medical equipment that tethered my friend, Patricia Young, to life.

Whirring, sighing, beeping.

Whirring, sighing, beeping.

'Golly,' I said, feeling overwhelmed.

'Awesome, isn't it?' Peter said. And after a moment, sounding surprisingly cheerful, he added, 'By the way, thanks for breakfast.'

I smiled. 'That was Paul. He's the early bird in the Ives household.' I turned toward the bed. 'How's she doing?' I whispered.

'Stable,' he whispered back. 'And they've cut way back on the sedation. This morning when I touched her shoulder and called her by name, Trish opened her eyes.'

My eyes cut from Trish to Peter and back again. Would Trish have responded if he'd called her Liz? I wondered, but quickly shelved the thought. 'Why don't you go get some lunch?' I said instead. 'I'll sit with her for a while.'

'Don't you—?' he began, but I cut him off.

'I've already eaten, but you can bring me a coffee when you come back. Half and half, one sugar.'

Peter stepped forward and wrapped me in a hug. 'Thank you, Hannah.'

I lay a hand flat on his chest, pushed gently and aimed him towards the doorway. 'Go on now. Take your time. I have nowhere else to be.'

I plopped down in the chair, still warm from Peter's body, and leaned closer to the bed. A bandage wrapped, turban-like, around Trish's head, swooped down on one side to cover her left ear and eyebrow. A mask resembling elaborate scuba gear was strapped to her face, covering her nose and mouth.

For a long time I sat there, watching Trish's chest rise and fall, rise and fall, as the ventilator breathed for her.

Shhhh . . . paah.

Shhhh . . . paah.

Shhhh . . . paah.

'She's doing well, considering.' A nurse appeared out of nowhere, quietly on little cat feet. She checked the settings on a couple of monitors, adjusted the flow on one of the IVs and seemed satisfied. As she turned to go, I asked, 'Is it all right if I hold her hand?'

She smiled. 'Of course it is. And talk to her, too. It helps speed recovery.'

'Do you think Trish will hear me?'

'I believe she will,' the nurse said. She gave my shoulder a gentle pat, and left the room as silently as she had entered.

Trish's right arm was immobilized, heavily bandaged where the IV lines fed into her veins. I dragged the chair to the opposite side of the bed, picked up her left hand and sandwiched it gently between both of my own.

Peter mentioned that Trish had responded to her name. Would she hear me, too? I wondered. 'Trish? Trish?' I said, as I stroked her palm gently with my fingers. 'Trish, it's Hannah.'

Shhhh . . . paah.

Shhhh . . . paah.

'Paul sends his love,' I said. 'He's tied up with classes at the academy, but what else is new,' I babbled on. 'We don't want you to worry about anything except getting better. Peter's staying at our house, so we're keeping him out of trouble.'

I was well launched into a one-sided discussion about the lavender border I planned for the side yard in the spring, and what on earth to do with the black-eyed Susans that were wending their carefree way across the lawn – Trish was a keen gardener – when her fingers began to twitch beneath mine. 'Trish?' I said.

Her hand moved again. Perhaps I hadn't imagined it.

'The lily of the valley is out of control, too,' I continued as I watched her face for any signs of consciousness. 'I'm thinking of pulling it up, especially now, because it's so poisonous and, well, we're taking care of Hobie.'

Her fingers twitched again.

I lifted her hand and carefully folded her fingers around mine. 'Trish? Can you hear me?'

Again, the barest movement.

'Trish, if you can hear me, squeeze my hand again.'

Trish's eyelid quivered and I felt gentle pressure on my hand.

I sat silently for a while, heart racing. When her fingers hadn't moved again for several minutes, I leaned closer and said, 'Trish, if you can hear me, squeeze my hand once now.'

She did.

Halleluiah! It was not an involuntary reflex, then. Although Trish's eyes were still closed, somehow, my words were getting through.

Meanwhile, my mind raced. Should I ask her some yes-or-no questions? Was that medically advisable? Earlier, the nurse had suggested that talking to trauma patients helped speed recovery, so I took that as a green light and said, 'Trish, I need you to squeeze once for yes and twice for no. Can you do that?'

Yes.

Because of her condition, I figured there was little time to waste, so I got right to the point. 'Do you know who shot you?'

Two slow, light but deliberate squeezes. *No.*

'You gave me a flash drive, Trish. I still have it. Do you still want me to give it to that reporter? The one at the *New York Times*?'

A long pause while I held my breath, then a single squeeze, firmer now. *Yes.*

'OK,' I said, wondering if I should go ahead with the questioning or let her rest. And yet . . . a faked suicide? A twenty-year-old woman on the run? Living out west under an assumed name? An apparently clueless husband? I had so many unanswered questions.

Paul had found it hard to believe that Peter knew so little about his wife's early life. And if Peter *were* in the know, I figured I could grill him. I wouldn't need to waste precious time asking Trish about it.

'Trish, please tell me. Does Peter know what's going on?'

Two solid squeezes in quick succession. *No.*

Ah, ha. Still holding Trish's hand, I paused to consider the implications of her answer while breathing in and out, slowly and steadily, in synch with the ventilator.

Shhhh . . . paah.

Shhhh . . . paah.

'One more question before I let you go back to sleep,' I said, leaning closer. 'I have to tell Peter about the flash drive. Is that OK?'

A firm squeeze which I took for *yes* until, a beat later, it was followed by another, far more feeble. Had Trish just told me *no*?

'What flash drive?' somebody growled. I turned my head. Peter Young stood in the doorway, holding a cup of coffee in each hand.

TWENTY-TWO

Using my free hand, I raised a shushing finger to my lips. Peter froze in the doorway, frowning.

'I'll explain in a minute,' I whispered. Stalling for time, I turned my attention back to his wife.

'Trish,' I said, raising my voice. 'Peter's here.'

Her hand stirred; I felt slight pressure. Again, was that a yes? A no? Or just an acknowledgment that she heard me and understood?

Peter closed the distance between us in three long strides, effectively tabling any awkward discussion about a flash drive. 'My God, Hannah. Is she awake?'

'She seems to be. I was holding her hand, droning on about gardening and suddenly she squeezed it.' I smiled up at him. 'Maybe that's Trish's way of saying "Oh, do shut up about the day lilies, already!".'

Peter beamed. 'I step out for a minute, and look what happens. What did I miss?' In his excitement, he'd forgotten about the coffee. One go-cup tipped dangerously sideways, dribbling coffee onto the tile floor.

'Forget the coffee and sit down,' I said, rising from the chair and moving to one side, but keeping a light hold on Trish's hand as if afraid of breaking the connection. Peter unburdened himself of the go-cups and assumed my place at Trish's bedside. 'Over to you,' I said, easing Trish's hand from mine to his. 'She can definitely hear us,' I said, my voice trembling. 'And I'm pretty sure she's processing what we're saying.'

'Trish, sweetheart,' Peter said, leaning in, clasping her hand to his chest, his voice soft, soothing. 'Can you hear me?'

He started, drew a quick breath.

'She's been squeezing once for yes and twice for no,' I explained when I saw him flinch. 'Did she just answer you?'

Peter stared at me, eyes wide. 'What? You . . . Oh, my God, yes. She said "yes!".' Turning immediately back to his wife, he asked,

'Darling, are you in any pain?' After a moment, looking more relaxed than I had seen him in days, he told me that Trish had indicated no. 'That's a relief,' he continued. 'They've got her loaded up to the eyeballs with pain meds, but with all these damn attachments . . .' His voice trailed off. 'They've even got an oximeter clamped to her toe like a giant clothespin,' he said, gesturing vaguely to the sheet-covered mound at the foot of Trish's bed. 'That's got to ache. How can I be sure she's comfortable if she isn't able to talk?'

'I wanted to ask her—' I began, but I was interrupted by the sudden appearance of a nurse wearing a dark blue sweater over her pink scrubs. A photo ID identifying her as Ruthie Mack – NURSE swung from a lanyard draped around her neck. Wispy, light-brown tendrils escaped from the containment of the bandana – decorated with familiar cartoon characters – wrapped around her hair.

'Is everything all right?' she asked, making a beeline for one of the machines that monitored her patient's vitals.

'All right? I'll say,' Peter chirped. 'Trish is awake, at least we think so.'

The nurse smiled. 'Her heart rate spiked a bit, so I thought I'd better see what was going on.'

'Is she OK?' Peter asked, sounding worried. 'Nothing's wrong?'

'Everything looks fine.' Ruthie smiled reassuringly. 'Heart rate and oxygen levels well within normal range.' She turned her attention to the IVs, flicked her finger twice against one of the drips, then, seemingly satisfied, she said, 'You say she's awake?'

Peter explained about one-for-yes, two-for-no.

'That's really remarkable,' she said with a calmness born of long experience. 'I'll be sure to let Dr Mayhew know,' she added, referring to the neurosurgeon who had performed the operating-table miracle on Trish. 'He indicated he'd be stopping by in an hour or so to check on your wife. He wants to talk to you, too, so if you're planning on leaving—'

'Hell, no, I'm not going anywhere. And if I need to step out for a moment, just send me a text.' He shot a sideways glance at me. I took the hint.

'Either Peter or I will be here until visiting hours are over,' I confirmed.

The nurse nodded, then shooed us to one side so she could bustle around Trish's bed, checking the IVs and drains, straightening the sheets, smoothing the covers. She logged onto a portable bedside computer, typed in some notes, then said, 'We're being told to prepare your wife for an MRI, either later today or early tomorrow, so it might be a good idea to let her get a bit of rest now. OK?'

From a corner near the opaquely shaded floor-to-ceiling windows Peter pouted but nodded in agreement.

I loitered near the doorway while Ruthie worked. Gnawing on my thumbnail, I worried about how much to tell Peter about the flash drive. Trish's answer to my question had been inconclusive. Ordinarily, I'd ask myself what *I* would do in the same situation, but Trish had shared only a handful of facts, so how could I know exactly what her situation was? *Trust your vibes*, sister Ruth would say. *Energy doesn't lie*. I hoped she was right.

I worried, too, about Trish's upcoming MRI. MRI machines are installed in dedicated areas of the hospital, often far from the patient wards. There, technicians slide patients' bodies into a long, narrow, claustrophobic tube and bombard them with radio waves. 'How . . .' I began. 'Trish is on a ventilator – all those monitors. How on earth do they—?'

'No need to worry,' Ruthie explained. 'We use transport ventilators. We've done it a few times before.' She indicated the cups of coffee that Peter had abandoned on Trish's rolling, bedside tray. 'Your coffee's probably getting cold, Mr Young. Why don't you take a quick break while I finish up in here?'

Peter nodded agreeably, snagged both cups and handed one of them to me as we scooted out of the room into the corridor. My eyes flicked right then left as if checking for traffic. 'Where to?'

'If we leave the floor, we'll have to go through the whole rigmarole with the escort again,' Peter said. 'Follow me.'

With me close on his heels, Peter turned left, heading back the way we had come earlier in the day. He mashed a balled fist lightly against a wall-mounted push plate and the double doors swung away, spitting us out into the elevator vestibule. There was no place to sit, so I leaned against the wall, half-perched on the handicap handrail. Peter stood nearby, sipping his coffee. His eyes narrowed. 'OK, spill. What's this about a flash drive?'

'What? No word of thanks?' I gently scolded, stalling for time. Peter flushed. 'Sorry. Everything seems totally surreal. That one-for-yes and two-for-no business is totally brilliant, even though it's straight out of a daytime soap. What made you think of it?'

I shrugged. 'Watched too many movies on the Hallmark channel, I suppose.'

'Well, I have to admit it's a real breakthrough. Trish couldn't talk even if she wanted to with that ventilator taking up all the real estate in her airway. But once she's able to breathe on her own . . .'

I reached out and touched his arm. 'It's hard, I know, to live with such uncertainty, but it was comforting for me to know Trish is still *in* there, working as hard as she can to get *out*.'

'Your mouth to God's ears,' Peter said.

'Amen, brother,' I said. After a quiet moment, I asked, 'Are you finished with your coffee? I could get rid of the cups.'

Peter surrendered his empty cup. 'Thanks.'

I had just returned from a successful search for a trash can when Peter said, 'Now, about that flash drive.'

I could no longer put him off. I took a deep, steadying breath and – trusting my gut – told him everything.

As the details of what Trish told me in the car unfolded, I watched Peter's face morph from curiosity to puzzlement to . . . what? Anger?

'I don't understand this at all, Hannah. If what's on that drive is so goddamn important, why did Trish give the flash drive to *you* and not to me? I'm her husband, for heaven's sake. You're just, just . . .'

'Chopped liver?' I said.

'That's not what I meant, and you know it,' he snapped.

'What *did* you mean, Peter?' I asked, trying not to feel wounded.

He wagged his head. 'I simply don't understand why Trish didn't trust me.'

'I don't think it's a matter of trust,' I said. 'I think she was trying to protect you.'

'Protect *me*? From what?'

'Isn't it obvious?' I said, jerking my thumb in the direction of Trish's room.

Suddenly, Peter – stoic, rock solid, cool as a cucumber Peter – began to weep. His arms dangled loosely at his sides while tears flowed unchecked down his cheeks, dripping onto his polo shirt.

I stepped closer, but he raised a hand, palm out, warning me off. He'd been leaning with his back against the wall. Sobbing openly now, he collapsed like a hot-air balloon, gradually sliding down the wall until he was sitting on the floor where he rested his forehead on top of his bent knees.

Feeling powerless in the face of such overwhelming grief, I sat down cross-legged on the floor next to him, leaned my head back against the wall and waited.

'You know what?' I said rhetorically, when his sobbing subsided and the worst seemed to be over. 'I'm *sure* she would have told you about that flash drive. She just happened to reach me first.'

Scrabbling in my handbag, I unearthed a travel pack of tissues that had last seen daylight on a red-eye flight home from Denver. I handed it over.

Peter extracted a tissue and used it to wipe his eyes, then gave his nose a good, honking blow. 'That *Times* guy you just mentioned?'

'What about him?' I said.

'When you deliver that drive to the *Times*,' he sniffed, 'I'm going with you.'

And suddenly, everything just felt . . . right.

'I'd appreciate the company, Peter,' I said, bumping his arm playfully. 'Your car or mine?'

TWENTY-THREE

Nearly two weeks had crawled by since Trish had been wounded. One evening before dinner, Peter reported that she was breathing on her own for short periods of time. Her doctors planned a transfer to the University of Maryland rehab hospital just as soon as they weaned her off the ventilator. There, undergoing extensive therapy, she'd learn how to eat, talk and walk again.

Peter, rumpled and looking exhausted, had joined me in the kitchen, where I'd spent the better part of the afternoon putting together a Salade Niçoise using tuna steaks – grilled not canned. Prep time forty-five minutes, *Bon Appétit* had claimed. Liars.

Before Peter even asked, I handed him a glass of wine. *(Pairs well with Chardonnay.)* 'She couldn't be in better hands,' I said.

'It just kills me,' he said after downing half the glass, 'that she has to relearn how to *swallow*. Honest to God, if we ever find out who did this to her, I'll tear him apart with my bare hands.'

'Can I watch?' Paul wanted to know, popping in suddenly from the basement.

'I'll sell tickets,' I said.

Peter snorted and helped himself to more wine. 'What would I do without you guys?'

'You'd muddle through, old man,' Paul said, snitching a green bean from the bowl where I'd left them to marinate. 'But you wouldn't be eating half so well.'

'Peter's been bringing me up to date on Trish,' I told my husband. 'She'll be going to rehab up at UM.' I rapped the last of three hardboiled eggs against the countertop, leaned over the sink and began peeling off the shell. (*Use quail eggs for an upmarket vibe!*) As if.

Speaking over my shoulder, I said, 'I know that hospital well, Peter. Until a couple of years ago, it was called Kernans.'

'That's right. I remember. You were visiting that guy who was sitting next to you when the Metro crashed.'

I nodded. 'Nicholas Aupry.'

'Whatever happened to Nicholas?' Peter asked.

'Last time I talked to his mother, Nick was working at the Applied Physics Lab in Laurel. Something to do with ionized rare earths. Way above my pay grade.' I wiped my hands dry on a paper towel. 'To hear Lilith talk, he's the world's foremost authority on energy efficient light bulbs.

'He still walks with a cane,' I continued as I rinsed purple fingerling potatoes in a colander. (*Dial up the color!*) 'Maybe for the rest of his life, but, honestly, if you could have seen him after the crash . . .' I shuddered at the memory. 'It was a miracle he survived.'

'Hannah, I was thinking. What about Nick's father, John Chandler?'

I knew immediately where Paul was heading with his question. John Chandler, host of the popular CNN television program, *To the Limit*, was Nicholas Aupry's biological father. When I first ran into John and his breathtaking, heart-quickening, million-dollar smile, he'd been a prime-time commentator for Lynx News, working out of their Washington, DC headquarters.

I'd been popping into the Naval Academy library off and on for a couple of days, taking advantage of their access to reference databases, searching for hints of any improprieties that might shed light on what happened to Trish. I learned that, by and large, Lynx and its many subsidiaries were poor corporate citizens, donating less than one tenth of one percent of their pre-tax profits to charity, while creative accountants devoted their energy to manipulating existing tax laws to minimize the company's tax liability. Other than charges of age discrimination in a case involving a female news anchor, and a plagiarism lawsuit that resulted in the ouster of a veteran reporter, nothing stood out – certainly nothing that would capture the attention of a United States attorney in the Southern District of New York. Selfish, shifty, a bit sleazy, but not criminals.

'If anybody has background information on what might be going on with Lynx,' Paul was saying when I tuned back in, 'it would be John Chandler. He spent years working for the network.'

'I thought about that,' I said, 'but Chandler's first and foremost a reporter. I promised Trish that I'd give the information to Reingold at the *Times*. She was firm about that. I can't just call up Chandler, tell him I want to pick his brains and then give the story – which for all I know may be a blockbuster – to somebody else.'

'I see your point, but the man owes you. If you hadn't gone searching for his long-lost son after that Metro crash, if you hadn't tracked down the owner of those love letters, he might never have reunited with Lilith Chaloux.'

'Lilith would probably still have a house, too,' I sniffed, 'instead of a blackened hulk.' After a moment, I added, 'Let me think about it.'

Lifting the platter with both hands (*Makes an eye-popping centerpiece!*), I turned my salade composée over to Paul. 'Now, go sit down, you two. Dinner is served.'

Over the previous week and a half we'd all been paying close attention to the nightly news which had so far failed to produce reports of any indictments. But the clock hadn't run out yet. I had four more days – until Tuesday – before I'd have to keep the promise I made to Trish – twice – that I'd find that reporter and turn the flash drive over.

As late as that morning, I still hadn't figured out how best to do it. It wasn't 1940, after all, and I was no Katherine Hepburn in *Woman of the Year*. I couldn't simply waltz into the *New York Times* newsroom and announce, 'Oh, boy, do I have a scoop for you' and expect them to drop everything. Besides, Reingold was a busy reporter. He might be off on assignment, dressed in cammies, tracking members of the Sinaloa drug cartel through the rain forests of Guatemala or something.

In the end, it turned out to be surprisingly simple. I sent Reingold an email, and by late afternoon I had a reply.

'I got in touch with Reingold, Peter,' I said as Paul began to clear our plates away. 'If nothing happens at the courthouse between now and then, we have an appointment this coming Tuesday. Eleven thirty.'

Peter straightened. 'Damn. What did you tell him?'

'Not much. Just that I had some information that might interest him.' Seeing the look of panic on his face, I added, keeping my voice steady, 'I can always cancel.'

'I don't want you to think I'm dragging my feet, but . . . I have to be honest with you. I'm afraid whoever did this to Trish will come back and finish the job.'

'If I can stick an oar in,' Paul said, 'it seems to me that once the information is with the Feds and out of Trish's hands, there would be no great need to silence her.'

'And she told me she'd already turned over the originals,' I reminded him.

'Sure,' Peter said. 'But do *they* know that? Whoever they are.'

'But even if Trish were still in the crosshairs,' I said, 'I can think of few places safer than the shock trauma ward. Even *I* couldn't get in without special clearance, and I was claiming to be her sister.'

I let Peter chew that over while I ducked out to the kitchen in search of dessert. I came back armed with a half-gallon of rum raisin ice cream, three bowls and an idea.

'I've decided to touch base with John Chandler,' I said. 'It's Friday night and he's likely to be spending the weekend with Lilith. If not . . .' I shrugged. 'No harm done.'

'What will you say?'

I waggled my eyebrows. 'Listen and learn, ducklings. Listen and learn.'

*   *   *

Around eight thirty, at her art studio near Cambridge on Maryland's eastern shore, Lilith picked up her phone. 'You sound out of breath,' I said.

'I was sitting out on the dock with Zan,' she said, calling him by his Czech nickname. John Chandler had been born Alexander Svíčkář. Impossible to pronounce and harder to spell, a journalism professor had recommended a change if the kid ever wanted to make the big time in broadcasting.

'I'm glad Zan's there,' I said. 'But isn't it a little late in the season for dock sitting? You must be freezing your buns off.'

Lilith giggled. 'No worries. I found a spectacular clay chiminea at a local craft fair. Dwight built a pad out of river rock and installed it at the T-head in front of that Adirondack bench you might remember.'

Dwight was Dwight Heberling of Heberling & Son Construction. Dwight and Rusty had done the renovations to Our Song, the eighteenth-century holiday cottage we'd bought on Chiconnesick Creek outside of Elizabethtown. Elizabethtown was about an hour's drive south of Woolford where Lilith had had her home, until an arsonist burned it to the ground.

'Dwight's done a fabulous job,' Lilith continued, as if reading my mind. 'I can't thank you enough for the recommendation. The new house is smaller and oriented more towards the creek. Quite modern, which upset some of the locals, but what the hell, we went ahead with it anyway. Our architect is simply brilliant, but you need the patience of Job to work with him. When he made a last-minute alteration to the truss design, it's a wonder Dwight didn't chuck him into the creek.' She laughed. 'I can't wait for you to see it.'

'We've already closed up the cottage for the winter,' I explained. 'Will your house be finished by spring? I'll look forward to stopping by on our way south.'

'It better be,' she said. 'I'm getting tired of sleeping on a futon.'

When she inquired, I brought Lilith up to date on my family, segueing as smoothly as possible from junior soccer, to Spa Paradiso, to our dinner club and, finally, to our missing neighbor.

'When she reappeared,' I told Lilith, 'she explained that her disappearance had something to do with Lynx Media Corp. If Zan is available, I'd like to pick his brain about Lynx.'

Mercifully, Lilith didn't ask why Trish couldn't tell me herself.

Rather, she clunked the receiver down and summoned John
Chandler to the phone.

'Sorry to interrupt your evening,' I said when he came on the
line.

'Always good to hear from you, Hannah,' he said. 'How can I
help?'

'I need to ask you something, but I can't tell you why I want to
know.'

'I'm listening.'

'I have a friend—' I began.

Zan chuckled. 'Where have I heard that before?'

'I'm serious!'

'OK,' he said, trying to temper the amusement evident in his
voice.

'So, this neighbor disappeared for about five days,' I began,
without naming names. 'And when she came back, she was totally
freaked out. Said something had happened in the past, and it had
to do with Lynx. Now, this woman's been married for more than
twenty years,' I barreled on, 'and her husband hasn't a clue what's
going on, so whatever scared her spitless must have happened in
the 1990s. Based on what I know about her background, most likely
in New York City.'

'How old is this woman?' Zan asked.

'Now? She's forty-three.'

'Why don't you just ask her?' Zan asked logically.

'She's won't talk about it,' I said. 'Not even to her husband. But
I'd really like to help, so I thought I'd call you for . . .' I paused,
trying to think of the term journalists used. 'For deep background
about Lynx.'

This made him laugh. 'OK.' I could hear steady breathing as he
paused, apparently to organize his thoughts. 'How far back do you
want me to go?'

'Start at the beginning,' I said.

Zan cleared his throat. 'It's pretty complicated, so I'll just hit the
high spots. Lynx started out in the late 1980s as Lynx Television
Group, marketing themselves as an alternative to Fox and CNN.
They targeted a demographic somewhere in the middle, policy-wise:
more conservative than CNN, more liberal than Fox. They started
buying up local television stations in major cities. New York,

Chicago, LA, Washington, DC. New York City was one of the first, I believe. Lynx8. In those days, it was news, weather, traffic and sports and they didn't even broadcast twenty-four/seven.'

'The good old days,' I said, grabbing a napkin and making frantic writing motions in the air until Paul handed me a pencil. 'Lynx8 was in DC, too.'

'Right. They tried to keep to the existing channel numbering scheme wherever possible. Before long, they started cutting deals with up-and-coming cable companies so they could get their fingers into smaller markets, and LynxNet was born. To give credit where credit is due, there was some innovative programming going on around then, too. They pioneered game and reality shows, but hit the jackpot big time with that fantasy series called *The Ninety-Sixth Thesis* . . . remember that?'

'How could I forget? Chloe was eight. Life was not worth living without a Raven Foster doll, but every toy store in the world was sold out weeks before Christmas. Raven was available only from scalpers on the Internet. I did score an obsidian blaster for my grandson, though, so I wasn't a total failure in the grandmother department.'

Zan snorted. 'God, what rubbish! Anyway, it didn't take Lynx long to realize that rather than buying programs from Hollywood studios, they could simply acquire a studio or two and churn out programs themselves. So, there you have it! NewsLynx, SportsLynx, BizLynx, KidLynx, ShopLynx, the Lynx Movie Channel . . .' His voice trailed off.

'Who was in charge back in, say '91, '92?' I asked, pencil poised over a napkin now ragged and littered with notes.

'Top level management, you mean?' Without waiting for an answer, he said, 'It's always been owned by Granville Conners, and the board is top-heavy with his blood-sucking progeny, some more competent than others. There's a plethora of CEOs, EVPs, and chiefs of this, that, and the other, the odd former politician . . .' He paused. 'Check out their website, Hannah. It'll all be laid out in their annual report.'

'That's now,' I reminded him. 'How about back then?'

'Other than family there's been a pretty steady turnover among top-level management. They come, shake things up, stay a few years to make their mark, then move on. I'm remembering that Calvin

Bishop was running Lynx8 in New York before he was put in charge of Lynx Entertainment. You might have read his book, *Lynxed Up*.'

'I must have missed that one,' I said, wondering if I could pick it up now for ninety-nine cents on Kindle.

'But, listen. From what you've told me, your friend was young then, what, eighteen, nineteen?'

'Thereabouts.'

'There would have been hundreds of people working for Lynx8 in New York City back then. Tight schedules, irregular hours. The nineties club scene. Wild. Anything could have happened.' He paused. 'Ever watch *Mad Men*?'

'First three seasons,' I said. 'Up until Betty finally divorces Don.'

Zan chuckled. 'Don cheats on Betty with Midge, Roger cheats on Mona with Joan, Peggy sleeps with Pete. Nowadays it's all Times Up and #MeToo, but back then . . .' He paused, and I could almost visualize the good-old-boy-so-what-ya-gonna-do shoulder shrug. 'Don't get me wrong, I'm not condoning that kind of behavior, but back then, that's just the way things got done in the entertainment business.'

And you should know. John Chandler had cheated on his wife with Lilith Chaloux. For years. The guy was a card-carrying expert in the field. I bit my tongue.

'My advice?' he continued. 'Talk to her. I'm betting she ran into somebody she used to know and the trauma, whatever it was, came rushing back.'

I stole a glance at Peter, hesitated for a fraction of a second, then came out with it anyway. 'Rape did spring to my mind, Mr Chandler, especially since she didn't confide in her husband.'

He grunted softly. 'I was imbedded with the 101st Airborne in Kunar. I had flashbacks for years after what went down at Barawara Kalay, but PTSD isn't limited to what happens on the battlefield, I can tell you that for sure.'

'Thanks, Mr Chandler, you've given me a lot to think about.'

'If anything else occurs to me . . . does Lilith have your number?'

'She does.'

'Good luck with your friend,' he said. 'Always good to hear from you, Hannah.'

*　*　*

'Jesus,' Peter said after I'd hung up the phone. 'Do you really think Trish might have been raped?'

'It's just a theory. And, if so, it's only part of the story. A couple of months ago, the governor extended the statute of limitations for prosecuting rape in New York state, up from five to twenty years.'

'That's good, isn't it?'

'For most victims, this is great news, yes. But whatever happened to Trish happened more than twenty years ago, so the new law doesn't apply. But even if Trish's case did fall inside the statute of limitations, the law says it would have to be tried in civil court.' I shook my head. 'No, whatever Trish is involved in is a federal issue, so it can't be rape.'

Peter drooped. 'I can't sit at Trish's bedside and ask her yes-or-no questions while she fades in and out of consciousness. Rape! Jesus.'

'You could, but this is what we're going to do. We're taking that flash drive to Reingold on Tuesday and even if we have to stage a sit-in, we won't leave his office until he tells us what's on it.'

For the first time that evening, Peter's face brightened. 'Sounds like a plan.'

TWENTY-FOUR

Keyed up and fidgety, Peter insisted on driving into DC. 'I have no idea where I'm going,' he admitted. 'But I'm a quick learner.'

Once we reached downtown, following my directions, he steered the Honda straight down New York Avenue, veered right onto Eye Street and pulled into a Colonial Parking garage just off 17th Street near Farragut Square. After self-parking deep on one of the lower levels, we discovered that the elevator was out of order. Five minutes later, mumbling curse words under our breath, we emerged, dazed and blinking, onto the northwest corner of sunny Farragut Square Park.

'That-a-way,' I said, pointing out the walk that cut kitty-corner across the park. Although it was only eleven fifteen, park benches were beginning to fill with office workers carrying brown bag lunches or takeaway containers from one of the restaurants, fast food joints or gypsy food trucks that ringed the park.

'Who's the dude?' Peter asked as we circled the central statue that gave the park its name.

'David Farragut,' I explained. 'The first admiral of the US Navy.' As we circumnavigated the statue, I said, 'The sculptor was a woman . . . sculptress, I mean. It's unusual in that it was cast from the bronze propellers of a sloop of war steamer and not from captured enemy canons.'

Although they didn't share an entrance, I didn't realize until after we exited Farragut Square that the *New York Times* occupied the seventh floor of the same building that housed the famous Army and Navy Club, whose far more elegant entrance directly overlooked the park. The Italian renaissance-style building – now a members-only boutique hotel – had been founded in 1885 by a handful of Mexican and Civil War veterans. It housed a 25,000-volume library, an extensive collection of military art and was home, it is said, to the first daiquiri served in the United States.

Channeling my inner tour guide, I pointed this out.

'Who needs Wikipedia when I have you?' Peter said with a grin.

'Nerves,' I said, fingering the flash drive, deep in the pocket of my coat. 'If I keep talking, it helps me relax.

'Paul and I attended a wedding here once,' I told Peter as we stood in front of the club, gawking. Cheerful baskets of chrysanthemums decorated iron railings under windows that stood tall and proud, wearing green awnings like bonnets. 'I remember an impressive wall of framed *Time Magazine* covers featuring prominent members. It's a mixed bag, politically speaking. Charles Lindbergh, Chester Nimitz, George Patton, Ted Kennedy, Ken Starr, Ollie North, John Glenn . . .' We rounded the corner onto Eye Street where I added, 'But I suspect you're more interested in the daiquiris.'

Peter turned to me and smiled. 'How did you guess?'

'At the 1912 dedication, or so the story goes, a Major General Humphrey arrived late, galloped up the steps of the building on horseback and rode straight into the bar, where he joined fellow club members for pitchers of daiquiris.'

'Hooah! Those army guys really know how to party,' Peter said, laughing, as he held the door open for me.

In contrast to the club, we entered the building through a comparatively non-descript entrance on the Eye Street side and rode the elevator – thankfully in service – up to the seventh floor. 'We're here to see David Reingold,' I told the receptionist. 'He's expecting us.'

After a two-minute wait, David appeared. I'd looked him up on the Internet, so I recognized him at once. The dark-brown hair, cut short on the sides, floppy on top, the hint of a goatee. He had a few more strands of gray than when his mugshot had been taken, but who doesn't? A single gold stud decorated his left ear.

After the introductions, Reingold led us, bobbing and weaving, through the busy newsroom, a vast space that took the term 'open-concept' to its logical conclusion. Desks sat row upon row, cheek to cheek, each hosting at least one, more often two, iMac computers. Some desks were piled so high with printouts that I wondered how the reporters who worked there could even see their screens. Television monitors tuned to CNN, MSNBC, Fox, Lynx and Bloomberg descended from the ceiling, which, even if their sound had been turned on, couldn't have been heard over the *clackety-clack-clack* of computer keys or the low murmur of voices talking to sources on their phones.

Cables and wires snaked everywhere. *New York Times* reporters were as hooked up to each other and to the outside world as Trish Young was to life support.

'This will give us a little privacy,' Reingold commented, opening the door of a small, glassed-in conference room and ushering us inside. 'Please, take a seat,' he said, as he closed the door behind us.

'So, how can I help you?' he asked, settling into a chair at the head of the table.

I chose the chair to his left, rested my forearms on the table and folded my hands. 'Perhaps you remember reading about a woman who was shot in her car at the Annapolis Mall?'

He considered me over the tops of his tented fingers. 'When was that?'

'Two weeks ago,' Peter chimed in from a seat to Reingold's right.

'Sorry, I apologize, but I was on assignment at the Pentagon. What can you tell me about it?' he said, leaning forward with apparent interest.

'The victim is Patricia Young, and I was in the car with her when it happened. This is Peter Young, Trish's husband.'

I paused, waiting for a reaction. Reingold said nothing at first, then raised an eyebrow. 'Is she going to be OK, your wife?'

'A long road ahead, but we're cautiously optimistic,' Peter said. 'Baltimore's shock trauma center deserves a whole sheet of gold stars.'

'Good, that's good,' Reingold said, nodding. 'Go on.'

'Before Trish was shot, she gave me this flash drive.' I reached into the pocket of my jacket, pulled out the drive and laid it on the table directly in front of me. 'Trish and Peter have been our friends and neighbors for more than ten years,' I explained, resting my fingers lightly on the drive. 'That's why she decided to confide in me, I suppose. She wanted to make sure this information got into the right hands. Into *your* hands. Trish told me that something big was about to go down in federal court. I was supposed to wait to hear about it, and if nothing happened, I was to bring this information to you.'

'Trish didn't trust the Feds,' Peter added.

'She named me specifically?' Reingold asked.

'She did. Said it was your work on that international adoption scam that impressed her.'

'This conversation is in confidence, right?' Peter said, keeping his voice low. 'You'll protect our identity?'

'Goes without saying, but I'll say it anyway. We always protect our sources.'

So, starting from the evening Trish ran away, I told the reporter everything I knew. As I talked, Peter slid photocopies of the newspaper articles about Elizabeth's suicide and even the rental car receipt across the table.

'But here's the real evidence,' I said, shoving the flash drive several inches in his direction.

Reingold stared at the drive, but didn't touch it. 'What's on it?'

'All I know is that it's big and has something to do with Lynx Media Corporation.' I paused, watching his face. 'It's encrypted.'

Reingold opened his mouth to say something, then apparently thought better of it. 'Naturally we looked at the files,' I confessed. 'Who wouldn't? We're pretty sure she used PGP and the private *Times* key posted to your website to encrypt the files.'

Reingold's head bobbed. 'Ah.'

'So, only the *Times* can decipher it,' Peter said.

'We've decided to give it to you on one condition,' I said, even though he didn't strike me as a man who welcomed conditions being placed on his work.

He frowned, and I worried that we'd lost him. 'What's that?' he said.

'You tell us what's on it.'

'I don't know—' he began, but I cut him off.

'That's the deal.' I kept my fingers on the flash drive, as if I intended to take it back, but I was hoping he wouldn't call my bluff.

Journalistic curiosity apparently won out. Reingold rapped the table twice with his knuckles, swept the drive into his palm, stood and said, 'OK. No promises, but let's have a look. Come with me.'

We followed the reporter to a cubicle at the far side of the news-room, tucked into a corner by a window overlooking 17th Street. Reingold appropriated two chairs from colleagues he said were out on assignment and invited us to sit down. As we watched, he donned a pair of wire-rim glasses, slid the flash drive into a slot on the back of his Mac, and clicked a few keys. We waited a long minute until he said, 'Yeah. She used our key. Give me a minute.'

Hardly daring to breathe, we waited.

'What's on it?' Peter asked as a series of folders gradually populated Reingold's monitor. 'Are they photographs? Documents? What?'

'They're photographs,' Reingold said, peering at the screen more closely.

'Compromising?' I wondered aloud.

'Taken by some two-bit dick with a hidden camera showing some hot-shot politician banging an intern?' Peter blurted.

I scowled at him until he squirmed. *Don't be a douche.*

'No, no,' Reingold said, seemingly unfazed. 'Not photos in the usual sense. These are photos of documents,' he explained, addressing Peter directly. 'I think your wife laid the pages out and took pictures of them with her cell phone.' He waggled a finger. 'You can even see the edges of a floral bedspread.'

'That's not one of ours,' Peter said, referring to the bedspread. 'I don't know where she took that picture.'

As we watched, Reingold leaned closer, adjusted his glasses. He opened another file, moused over the magnifying glass icon and clicked twice to enlarge the image. From where I was sitting, we appeared to be looking at the photo of an appointment book, like the one Karen James used at her salon before her son swooped in and computerized everything. Or, it could be an old-fashioned teacher's lesson planner. Days were laid out in grids, hour by hour. No year appeared at the top of the page, but there were only so many years when June the third fell on a Monday. An Internet search would quickly sort that out.

I was leaning close to the reporter, studying the document, so I nearly went deaf when Reingold said, 'Holy shit!'

Peter jumped. 'What?'

'Just a minute.' Reingold closed the document he was reviewing, opened another file and enlarged it until the writing grew so large that even I could read it. 'Names,' he said, 'and times.' He tapped the screen with a long, slim finger. 'This column here appears to be clients. Whoever was keeping the book even wrote down their phone numbers.' He looked up, his dark eyes enormous behind his glasses. 'You said this had something to do with the Lynx Network?'

'That's what Trish told me.'

He turned to Peter. 'Where are the originals?'

'According to Trish, the FBI has them. That's her backup,' Peter added. 'As I said before, she didn't entirely trust the Feds.'

I didn't mention that I'd backed up the flash drive, too, both to my hard drive and to the Cloud.

I flapped a hand, indicating the screen. 'So, what do you think?'

'It's definitely an appointment book.' He swiveled in his chair, turning his back to the screen. 'Women's names. Guy's names. Phone numbers. What does that suggest to you?'

Peter, suddenly nose to nose with Reingold, rumbled, 'You think my wife was a *hooker*?'

'Not necessarily,' Reingold said more calmly than I would have under the same circumstances. He fingered the photocopy of the newspaper article about Liz's suicide. 'Back in 1997. She was young, right? Naïve? It's possible she got caught up in something, realized what was going on and got out of Dodge, taking this with her.'

'Are we talking about a Mayflower Madam?' I asked, referring to a socialite who, years before, had famously pleaded guilty to running an exclusive call girl service. 'And Trish ran away with her Little Black Book?'

'If so,' Reingold said, 'this stuff is dynamite. And in the wrong hands . . .'

'Trish would never stoop to blackmail,' Peter said defensively. 'This was her insurance policy.'

'It will take a while to cross check all those names and telephone numbers. It's been twenty-some years, so people will have died, and I imagine most of the phone numbers will lead to landlines. We'll have to weed out the podiatrists and the dog-walkers. It's a tedious job, but straightforward. At the end of the day, it's a safe bet there'll be people on the list whose names everyone recognizes. I already noticed a name that could be someone I know,' he said, jerking a thumb at the monitor. 'A Wall Street banker. Pompous shit. Married, of course.' He paused. 'So, you'll let me have it?'

I looked at Peter, who nodded mutely.

Reingold ejected the flash drive and physically removed it from the slot. Waving it like a trophy, he said, 'This is probably why somebody shot your wife.'

'Everything was OK as long as Trish was dead,' Peter murmured. 'But once somebody found out she wasn't . . .'

I finished the sentence for him. 'Dead girls don't talk.'

TWENTY-FIVE

The Alexander sisters have a reputation for inclusive, easy-going, all-day Thanksgiving celebrations. We – Ruth, Georgina and I – host on a three-year rotation. Come one, come all, we say, welcoming husbands, children, grandchildren, our father and his girlfriend, as well as assorted strays – midshipmen, grad school students and interns fresh out of law school – all stranded far from home over the holiday weekend. Peter was already spoken for by the Collins' or we would have dragged him along with us, too.

Typically, guests begin to arrive around ten to visit, watch TV or play games, snacking and drinking off and on for hours, until

dinner is served around four. Folks generally begin to waddle home
after dessert, but the hostess can't haul her exhausted ass into bed
until the last football game winds up just before midnight.

'Let me host this year,' Ruth had said in October. 'I know it's
not my turn, but so soon after Scott . . .'

'No way,' Georgina had insisted. 'It'll take my mind off things.'

Her first Thanksgiving without Scott could have been difficult
for her, but she surprised me by making light of the effort. 'Are
you kidding? I did all the work while Scott vegged out in front of
the television watching football with the boys. And he was hopeless
at carving the turkey.'

Everyone could attest to that. My late brother-in-law didn't take
well to instruction. Although coached with infinite patience by Ruth's
husband, Hutch – who was so skilled at dissecting a bird that he
should have trained as a brain surgeon – Scott, invariably using a
dull knife, tended to hack the drumsticks from the thighs with all
the precision of a Mafia hit man. Furthermore – horrors! – he
preferred to cut the breast meat across the grain, which never seemed
like a federal crime to me, but it annoyed the hell out of Georgina.

I stuck up for my late brother-in-law. 'He was an accountant, not
a chef.'

We were down several regulars this year. Under the circumstances,
it was just as well. Daddy planned to spend the holiday in Dallas with
Neelie and her daughter. Although Dylan would grace us with his
presence, his twin, Sean, had taken off for Long Island to meet
his girlfriend, Lacey's, parents for the first time. And Julie, of course,
was busy running a buffalo hunt on the Pine Ridge reservation.

Just before nine thirty on Thanksgiving morning, Paul and I found
a parking spot next to the garbage bins in the alley behind Georgina's
house, wandered across her backyard, and let ourselves in through
the kitchen door. We were carrying a six-pack of beer, two bottles
of Sauvignon Blanc and my famous cheesy broccoli-cauliflower
casserole, still hot, swaddled in a beach towel.

We found Georgina in her spacious kitchen, wrestling stuffing
into the rear end of a twenty-four-pound turkey. With one hand
grasping a drumstick and the other up to her wrist inside the bird,
she acknowledged our arrival by a jerk of her head that sent damp,
apricot tendrils dancing. 'Put it down on the counter over there,'
she said, referring, I presumed, to the casserole. 'Dylan's in the rec

room putting ice in a tub, or at least that's what he's supposed to be doing, but he's brought a friend along from Hopkins, so who knows what they're up to down there.'

'Dylan's got a girlfriend?' I asked as I relieved myself of the casserole.

My sister shrugged. 'It's a guy. They play ultimate Frisbee together.'

Paul hefted the cooler bag. 'I'll take these down then. Keep 'em cold.'

'While you're downstairs, will you dig the green beans out of the freezer?'

'Green bean casserole?' Paul asked, looking hopeful. I'd noticed two cans of cream of mushroom soup and a bag of crunchy French-fried onions on the countertop, so I suspected that the traditional dish would be on the menu.

Georgina grinned. 'Does the sun rise in the east?'

'I'll fetch the green beans,' I said, eager to greet my nephew and meet his friend.

We found the two young men sprawled on the faux leather sofa, Nikes propped up on the coffee table, watching the Macy's Thanksgiving Day Parade. We appeared just as a Sponge Bob Square Pants balloon floated across the sixty-five-inch television screen in my sisters' home theater.

'Hey, there,' I called out.

Dylan sprang to his feet, looking guilty. 'Hi, Aunt Hannah.'

I crossed the room and gave him a hug. 'The ice tub better be ready or there'll be hell to pay.'

'All set,' he said, gesturing with his thumb. 'Behind the bar.'

The guy sitting next to Dylan rose to his feet, smiling shyly, long arms dangling. Like my nephew, he wore jeans and a long-sleeved Johns Hopkins T-shirt, although he'd pulled a fleece hoodie over his.

'This is my friend, Lorenzo Ramos,' Dylan said. 'From El Paso.'

Lorenzo's hand shot out, so I gave it a welcoming squeeze.

'They call me Enzo.' Dylan's friend considered me with startling blue eyes. His dark hair was gathered into a curly topknot and secured with a fat, red rubber band at the crown of his head.

'My sister tells me you and Dylan are teammates,' I said. 'Ultimate Frisbee? Perhaps you can explain it to me sometime.'

'It's like soccer, except with a Frisbee instead of a ball,' Enzo said. 'No net, though, just an end zone like you have in football.'

'Flying disk,' Dylan corrected. 'Wham-o owns the Frisbee trademark, so officially the sport's called Ultimate.'

'Ultimate Frisbee, ultimate tag, ultimate paintball . . . what next? Ultimate Quidditch?'

'Don't scoff, Auntie. We're petitioning for the sport to be accepted at the 2028 Olympic games in Los Angeles.'

'I'm not scoffing!' I said. 'I'm impressed. I can never catch a Frisbee.'

Rapid thumping overhead – it had to be my grandson Timmy – indicated the arrival of Emily and her brood. Timmy lived life at full speed. His older brother, Jake, moved more deliberately. Chloe had travelled home from college with one of her friends.

'I'd better go see what they're up to,' I said, pointing a finger at the ceiling. 'Welcome to our crazy family, Enzo. And don't forget the green beans,' I called back to Paul from the foot of the narrow staircase.

With one foot on the bottom step, I paused.

Somebody was on the way down.

Well, OK then.

Zachary Curtis's picture hadn't done him justice. If anything, he was better looking in person. Georgina's boyfriend had the raw-boned good looks of a Texas rancher. His salt-and-pepper hair was trimmed close on the sides, but he styled it longer and swept back on top, the kind of cut that wouldn't get messed up if he had to put on a Stetson. Laugh lines crinkled at the corners of his gray eyes. 'I come bearing gifts,' he said, meeting up with me at the bottom of the staircase, carrying a six-pack of beer in each hand. He hefted them, like a pair of dumbbells, and his biceps rippled, straining the fabric of his sweater.

'You must be Hannah. Gina told me you might be down here.'

It took me a moment to figure out he meant Georgina. My sister had never gone by a nickname.

'And you must be Zack. We can shake hands later.' I grinned, pointing at the beer. 'Paul's manning the bar over there. The beer will be safe with him.'

Zack's presence at our family dinner caught me completely by surprise. Typical Georgina: easier to apologize than to ask permission.

I was feeling annoyed, but didn't want to spoil the holiday, or take it out on the poor guy. Zack had obviously been given a heads-up on our holiday dress code. He was dressed – similar to Paul – in slim jeans and a turtleneck sweater. In Zack's case, though, the sweater was lush, black and cashmere. I resisted the urge to reach out and pet it.

'I'll look forward to talking to you later, Zack, but right now, I think my services are required upstairs.'

I found Georgina in the kitchen. Somehow, the turkey had been shoehorned into the oven and she had transferred her attention to a ten-pound bag of potatoes.

'Let me do that,' I insisted as she upended the bag over the sink.

Georgina swept a strand of hair off her forehead with the back of her hand. 'Thanks,' she said.

I rummaged in the cutlery drawer until I found the potato peeler. 'He's very handsome.' I aimed the potato peeler at my sister like a gun. 'Gina.'

Georgina flushed.

'I thought you hated nicknames,' I said, turning my attention to the spuds.

'I do, but at least it's better than Georgie Girl or' – she mimed sticking a finger down her throat – 'Gigi.'

'Children can be cruel,' I said, recalling playground taunts of 'Hannah Banana'.

'Why didn't you tell us Zack was coming?' I asked after a few beats of silence.

She side-stepped the question. 'We both thought it was time to meet my family.'

I cocked an eyebrow. 'Aren't you rushing things a bit?'

My sister skewered me with a death ray. 'I'm pushing fifty, Hannah. I have four kids, three of them grown and flown. And Scott. Is. Dead.'

'I get it,' I said. 'If not now, when? Right?'

'Hannah, look. I honestly think I'm in love with the guy.'

Ah ha, I thought. No wonder Georgina had insisted on hosting the dinner this year.

'Well, he better not break your heart, that's all I can say.' I brandished the potato peeler like a lethal weapon. 'Or, the son-of-a-gun will never know what hit him.'

*   *   *

Five hours later, in the extended intermission between dinner and dessert, feeling mellow – the natural result of combining wine with the tryptophan in the turkey – I trailed lazily after Emily into the sunroom. My daughter and I melted into the pluffy cushions of the floral chintz-covered sofa. The windows overlooked the backyard where Timmy, Jake and Colin had ditched the jackets their mothers had insisted they wear and were giving the trampoline a workout, with Dylan and Enzo serving as spotters.

'Wish I had their energy,' I mused as the boys leapt and tumbled like acrobats in training for *Cirque du Soleil*.

'Don't we all?' Emily said. 'We're getting FreshChef deliveries three times a week now, but I'm such a slug I can barely muster the energy to unpack the box, let alone prepare it.'

'Put the boys to work,' I suggested. 'They're old enough.'

'Oh, I do, I do,' Emily said. 'Jake is pretty good at it, too, once he learned the difference between onions, scallions, garlic and shallots.'

As we watched, sipping quietly, the budding chef took a solo turn, executing a perfect aerial with a half twist, landing on his knees before rebounding into the stratosphere.

'That's my boy,' Emily said with a grin. 'Olympic-bound.'

'He can go with Dylan,' I said. 'On the Ultimate Frisbee team.'

'Call me when the Olympic Committee approves croquet,' Emily said, gazing at her son with affection. 'Jeesh! After all the mashed potatoes he put away, I'm surprised he doesn't puke.'

'The resilience of youth,' I said, lifting my glass. 'I'm surprised they aren't freezing to death without their jackets.'

'There you are!' Paul wandered into the sunroom, closely followed by Emily's husband, Dante. 'Who wants to take a tour around the block?' Paul asked, patting his stomach. 'I need to walk off the turkey. Make room for pie.'

Although the day was sunny and delightfully crisp, I wasn't in the mood for a stroll. Thankfully, before I could answer, my cell phone sprang to life in the pocket of my skirt, vibrating impatiently against my thigh. 'Sorry,' I said as I retrieved the phone and checked the display.

Emily glared. 'Excuse me? Why do you still have your iPhone when everyone else is required to "Deposit All Electronic Devices" in a basket at the door?' She drew quote marks in the air with her fingers.

'I promised Peter I'd be on call,' I said, shading the truth just a tad. 'Trish has been taken off the ventilator, but it's still a bit of let's wait and see.'

Emily's face softened. 'Sorry, Mom. But that actually sounds promising.'

'So far so good,' I said.

The call originated from a 680 area code. Definitely not Peter, and with Emily watching with a critical eye, I let the call go to voicemail.

'Where's Peter spending the holiday?' Emily asked.

'Right now, he's with Trish,' I said, easing the phone back into my pocket. 'Later tonight he'll head back to Annapolis. Bobbie and Ed Collins have invited him for dinner.'

'Lucky him! Bobbie's cherry pies are legend.'

'Speaking of pies,' I said, leaping to my feet. 'It's time to get ours out of the oven. Stay put,' I ordered as I hurried out of the room, hoping that no one would notice my detour to the powder room tucked under the stairway. Once inside, with the door locked behind me, I sat on the toilet lid and checked my voicemail.

The message was simple. 'OK. Let's talk. In person, not on the phone.'

The caller was Mary Goodrich.

After excusing the children from the table, the adults lingered over second helpings of pie, sipping glasses of brandy, cognac, malt whiskey and Bailey's Irish Cream. Feeling tipsy, and a bit giddy over the message from Mary, I opted for club soda with lime.

During dinner, Zack had been relatively quiet, but his eyes had been active, following our conversation, probably sizing us up. After Georgina excused herself to supervise the washing up, Zack turned to me and said, 'Gina told me about your friend, Trish. How's she doing?'

'I was about to ask the same thing,' Ruth said.

So, blow by blow, I brought the whole table up to date. 'I finally tracked down the woman who rented the car Trish drove to Annapolis,' I announced.

'Doesn't surprise me one bit, Nancy Drew,' Hutch said. 'How'd you do it?'

'I found the rental car receipt, so a couple of days ago, I telephoned the rental car agency. I identified myself as Mary Goodrich and reminded the agent that they were supposed to email me a copy of the receipt for the rental, but it still hadn't come. Then I asked them if they'd sent it to my home or my work email account. To my utter astonishment, she read the address right off to me. Tah dah!' I crowed, raising both arms overhead in triumph.

'And you emailed her?' Dylan asked.

'Of course, she did, silly,' Ruth chided.

Undaunted, Dylan pressed on. 'Well?'

'I left my mobile number on the email and she just got back to me.'

'Wait a minute!' Paul snapped to attention. Until that moment, he'd clearly zoned out. 'You said this Mary person got back to you?'

'About an hour ago, Paul.' I bopped him with my napkin.

'What did she say?' he wanted to know.

'She's willing to talk to me, but says it has to be in person.'

'Where does she live, Mary?' Ruth wondered.

'The number's in a six eight zero area code. I looked it up. Could be anywhere in the Syracuse area.'

Paul touched my arm. 'So, did you answer? What did you say?'

'Nothing, yet, my dear. It's not like I can just pop over to her house with a fresh-baked batch of cookies for a good, old-fashioned chinwag.' I paused, my thoughts spinning. 'As far as I can tell, the investigation is going nowhere, so nothing's tying me down here. It's frustrating, but every time I check in with Detective Fogarty, I get the runaround.' After a moment, I added, 'It's a long drive.'

'That's never stopped you before,' Ruth said. 'Oregon? Colorado? South Dakota?'

Ruth had a point.

'I have half a mind to—' I began.

'Half a mind to what?' Georgina asked, joining the conversation in midstream. She stood behind Zack's chair, rested her hands lightly on his shoulders.

'I was just saying that the cops seem to be doing diddly-squat—'

Paul said, 'It's not that they aren't working on the case, sweetheart, it's just that they aren't talking to *you* about it.'

I felt my face grow hot. 'Well, they ought to be talking to me! It's not like I'm not involved!'

'Why drive?' Zack surprised me by saying. 'I can fly you there.'

'You have a plane?'

'A Piper Aztec. Two props. It's a honey.'

Standing behind him, Georgina flushed. 'It's really nice. It seats five passengers.'

'You've been up in it, Georgina?' Ruth asked.

Georgina nodded.

'Where did you go?' I asked, genuinely curious.

'Oh, up and around,' Zack said modestly.

'Zack flew me down to Carthage, North Carolina for the day. There's an awesome barbeque place there called the Pik N Pig smack dab in the middle of an airfield.' Georgina glowed. The jet-setting life was seductive.

'Here's the deal,' Zack said. 'Georgina and I are flying up to Niagara-on-the-Lake for a couple of days. No problem to drop Hannah off in Syracuse and pick her up on the way back.'

I stole a sideways glance at Paul. We'd been married long enough that he could read my mind. 'When are we talking about?'

'Next week,' Zack replied. 'Weather depending, of course.'

'You'll come, too, of course,' Georgina said, addressing Paul. 'Plenty of room.'

'Sorry, Georgina, but that's the worst possible time for me.' He turned to Zack. 'Georgina probably told you I teach at the Naval Academy. Exams are coming up in the next couple of weeks. But I encourage Hannah to take you up on your offer. Besides,' he added, with a smile aimed at me, 'if I don't, I'll be sleeping with the cat.'

'You already sleep with the cat,' I teased. 'I feed him,' I added, addressing the table, 'but the ungrateful beast prefers Paul's side of the bed over mine.'

Paul raised his glass. 'As a famous Naval Academy graduate, Robert A. Heinlein once said, "Women and cats will do as they please, and men and dogs should relax and get used to the idea."'

TWENTY-SIX

As luck would have it, our departure was scratched by a blizzard that roared in from the Pacific northwest, gathering strength as it swept across the Great Lakes, burying the northeast in several feet of snow. Temperatures plummeted across the region. Flights were cancelled and children let out of school.

Even before Georgina called with the bad news, I had set my overnight bag aside and begun to fill my days alternating between visiting Trish and playing citizen detective.

On Wednesday, while pounding rain performed a magic disappearing act on the accumulated snow outside her window, I sat at Trish's bedside working on the sweater I was knitting Paul for Christmas.

'Morning, Hannah,' Glory suddenly whispered. 'How's our sweet girl doing today?'

She'd snuck into the room so quietly that I started, sending my cable needle clattering to the floor.

Glory stooped to pick it up. 'Sorry to spook you,' she said, handing the needle back.

'It wasn't you, Glory. I'm always dropping the darn thing.'

'Can't stay for long, I'm afraid. Got to get to the doctor myself,' she said. 'I've got the sugar and my pills have run out.'

Glory, I knew, had been diagnosed with diabetes several years before, but so far, she kept the disease under control with pills, diet and exercise.

Glory wore a leather fanny pack embroidered with tropical flowers strapped around her waist. She reached into it and pulled out an object wrapped in tissue paper. 'I wanted to bring this by. I know Trish would want to have it.'

The gardener peeled the tissue paper aside, revealing the locket that I'd last seen hanging on a hook in the Youngs' bathroom. Glory had removed the chain, replacing it with a small gold safety pin. As I watched, she tiptoed to the opposite side of Trish's bed, bent over and pinned the locket to Trish's hospital gown, directly over her heart. With her hand covering the locket, Glory closed her eyes. Her lips began to move in silent prayer.

I teared right up.

'And all the people say amen!' Glory exclaimed.

'Amen,' I sniffled.

As Glory turned to go, I said, 'How are *you* holding up?'

'Keeping busy, especially now that Peter's back home.'

'I'm glad we could help during such a stressful time, but I think he's more comfortable sleeping in his own bed, don't you?'

'Yes, ma'am, I sure do.' Suddenly, she grinned. 'Glad your keeping that old cat, though. Gives me the willies, hanging round like some jumbie.'

'Jumbie?'

'Like a ghost. He's always watching.'

Two days later, three-hundred and fifty miles south of Syracuse, New York, I arose on a sunny Friday that, according to the weatherman, promised to be relatively warm, with predicted highs in the mid-fifties. I was knocking the top off a soft-boiled egg when Georgina called. 'We have lift-off,' she chirped. 'Can you be here by nine?'

'Here' was Martin State Airport in Middle River, a community about a dozen miles northeast of downtown Baltimore, where Zack kept his plane. 'If I leave now, I can make it. What time does the flight leave?'

'As soon as you get here,' Georgina said.

'Don't I need time to check in and get through Security?'

Georgina giggled. 'Clearly you've never flown private before.'

'Not true! We took a five-seater to the Bahamas when Paul went on sabbatical. Remember? The plane was so small they weighed both the luggage and *me*.'

Georgina snorted. 'Back then, your bag probably weighed more than you did.'

'Chemo does that to you,' I said. 'I don't recommend it as a diet plan.'

'You're a riot,' Georgina said. 'Now get your skinny butt up here.'

It's a fairly straight shot from Annapolis up Interstate 97, through the Baltimore Harbor Tunnel to the Eastern Boulevard exit off 895. Three miles later I steered the battered VW I'd borrowed from my daughter onto Wilson Point Road, a divided, tree-lined highway that skirts the Lockheed-Martin campus and, a short two minutes after that, pulled up to the guardhouse at the airport gate.

'Been expecting you,' the uniformed guard said, giving my battered vehicle the critical eyeball.

'My other car's a Mercedes-Benz,' I said, flashing a disarming grin.

He frowned skeptically, but lifted the barrier and waved me through, directing me to park my heap in one of the spaces to the left of the terminal. I slotted Emily's car between a Tesla and a Cadillac Escalade, like a poor relation.

Martin State Airport terminal was built around 1940 in the Modern Movement style, although what Gropius would have made of the architect's modifications to an otherwise simple design is anyone's guess. It reminded me of a three-tiered wedding cake – if you like butterscotch icing – topped by a control tower instead of a bride and groom.

After dropping my bag off on a rolling luggage cart just inside the door, as Georgina had instructed, I found my sister watching CNN in the Signature Flight lounge, relaxing in a leather recliner, hands wrapped around a cup of coffee.

'Brrrr,' I said, rubbing my hands briskly together. 'I could use some of that coffee right now, if there's time.'

Georgina aimed her cup at an urn sitting on a sideboard by the window, surrounded by all the usual fixings. 'Zack's having the plane fueled up and de-iced. Shouldn't take too long.'

My stomach did a flip flop. 'There's ice on the plane?'

'Just a precaution,' she said pointing toward the sky, 'in case it gets cold up there.'

'Georgina, are you sure—?'

'Chill. Zack has been flying airplanes since he was fourteen,' she said with a comforting smile. 'When they lived at Wright-Patterson, his dad used to take him up in an old Stearman biplane. One day he said, "Son, how would you like to learn to fly this thing?" There isn't a cornfield in Ohio that boy hasn't buzzed.'

'How reassuring,' I said, settling into the recliner next to her, leaning back to engage the footrest. 'Where have you stashed Colin, by the way?' I asked, shifting the Tiffany-style lamp on the table between us so I could see her face. 'Most sixth graders I know are in school today.'

'Dylan,' she said simply. 'He's writing a paper on John Milton and Satan, and before you ask, no, I haven't a clue, except it has something to do with *Paradise Lost* and the Book of Revelations. Dylan jumped at the chance to get away from his housemates for a few days so he could finish it up.'

One could live a long and happy life and never read one word from John Milton, but I decided not to say so. 'Fascinating,' I commented instead.

'It's called War in Heaven, colon, blah-blah, something-or-other.' She waved her hand vaguely. 'At Church of the Falls, I heard enough to last a lifetime about sinners burning in the fiery pits of hell, thank you very much.'

I was saved from making intelligent conversation about apocalyptic visions of the afterlife by Zack's arrival. He opened the door to the lounge, stuck his head in, flashed a toothy grin and announced, 'Ladies, your chariot awaits.'

Zack was dressed in jeans. He'd pulled an off-white V-neck sweater over an open-necked, button-down shirt. A classic bomber jacket and boots completed the ensemble.

Georgina eased gracefully to her feet. When she noticed me struggling to rise from the fully deployed lounger with all the elegance of a woman in her ninth month of pregnancy, she smiled, extended her hand and helped me transition from a horizontal to vertical position.

Once on my feet, I watched Zack leave, appreciating the view. Long-limbed and lean, he strode ahead, dragging the luggage cart behind him. He exchanged pieces of paper with a cheerful redhead named Nancy behind the Signature service desk, saluted, then motioned for us to follow him outside.

Zack's Piper Aztec sat waiting not far from the yawning doors of a massive hangar. While Zack stored our bags in a compartment under the fuselage, a uniformed mechanic helped Georgina climb into the co-pilot's seat, then turned his attention to me. With his hand firmly on my arm, I mounted a step stool, then transferred my weight to the wing of the plane, before easing through an open door and plopping down in the passenger seat directly behind my sister.

'Holy cow!' I said, stroking the leather upholstery, as soft and creamy as French vanilla ice cream.

Zack had completed his pre-flight safety check and had hopped into the pilot's seat. He donned an aviation headset that made him look like a matinee idol, just stepped out of a World War II movie poster. As he helped Georgina with a similar headset, she beamed up at him adoringly. My sister was clearly smitten. 'Fasten your seatbelts,' he instructed. 'Life preservers, should you need one, will be found under your seat.'

Swell, I thought as I reached down, reassuring myself that it was actually there.

As Zack fiddled with the controls, my eyes followed the airport's single runway all the way to where it seemed to vanish into the river. 'Is the runway long enough?' I asked, then quickly added, 'Sorry. That was a dumb question.'

Zack chuckled, toggled a couple of switches, punched a touch screen, then eased forward on the wheel. 'Relax, Hannah,' he said as we taxied away from the hanger. 'It's a longer runway than at Reagan National in DC.'

'No kidding,' I said, relaxing a fraction as he turned the airplane, bringing it to a halt at the head of a runway marked thirty-three in numerals so large they could be read from outer space.

'And the Blue Angels have staged air shows from Martin,' he added. 'They fly F/A-18 Hornets.'

Georgina swiveled in her chair. 'Big-ass jets.'

'Duh!' I shot back. As a decades-long observer of Commissioning Week air shows at the Naval Academy, I didn't need Georgina to explain an F/A-18 Hornet.

Zack began a conversation with the control tower consisting entirely of letters and numbers, so I shut my mouth and sat back, dissolving into the plush leather, feeling like a rock star.

The propellers spun faster, revving up. The plane began to vibrate, quiver, bounce on its wheels, as restive as a racehorse at the gate, in anticipation of take-off. Suddenly, as if shot from a rubber band, the plane surged forward. We taxied down the runway, gathering speed, then lifted up and up and up, flying over waterfront homes and marinas, following the path of Middle River out over the Chesapeake Bay.

Zack banked the plane high and to the right, heading south, making a lazy pass over the double span of the Chesapeake Bay Bridge before looping north again.

'How high will we fly?' I shouted over the roar of the engines as I eyed the complicated control panel, watched the hand of what I assumed was an altimeter inch upwards from zero to point five.

'We cruise at around ten thousand feet,' Zack shouted back. 'Sit back and enjoy the view.'

As he steered the plane around Hart-Miller Island and over the pink-stained ruins of Sparrows Point and its abandoned steel mills, I realized that casual conversation would be impossible over the howl of the engines. Resigned, I leaned back and took Zack's advice, spending the next several hours gazing out the window as the earth below reeled past at 170 miles an hour. Over the farms and bone-brown fields of rural Maryland we flew. Above the russet, snow-dusted patchwork that was central Pennsylvania until it merged with the white blanket of snow that still covered most of New York state.

Over Syracuse, the skies became dotted with clouds like dollops of meringue. In the far distance, when Zack pointed it out, I could see the cold expanse of Oneida Lake, its surface glazed with ice, reflecting the sun like a mirror into my eyes. Even at this altitude, I noticed that the snowplows had been busy. Interstates, highways and most of the suburban streets crisscrossed like glistening black ribbons through the otherwise stark-white landscape.

As Zack prepared us for landing, residential neighborhoods gave way to the scrubby pine forests that surrounded the airport. 'Heading one niner zero for five seven two,' he said as the runway gradually rose to meet us.

'Twenty-eight taxi via echo alpha cross runway three three,' the control tower replied.

The wheels kissed the ground, hopped, squealed against the tarmac.

Safely landed. I texted Paul. *Full report later.* ♥

TWENTY-SEVEN

K yle at Signature Flight Support in Syracuse had arranged for a courtesy car to meet me.

I could get used to this.

Although the main terminal at Hancock International was just a stone's throw across the tarmac, unless I wanted to get run over by a taxiing Airbus A320, I had to rely on the driver to circumnavigate

the airport and drop me off at the airport's rental car area near
baggage claim.

Ten minutes later, I drove away in a sporty red Mustang from
Hertz. It probably never occurred to Kyle that his customers would
deign to drive anything less flashy.

First a Mercedes, now a Mustang. In the car rental department,
I was being spoiled rotten.

I'd reserved a room ahead of time at the Hampton Inn and Suites
near Carrier Circle because, from the map, it looked like a straight
shot from the motel up Country Road 82 to Lakeshore and the
community where Mary Goodrich lived.

I checked in, unpacked, ran a warm washcloth over my face and
a brush through my hair, then hit the road again.

Following my Waze app and the directions Mary emailed – 'if
you get to the overhead power lines you've gone too far' – it took
only twenty minutes before I pulled into her driveway on Snowshoe
Trail, a neighborhood of modest, well-kept, two-story bungalows.
An American flag hung from a stanchion over Mary's garage door,
flapping wildly in the brisk breeze. Keeping my head down, I hurried
up the walk and rang the doorbell.

'I figured the past would catch up with Liz eventually,' Mary
said as she invited me into her living room. 'How did you find me?'

I explained about the rental car receipt. 'And it helps that you
kept your maiden name,' I added, not wanting to fess up to the trick
I had played on the car rental company.

'Would you like some coffee?' she asked.

'If it's no trouble.'

Mary smiled. 'My son gave me a fancy espresso machine last
Christmas. Does everything but wash out the cups and put them
away.'

I followed her into a bright, spotless kitchen where a stainless-
steel coffee maker, equipped with enough levers, dials and pressure
gauges to drive an ocean liner, stood in sharp contrast to 1970s-style
pale aqua cabinets, stark white appliances and a red brick linoleum
floor. It occurred to me as Mary was bustling about, brewing cappuccino, that for a woman in a hospice, dying of cancer, she seemed
in exceptionally good health. Her chestnut curls, abundant
and professionally highlighted, were twisted into an untidy knot and
secured with a red plastic claw.

Perhaps she'd rallied.

'Forgive me for asking,' I said, 'but Peter led me to believe that Trish went to Cicero to spend time with a critically ill high school friend.'

Mary frowned. 'Peter must have misunderstood. It's Liz's father who was dying. Sadly, he passed away two weeks ago Tuesday, so she got here just in time.'

'I'm sorry to hear that,' I said. 'Had he been ill long?'

'COPD and dementia,' she explained. 'He'd been in a care center called Lakeview for a couple of years. It was important to Liz that she saw him before he died.'

'Do you think he recognized her? Did he know she was there?'

'It's hard to say,' Mary replied thoughtfully, 'but Liz certainly thought so. Sugar?'

'Yes, please.'

'Did she visit her mother, too, while she was here?'

'Oh, no, I hardly think so. You're probably thinking it was cruel for Liz to run away like that, without a word, letting everyone believe she was dead. But look, she had to go into hiding, and she knew her mother would never be able to keep it secret, especially if pressure were brought to bear.'

'Brought to bear by whom?' I asked.

'Honestly, I don't know.'

'So, she's still trying to protect her family, then? Her mother, her sister?' I asked as I accepted the cup of coffee. Mary's fancy machine had drawn a heart on top of the cream. Somewhere on the control panel, it probably had a button labeled 'latte art'.

'Liz told me, and I totally believe her, by the way, that I was the only person who knew she hadn't really jumped off that bridge. But we hadn't spoken in years. She always knew where to find me, though. Have a seat,' she said, pointing to the kitchen table, fashionably retro in chrome and red vinyl.

'How was that?' I asked as I sat down.

'A post office box. She'd send me postcards from time to time, and we'd exchanged phone numbers, but I was under strict orders never to use it, except for emergencies.' She shrugged. 'Until her father grew so ill, I never did.'

'Facebook would have been easier,' I mused.

Mary's jaw dropped. 'You're kidding, right? Liz would never

have done Facebook. If you were trying to keep a low profile, would *you* go on Facebook?'

'Of course not,' I said, feeling sorry I mentioned it. 'But she could have set up a fake account, like all these military guys who seem eager to date me.'

'Move over, me, too. Well, she didn't.'

'About her rental car—' I started to say.

'Yeah, even I had to admit that was weird. I was planning on running Liz back and forth from the care center. I didn't mind doing that one bit, you know. But on the day after she got here, Friday, I think it was, something spooked her. As I drove, she kept looking over her shoulder, saying she thought we were being followed. I checked in the rear view and noticed a guy in a maroon car. He looked totally harmless – what kind of hitman wears a ball cap, I ask you? – but I decided to humor her. Drove around for a little bit, entered a bank drive-through by the exit, took a hard right down an alley. Real Cagney and Lacey.' She laughed. 'Either he was just some guy out to pick up some cigarettes and a six-pack, or we lost him.

'Anyway, before we came back here to collect some stuff I'd been keeping for her, since, you know, just before she supposedly jumped, she asked me to take her to Penn-Can. That's where I rented the car for her. She paid me back. In cash. Liz was always good that way. Back in the day, she'd borrow money for lunch when the cafeteria was serving pizza, then toss the bologna and cheese her mom packed in the trash. Pay me back the next day.'

'What were you keeping for her?' I asked.

'It was a box, about so big,' she said, indicating an object about two feet by three feet with her hands. 'There were scrapbooks in it, she said, and diaries. We all kept diaries in those days, with locks and tiny little keys, although I don't know why anybody bothered with the keys. You could open them pretty easily with a bobby pin.'

'Do you know what was in the diaries?' I asked.

Mary shrugged. 'The usual, I suppose. "I saw BT at lunch, he's so dreamy! If he asks Stacey to Homecoming, I'll just die."'

'You didn't read them? If it were me, I'd be dying of curiosity.'

'Liz made me promise not to look inside, so I didn't.'

'I can see why she trusted you with her secret,' I said, selecting one of the cookies that had mysteriously appeared on a small platter between us. 'Do you have any idea why she faked her own death?'

'How much time do you have?' Mary asked.

'As much time as it takes.' I bit into the cookie, chewed thoughtfully, waiting.

Mary stared silently at the cookies, chocolate chip and obviously homemade.

'Mary?'

She looked up. 'Sorry, I was just trying to organize my thoughts. Give me a minute.'

'You can trust me, Mary, I promise. As I explained in my email, Trish is a dear friend. She can't speak for herself right now, so I'm trying to help her husband figure out what the hell is going on. Peter says he is completely in the dark, and I believe him.'

Mary pressed her palms together, almost prayerfully. 'OK. Good. More coffee?'

'Yes, please.' I would be wired, but I wanted to stay alert.

With a shamrock staring up at me from a fresh cup of cappuccino – I must have been right about the latte art – Mary sat down and finally began to talk.

'The first thing you need to know is that when Liz ran away, I ran away with her.' She held up a hand. 'Stupid, I know, but we were only fourteen. What did we know?'

'And you went to New York City. Trish managed to tell me that much.'

'Right. We got a room at the Y and I started waiting tables at Bernie's Kitchen, one of those all-day breakfast places down near the Battery. Liz got a job behind the counter at Izzy's Deli on the Lower East Side. It was all very grown-up and exciting.

'So, one day, this woman comes into Bernie's, hair all Vidal Sassoon, dressed Ann Taylor-ish and professional, and sits down by herself in a booth. Comes back several times a week – always ordering the same thing. I'll never forget: two dots and a dash, eighty-six the toast, a short stack on the side. Says she's new in town, making desserts for a caterer. One day, she asks if I'd like to make some extra money. All I'd have to do is walk around looking pretty and hand out hors d'oeuvres at a party for some bigwigs in Brooklyn. I said, sure, and did she need anyone else, because I had this friend.' Mary paused to come up for air. 'That would be Liz.

'We say OK, so she sends a car to pick us up at the Y. The guy drives to this mansion somewhere on Clinton Street. They'd just rehabbed the place, and it was a house-warming party, I suppose, because the architect was at the party, and the decorator. Tons of rooms, all beiges and tans, leather and twisted metal, chandeliers like geodesic domes. Way too modern for my taste, but you know the guy must be oozing money to afford all that.

'And the kitchen! Shee-it! Stainless steel up the wazoo way before it was fashionable, and a wine cellar that could accommodate the New York Jets. Seriously.'

'Who owned the house, do you remember?'

'Yeah. Guy owned one of the big New York television stations. Cal somebody or other. Super good-looking, I have to say, like that actor in the *West Wing*, what's his name? Rob Lowe?'

Cal. I'd have to check my notes, but hadn't John Chandler mentioned a Calvin Bishop at Lynx in New York?

'Liz and I worked a couple of more parties in the weeks after that, always at Cal's house,' Mary continued.

'What was the woman's name, the one who hired you?'

Mary squeezed her eyes tight, chewed her lower lip. Seconds later, she looked at me and I heard her say, 'Shuh-von.'

'Yvonne?'

'No, it's this weird Irish name.' She spelled it for me. 'S-I-O-H-B-A-N. I don't remember her last name, sorry. It's been a long time.

'Doesn't matter anyway, because shortly after that, all hell broke loose. My dad found out where we were and went all caveman on me. Dragged me home by my hair.' She leaned closer. 'He hired a private detective. Can you believe it?'

I could but didn't say so. At least Emily had waited until she graduated from college before running off to become a travelling groupie for the rock band, *Phish*.

'Once they knew where you were, didn't anyone come looking for Liz?' I asked.

Mary wagged her head. 'Nope. Her parents had pretty much washed their hands of her. To be fair, though, Liz could be a pain in the butt.

'Anyway, she eventually got a job working as an au pair for some fancy-pants lawyer in Greenwich Village. They were sending her to high school, too, so she had access to AOL on the library computers. For a while, that's how Liz and I stayed in touch.'

'Tell me about Dicey,' I asked.

She smiled coyly. 'Liz's baby sister?'

'Is there another one?'

'I suppose you'll find out eventually, so I better tell you. Dicey wasn't Liz's sister. She was her daughter.'

I nearly dropped my coffee cup. 'Her daughter?'

'Yup. Liz never got along with her mother, but when Liz came home pregnant, I have to hand it to her. Mrs Stefano stepped up to the plate. Big time. Whisked Liz away to the Catskills for a few months, came back with a baby. 'Course, I thought Mrs Stefano was old as the hills, but she was probably only thirty-four or thirty-five when Dicey was born. Complicated pregnancy, everybody said, at some hospital upstate, yadda yadda. Nobody suspected that the baby wasn't hers. Nobody.'

'How old is Dicey now?' I asked.

Mary knit her brow. 'Twenty-six, I guess. Maybe twenty-seven.'

'But that means . . .'

'Well, yeah. Liz was sixteen when Dicey was born.'

'And fifteen when—'

Mary snorted. 'Yeah. Sucks. Statutory rape is about the best spin you can put on that.'

'Do you know who the father was?'

'Don't know, and don't care,' she said. 'Somebody she met in New York, obviously. But I always thought it was a good thing that Dicey came along, especially after Liz . . .' She shrugged. 'You know. Dicey was a gift from God, truly. She gave the Stefanos something to live for.'

'Where is she now, Dicey?'

'Girl's super smart. Last I heard, she was working on her PhD at Cornell, but I don't know where she's living.'

'I tried to locate the Stefanos at an address I found for them on South Collingwood in Syracuse, but they must have moved. Do you know where I could find Mrs Stefano now?'

'They used to live in Eastwood, but after Dicey graduated from Smith, they downsized to a condo near Cayuga Lake. I've never been, but they say it's really posh. I have their address in the kitchen somewhere. Let me get it for you.'

When she rose from her chair, I stood up, too. 'While you're looking, could I use the bathroom? I'm getting an urgent message from that second cup of coffee!'

Mary grinned. 'Sure. Down the hall, second door on the right. The tap drips, so make sure it's screwed down tight after you're done.'

On my way to the bathroom, I breezed past what must have been the guest bedroom, screeched to a halt, took two steps backwards and peered in. Mary had furnished the room with a five-piece maple bedroom suite á la 1940 that might have been inherited from a maiden aunt. Curtains of Irish lace hung at the windows, allowing sunshine to flood the room. But what brought me to attention was the four-poster bed and its eye-popping duvet, splashed with enormous sunflowers. Unless everyone in the Syracuse area shopped at the same bath and bedding store, this had to be the room where Trish had laid out her documents in order to photograph them.

When I returned from the bathroom, Mary was back in her chair. 'Here you go.' She waved a folded piece of paper in my direction.

I plucked it from her fingers, then reclaimed my seat. 'Tell me something, Mary. Have the Maryland police contacted you at any point? The FBI?'

'The FBI? Crap, no. Why?'

I explained my frustration about the lack of progress on the investigation into the shooting. 'The Annapolis police are supposed to be working as part of a joint task force with the FBI. If I were running the show and my attempted murder victim had been living for years under an assumed name, I'd want to look into it thoroughly, wouldn't you? Track down the rental car? Dig into her past?'

'Maybe they already know who did it, and they just aren't telling you.'

I mulled that over. 'That's possible, I suppose.'

'You know, I just thought of something,' Mary said.

'What was that?'

'That box of things I'd been saving for Liz? She didn't have it with her when she left.'

'Are you sure?'

'Positive. It was in the trunk of my car, and I helped her transfer it to the rental. But the day she left? When she tossed her overnight bag in, the trunk of the rental was empty.'

I could guess what happened to it, because I'd already checked the Internet. Syracuse didn't have an FBI office, but its agents hung out at the US Attorney's Office there. Somewhere between Mary's house and the care center, Trish had made a pit stop to turn the box over to the Feds.

'There's no way she would have gotten rid of it,' Mary insisted. 'She told me it was her insurance policy.'

'Insurance against what?'

'It was a long time ago, but when she came back to Syracuse, just a few weeks before she supposedly jumped off that bridge . . . that's when she came over to leave the box with me. She was worried that this girl she used to work with had disappeared. To hear Liz talk about it, you'd think the girl had been murdered, but back then, you know what? Girls were coming and going from the city all the time. Like me, for example. There one month, gone the next. I thought Liz was over-reacting and I told her so.

'But she said, "They made Susie disappear, they could do the same to me. I'm not going to make it easy for them."' Mary closed her eyes, took a deep breath, then let it out slowly. 'For a long time, I thought she'd actually done it. Jumped off the bridge, I mean. But she promised me she'd come back for the box. If she planned to kill herself, that doesn't make a damn bit of sense, does it? So then, of course, I thought she'd actually been murdered like this girl, Susie. Then, thank God, Liz sent me a postcard from somewhere in California, so I forgot about all the rest of it.'

Another thought suddenly occurred to me. 'Did you help Liz cut and dye her hair?'

Mary flinched. 'Are you kidding me? No.'

'That's another odd thing, then,' I said. 'Somewhere between Cicero and Annapolis, she turned into a cropped-top blond.'

TWENTY-EIGHT

As Mary had told me, Nora Stefano lived in a modern condo overlooking Lake Cayuga. I'd called ahead, so the security guard was expecting me when I pulled up to the gate at the complex on Saturday morning.

Unlike some of her neighbors, Nora had scored an end unit with an unobstructed view of the lake. I parked in a space marked 'Visitor' and walked up the short flight of steps that led to the door of her unit. Snow still dusted the 'feathers' of the preposterous Thanksgiving turkey wreath woven of grass, twigs, dried leaves and corn husks that decorated the door.

The woman who answered the doorbell did not speak at first, but considered me with blue eyes so faded they might have been bleached by the sun.

'I'm Hannah Ives,' I said. 'I called earlier. To talk to you about your daughter?'

Her eyes narrowed suspiciously. 'Liz? It's been a long time since she died. Did you go to school with her? I don't recognize you.' She raised a dark, neatly drawn eyebrow. 'Perhaps you knew her when she worked in New York?'

'Do you mind if we talk inside?' I said, scraping snow off my boots on the doormat. 'I'm from Maryland and I'm not used to being so cold.'

Nora smiled and stepped aside. 'Of course. Sorry. Come in. Please. You can hang your coat on that hook,' she said, indicating the dark Victorian-style hall tree that dominated the tiny vestibule.

'Thanks, but I think I'll keep it on for a while,' I said as I removed my gloves and tucked them into the pocket of my parka.

'I'll turn up the heat, shall I?' she asked as she led me into the living room.

'Not for me,' I assured her with a smile. 'It's wonderfully toasty in here. I'll be fine.'

Nora sat down in a Queen Ann chair that could have accommodated two women her size and indicated I should sit diagonally across from her on one end of a tufted, rolled-arm sofa. As I settled into the pink velvet upholstery, surveying my surroundings, it became clear that the only thing Nora had downsized in the move was her house. How the movers had managed to manoeuver the massive slant-front secretary or the neo-Renaissance dining room suite through the front door and down the narrow hallway was a mystery I'd have to solve another day.

Bare space, too, was apparently anathema. Nora had decorated the walls with the kind of 'fine art' I associate with cruise ship auctions. She'd cluttered every surface with eclectic arrangements of tchotchkes including, inexplicably, a vase shaped like a woman's roller skate with neon pink wheels that took pride of place on a Bombay chest centered between the two windows. The wax-headed doll staring at me from the windowsill like a Dickensian orphan, glassy-eyed and vacant, would give anyone nightmares.

No wonder Trish's taste ran to clean, minimalistic, Scandinavian décor. The only way to keep most of this stuff dusted would be with a Q-tip.

Nora sat stiffly in her chair, hands folded in her lap, as we silently sized each other up. I figured she was in her early sixties, but she appeared much younger. Her silver hair was cut in a classic A-line bob with pin-straight bangs that met her eyebrows, perfectly framing her face and the no-nonsense, clear-plastic eyeglasses she wore. Except for the tip-tilted nose, I could see little of Trish in Nora. Perhaps Trish had favored her late father.

'So, why are you here?' she asked.

'Mrs Stefano, I'm not sure how to tell you this, but Liz didn't jump off that bridge all those years ago. She's still alive.'

Nora closed her eyes, gasped and pressed a hand, fingers splayed, to her breast. I leapt to my feet, thinking I'd given the woman a heart attack. 'I'm sorry to shock you like that. Can I get you something? A glass of water?'

With her hand still pressed to her chest, she glared up into my face. 'Who *are* you?'

'My name is Hannah. Your daughter and her husband live across the street from me in Annapolis, Maryland.'

She took three deep, steadying breaths, then snapped, 'I don't believe you.'

I reached into my handbag and handed Nora a photograph of the Youngs taken at a Christmas party at our house the previous year. 'This is a picture of the woman I know as Patricia Young, and this is her husband, Peter.'

Nora took the photo from my outstretched fingers and stared at it for what seemed like an eternity, shaking her head gently from side to side. 'That's her. That's my Liz, all grown up and so, so pretty.' Tears spilled over and began to trickle down her cheeks. 'If only . . .' She sobbed. 'If only Greg had lived to see this.'

'I believe he did, Mrs Stefano. Liz found out her father was critically ill and was able to visit him in the care center just a few days before he died.'

'She was really *there*?'

I nodded.

'And I didn't believe him.' She laid the photo in her lap, but kept one hand on it. 'Greg had dementia, so naturally I thought he was hallucinating. "She's back, Nora," he said, "she's back," over and over. "Our Liz came back."'

We sat in silence for a moment, then her head shot up, eyes wide and glistening. 'Wait a minute. How do you know all this?'

'Before she left for Syracuse, Liz told her husband where she was going,' I explained, shading the truth a bit. 'And Peter told me.'

Her gaze suddenly turned icy. 'Why didn't she speak to *me*, then? Why didn't she put her mother's mind at ease, not to mention her daughter's? Oh, sweet baby Jesus, I have to tell Dicey!' Her voice hardened. 'Or does Dicey already know?'

'If she knows, Mrs Stefano, she didn't hear about it from me.'

'So, it wasn't a suicide!' She seemed to droop in her chair. 'But as far as we were concerned, it might as well have been. Disappearing like that, without a word. Dicey was only four. She cried every night for months! What kind of mother does that to her own child?'

'I believe she was protecting Dicey. You and your husband, too,' I said.

I explained to Nora that Liz had been providing evidence to the federal government about a very important case. 'Something happened a long time ago, probably while she was working in New York City. As long as whoever Liz had evidence on believed your daughter was dead, her family would be safe. She even kept her husband, Peter, in the dark.'

'This case you mention, is it over yet?'

'No, not yet.'

'She's still hiding out, then? That's why you're here?'

'In a manner of speaking, yes. Liz was right, you see. For years after her disappearance, she lived under an assumed name, first in California, then in New Mexico before finally settling down in Annapolis with Peter. Liz risked her life by visiting that care center to say goodbye to her father, and I think somebody must have seen her there, and recognized her.'

I reached across the space that divided us and took Nora's hand. 'Somebody shot her, Nora. Somebody shot Liz. She's in intensive care at a Baltimore hospital. She's expected to live,' I added hastily, 'but the doctors can't say if she'll ever fully recover.'

Nora began to sob. 'Wake me up, please. Tell me this is all a bad dream.'

'I'm sorry, Mrs Stefano, but it's true. Peter is there with her now, and I visit her every chance I get.'

'First I have a daughter, then I don't,' she gasped, hiccupped. 'Then just when I find out she didn't die, you tell me she almost did?'

'How old is Dicey now?' I asked, hoping to take her mind off Liz's condition.

'Twenty-seven,' she sniffed. 'We raised her, Greg and I, from the very beginning.'

'Tell me about it,' I urged gently.

'Liz was only sixteen when she had Dicey. She ran away from home when she was fourteen, but you probably know that. When she came back a year later, she was five months pregnant. Never did say who the father was. Liz stuck around for a couple of months after the baby was born, then ran off again.'

'She was just a baby herself,' I said in defense of my friend.

'Let me show you something.' Nora rose from her chair and disappeared down the hallway. When she returned, she was carrying a wad of tissues in one hand and a photograph in a silver frame – a five-by-seven copy of the miniature Trish wore in her locket.

'Is this Trish?' I asked.

'No, that's my granddaughter, Dicey, but she's the mirror image of her mother at the same age.'

Nora propped the photograph up on the table between us, then reclaimed her chair. 'Liz was too irresponsible to have children, that's what Greg always said. He wrote her off. Took her right out of his will.' After a moment, she added, 'But then I was, too.'

'Was what?'

'Too young and irresponsible to have children. I married Greg straight out of high school. I was only nineteen when Liz came along.' She stared down at her hands, folded in her lap, fingers tightly laced. 'Greg finished college, of course, but I was stuck in a crappy studio apartment . . .' She paused while dabbing at her eyes with one of the tissues. 'I was a terrible mother.'

I was about to protest, when she looked up at me, eyes moist, and said, 'I like to think we made up for it with Dicey.'

'Did you have any suspicions about who Dicey's father was?' I asked.

'She told us it was some art student she met from NYU. She said it wasn't a serious relationship. She didn't even tell him she was pregnant.

'I think she was afraid Greg would go after him.' She smiled sadly. 'He would have, too. Grabbed him by the collar and marched him down to the nearest police station. Liz was only fifteen. She looked older, sure, but if the guy was going to NYU, he had to be at least eighteen, and that would make what he did to Liz rape.'

'We pressed her,' Nora continued, 'but she always said it was no big deal. Easy for her to say! We were taking care of her daughter while she went gallivanting around New York City getting into who knows what. Booze. Drugs. Raves. Orgies—'

I held up a hand, interrupting the litany of evils that could have been leading their daughter astray. 'Wait a minute. She went back to New York after Dicey was born?'

Nora bobbed her head. 'She did. She got a job working as a receptionist for a talent agency. I might have the name written down somewhere. She'd come home for birthdays and holidays, but we – that's Greg and me – didn't feel that New York City was the proper place to raise a child, so we kept Dicey with us.'

'Where did she live in New York?'

'In Brooklyn, I think, with three other girls. We never visited her there.'

'Does Clinton Street ring any bells?' I asked, remembering what Mary had told me.

'That sounds right,' Nora said. 'That job lasted for several years. Liz came home for Dicey's fourth birthday party, stayed for a week then . . .' Her voice trailed off. 'That was the last time we saw her. The next thing we knew, the police came knocking on our door carrying Liz's shoes and handbag wrapped up in a paper evidence bag. Ripped the heart right out of my chest.'

'You can visit your daughter any time, you know.'

'I can't think about that right now,' she sobbed quietly. 'I need time, time to wrap my head around this. If only Greg were here. He'd know what to do.'

Silence grew between us, the only sound being the steady *tick-tock-tick-tock* of the grandfather clock towering over us from the corner of the room. The clock began to chime four, startling us both.

Nora looked up. 'I have to tell Dicey, but I don't know how.'

'Would you rather I told her?' I asked. 'Do you think it would be better coming from me?'

Nora pondered my question for a while then with both hands on the arms of the chair, levered herself into a standing position. 'You know all the details. I don't.'

I stood up, too, facing her.

'Dicey's in graduate school down in Ithaca,' Nora said, beaming. 'Let me write down her phone number for you.' She reached out and took my hand, sandwiching it between both of hers, squeezing it firmly. 'Thank you, Hannah. Thank you for bringing my daughter back.'

TWENTY-NINE

Sunday morning dawned sunny, but cool. Following turn-by-turn directions from the British aristocrat living inside my Waze app, I drove south on I-87 to Ithaca, entering the town from the east on Dryden Road. At College Avenue, I turned right and slotted the Mustang into a Park-and-Pay spot in front of the UPS store. After displaying the parking receipt on my dashboard, I wandered a short distance up the street, past the Bike Rack and a small 7-Eleven to Collegetown Bagels where Dicey had suggested we meet.

Over the phone, Dicey had said she'd be wearing a bright red coat and carrying a backpack. When I turned the corner, I spotted her immediately, loitering next to an outdoor picnic table. Dicey was a younger version of her mother, but quite a bit taller. She had the same dark hair, hazel eyes, and tip-tilted nose. Even the smile she greeted me with reminded me, with a pang, of my friend, Trish.

'Hi,' I said, waving. 'You must be Dicey.'

'And you must be Hannah.' She took a deep breath. 'Now we've gotten the formalities over with, let's get something to eat.'

Collegetown Bagels appeared to be a popular campus hangout where the specials were written on a blackboard in colored chalk.

'What do you recommend?' I asked Dicey as I studied the menu.

'I'm a vegetarian, so I usually get the tofu scramble, but if you're into meat, the Autumn Sky is supposed to be pretty good. Smoked turkey with bacon, spinach, apple and cheddar cheese.'

'Sounds yummy,' I said.

While we waited for our food to arrive, we sat down at a table for two by a window overlooking College Avenue. After several minutes of nervous, time-biding small talk during which Dicey learned that my flight up had been uneventful and I learned that she was close to finishing her PhD in Classical Philology and Literature at Cornell, Dicey was the first to get to the point. 'In your email, you said you used to know my mother.'

'I still do,' I said. 'Dicey, I came to tell you that your mother is still alive.'

Dicey froze, staring at me hard, as if I had a disfiguring wart on the end of my nose.

I pulled a photograph out of my pocket and slid it across the tabletop, the same photo I had showed to her grandmother the previous afternoon. 'This picture was taken at a party in Annapolis, Maryland about a year ago.' I tapped the image. 'That's your mom on the right. She calls herself Trish now. That guy standing next to her wearing the ugly Santa sweater is her husband, Peter.'

After a moment of shocked silence, Dicey began to weep quietly. I pulled a couple of napkins out of the tabletop dispenser, handed them over, and waited. Eventually, she dabbed her eyes dry, blew her nose. 'So she didn't jump off that bridge because I didn't eat my peas?'

'No,' I said gently.

'Or because I broke the ballerina off her jewelry box?'

I smiled. 'Not even for a crime as heinous as that.'

'I was four when Mom went away,' Dicey snuffled. 'I thought she was my sister, of course. Gram told me Liz had been accepted at a gifted and talented school in New York City. She got a job taking care of some rich people's kids. She'd come home to visit every so often. Then one day, she didn't.'

'That must have been hard,' I said.

'It was torture. It was years before they told me she had killed herself, and I had to hear about it from a well-meaning neighbor.'

The arrival of our food gave us both the time we needed to

regroup. Dicey ground pepper over her scramble, but seemed otherwise uninterested in eating, idly pushing the mixture around the plate with her fork as I tackled my sandwich.

'I'm no detective,' Dicey said at last, 'but if she's still alive, living under an assumed name, she must have been running away from something?'

'I believe so. And, sadly, that something caught up with her.' I chose that moment to break the news, as gently as possible, that her mother had been shot and was in intensive care. 'But she's expected to survive.'

'My God! Who did it? Who shot her?'

'That's what I'm trying to find out.'

'Do you think she wants to see me?' Dicey choked on the words.

'I'm sure of it, sweetheart. She carried a picture of you everywhere. Wore it in a locket around her neck. Even now, the locket is pinned to her hospital gown.'

'So all this time . . .?'

'I don't know where she was *all* that time, Dicey. She's lived across the street from me for about ten years, but when you were around six, she lived in Santa Fe, New Mexico under the name Patricia Tucker. She met a young professor—'

'Wait a minute!' Dicey's hand shot up so suddenly I nearly knocked over my latte. 'I know that name!' She unzipped a pouch on the side of her backpack and pulled out a cell phone. 'I've been fooling around with my ancestry lately,' she said, her eyes flashing from the cell phone to me and back again. 'Ah! Here it is.' She turned the screen in my direction, thrust it forward.

I recognized the app immediately – GenTree, the same popular genealogical research database I'd been using to build my own family tree.

'Patricia Tucker was my second cousin once removed. Her great-grandfather was my great-great,' Dicey explained, her voice rising in excitement. 'But, listen to this! Patricia lived in Tanneryville near Johnstown, Pennsylvania. She drowned in July of 1977 when the Laurel Run Dam overtopped and failed.'

'I remember that flood,' I said. 'More than eighty people died.'

'Way before my time, of course,' Dicey said, 'but I heard Gram talk about it. Patty was just a baby. She and her mom had sheltered on the second floor of their house with the dog when it was totally swept away.' She laid the phone face down on the tabletop and sighed. 'Golly. Mom stole her dead cousin's identity.'

'Apparently. It must have been easier to do back then. Write for a birth certificate for someone close to your own age, then use it to apply for a social security number. Nowadays babies get social security numbers at the hospital when they're born, but I don't remember it being a requirement until sometime in the 1980s.'

'Anybody with enough money can do it now,' Dicey mused. 'Surf on the Dark Web. Throw some BitCoin around.'

I had to laugh.

'Are you familiar with Ancestry, 23andMe or GenTree?' Dicey asked cautiously, as if I were over the hill and hopelessly out of touch.

'I am,' I admitted. 'We signed up with GenTree and got our DNA tested. When the results came back, we were totally shocked to learn that our mother was half Lakota Sioux. Reunited isn't exactly the right word because we'd never met them before, but since we first made contact this summer, I've met my first cousin, some second cousins and a half-great aunt who turned one-hundred-and-four on her last birthday.'

'Awesome!' Dicey said.

'It is, isn't it? My sister, Georgina, is still trying to take it all on board, but the rest of the family is, like, bring it on. My niece is working as a teachers' aide on the Pine Ridge reservation right now,' I said with a grin. 'She's helping with the annual buffalo hunt.'

'Kinda turns your world upside down, right?' she said.

'Indeed. One minute Julie's worrying about what to wear to the senior prom, and the next, she's learning how to say *Julie emáčiyapi. Ȟ'ahíya wóglaka ye.*'

Dicey chuckled. 'What does that mean?'

'Julie tells me it means, "My name is Julie. Please speak more slowly", but knowing Julie, it could just as easily mean, "My hovercraft is full of eels".'

We shared a laugh, after which Dicey said, 'As you just saw, I signed up with GenTree, too.'

When she didn't go on, I said, 'You were trying to track down your father.'

Dicey stared out the window, watching pedestrians trudge by, heads bowed into the brisk December breeze. 'Gram claimed she didn't know who my father was, that my mother never told her, and that it could have been one of any number of guys.' She paused, then added almost in a whisper, 'I don't believe my mother was a prostitute, do you?'

'No,' I said gently. 'I'm pretty sure she wasn't.' After a moment, I asked, 'Were you able to find him, your father?'

'I think so. Once I started building the family tree I just showed you, it all started to make sense. On the genetic matches, I kept turning up close relatives with names I'd never heard of.' She turned away from the window, waiting until she caught my eye. 'You know what a centimorgan is, right?'

'I do. It's a measure of the number of genetic links two people have in common.'

'That's right,' she chirped, as if praising a precocious tot. 'There were a slew of names on my match list, about a dozen. We all shared around sixteen hundred, seventeen hundred centimorgans which is smack dab in the half-sibling range. I found a couple more in the six to eight hundred range who could be my cousins, and that's how this other guy, Mike, and I connected and eventually tracked our biological father down, through the cousins we had in common.' She took a deep breath, then let it out slowly. 'Long story short, there was only one common denominator, a man named Nathaniel Flannigan.'

The way she delivered the name 'Nathaniel Flannigan', eyes wide, deliberately emphasizing every syllable, I realized she expected me to recognize him.

'Nathaniel Flannigan,' I repeated, my synapses not firing on all cylinders. '*That* Nathaniel Flannigan?'

With her mouth set in a firm line, she nodded, then immediately put me out of my misery by saying, 'You got it. Congressman. Twenty-eighth congressional district. New York state.'

'Sheeee-it,' I said, when I realized exactly who she must be talking about. Flannigan, an outspoken member of Congress since, like, forever, serving over the years on several important committees. I'd seen his over-Botoxed face on television, questioning witnesses during the infamous Benghazi hearings, but his tenure in Congress went back a lot further than 2014, maybe as far as all the hoo-hah over Iraqi weapons of mass destruction.

Dicey took two bites of her long-neglected scramble, then set down her fork. 'Yeah. Exactly!'

'Did you consider the possibility Flannigan could have been a sperm donor?' I asked. I spent several minutes telling Dicey the story of my late brother-in-law, Scott Cardinale, who had been a sperm donor in college, a help-pay-the-tuition sideline that resulted in at least seventeen children – and still counting – in addition to the four he had sired in the traditional way with Georgina.

'We did, at first,' she said, 'but eventually Cousin Mike and I decided he'd just been a randy dude with a pathological aversion to condoms.' She shot me a wicked grin. 'There's nobody special in my life right now, but whenever there is, I'm all "Whoa, dude. No raincoat, no sunshine."'

I had to laugh.

'The mothers we've identified so far were a Congressional intern, a legislative assistant, a waitress at a Capitol Hill restaurant, a fellow student at City College New York . . .' She'd been ticking them off on her fingers. 'You connect the dots. So, one kid named William with his current wife, two with his ex, and three oopsies, four if you include me, so seven kids and change.'

'I'm surprised the girls didn't opt for abortion,' I said. 'Particularly right after *Roe v. Wade*.'

'Believe it or not, if you listen to the political ads Flannigan runs every election year, he actually believes all that life is sacred from conception to the grave crap.' She leaned closer, resting her forearms on the table. 'They were all good Catholic girls,' she explained quietly. 'Makes you wonder, doesn't it? It's bad enough that he liked 'em young, but did he actually *target* girls he knew wouldn't use birth control? Girls who might be unwilling to admit they had sinned? How creepy is that?' She shivered. 'The gal at CUNY put her daughter up for adoption, the waitress was already married, but the others just went ahead with the pregnancies.'

'Like your mother,' I said, stating the obvious.

Dicey blinked away sudden tears. 'Like my mother, yes. I didn't find out until I was thirteen that Gram and Pops weren't my actual parents.'

'How did you find out?' I asked, genuinely curious.

'I overheard them arguing one night,' she said. 'That's when I learned that before she killed herself, my mother wrote a note and addressed it to me. Pops wanted me to have it. Gram didn't.'

'What did the note say?' I asked, then quickly added, 'You don't have to tell me if you don't want to.'

'No, no, it's OK. I carry her words with me everywhere. Right here,' she said, leaning back and laying a hand flat over her heart. She cleared her throat, then swallowed. '"Leaving was the only way to keep you safe. Someday you'll understand why. I love you, forever and ever and ever. Mom."'

'That breaks my heart.' We sat in silence for a long while.

'Dicey is an unusual name,' I said after a bit. 'Where did it come from?'

'It's my nickname,' she told me. 'Short for Eurydice. Isn't that a hoot?'

'It's a beautiful love story, Orpheus and Eurydice,' I mused. 'She dies, and he journeys all the way down to Hades to bring her back.'

'Playing the lute,' Dicey said with a grin. 'Don't forget about the lute.'

'Father Donovan always told me that Jesus had taken my sister up to heaven,' she continued. 'I hated Jesus for that. Still do. I dreamt of flying up to heaven to fetch her, bring her back. Not so different from Orpheus, when you come to think about it. Now, here you are. You're my Orpheus. Bringing my mother back.'

'Do you remember your mother?' I asked.

'She sometimes read to me at bedtime, I remember that. *Goodnight Moon* was my favorite, but I'd settle for *Where the Wild Things Are* in a pinch.

'When can I go to see her?' she asked, suddenly shifting gears.

'You have your studies,' I said, knowing from personal experience how busy it was at universities just before the Christmas holidays.

'No problem. I'll just need to let Christine know, and then—'

'Christine?'

'Dr Thomas. My thesis advisor. I'm supposed to meet with her on Friday, but she's always been flexible.'

'What's your thesis about, Dicey?'

She grinned. 'Sure you want to know?'

'Yes, I'm genuinely curious. I wouldn't have asked otherwise.'

'The title's rather ponderous. *The Girl He Left Behind: Views of*

War on the Homefront in the Greek Tragedies.' She paused to take a sip of her orange juice. 'Want it in five words or less? Feminist theory meets PTSD.'

'Better you than me,' I said, smiling. 'When do you think you'll be free?'

Dicey consulted her watch. 'Give me ten minutes?'

I laughed. 'You finish your scramble. Let me make a call.'

While Dicey dug into her scramble with fresh enthusiasm, I texted Georgina's cell: *Ask Zack if he has room for one more. Trish's daughter needs a lift.*

I had almost finished my sandwich when Georgina texted back a thumbs up emoji.

As we struggled into our coats on our way out of the coffee shop, Dicey asked, 'What time does your parking run out?'

I checked my watch. 'I've got thirty-five minutes.'

'Time for a short walk?'

'Sure,' I said.

I followed Dicey around Oak Street's semi-roundabout to the foot of the massive stone arch bridge that carries College Avenue across Cascadilla Creek. At the center of the bridge, she paused and waited for me to catch up with her. 'Quite a view, isn't it?' she said.

We stood silently for a few minutes, peering over the chest-high stone wall into the rapids more than a hundred feet below. Snow still weighed heavily on the branches of spindly trees clinging desperately to the steep banks, while water cascaded furiously over the waterfalls, the rocks rimmed with ice.

'They've suicide-proofed all the bridges like this,' she said, indicating the web of tensile steel netting just below.

With my forearms resting on the wall, I turned my head away from the view to look up at her. 'Was suicide a problem?'

Eyes still on the water, she nodded. 'In the past thirty years, twenty-seven people have committed suicide along the gorge. There were six in the 2009-2010 academic year alone.' She paused and caught my eye. 'The students call it gorging out.'

I shivered.

'I come here a lot,' she said in a quiet voice. 'It's so far down, and it's water, you know? I always wondered if Mom found it a beautiful way to die, to drift gently down and go out with the water.'

I reached around Dicey's shoulder and drew her close. 'But she didn't.'

'No.' She rested her head on my shoulder. 'Sometimes life gives you a second chance.'

THIRTY

On my way back to the Hampton Inn, I called ahead for a pulled pork sandwich and an order of fried pickles from the Bull and Bear Road House, then carried it back to my room. I filled the bathtub with hot water, dumped in the entire bottle of complimentary shampoo and, using my hand, whipped up a few desultory bubbles. No one was there to tell me not to, so I ate my dinner in the tub, thinking what an improvement warm bath water was over paper napkins when barbeque sauce dribbles on your chest.

After the last of the ranch dip that came with the pickles had been rinsed from my fingers, I closed my eyes and tried to relax, but my mind was a kaleidoscope of facts, whirling, shifting, ricocheting off one another and vying for my attention. I must have drifted off, because when I opened my eyes again, the water had grown cold. I climbed out of the tub, wrapped myself in a towel and crawled into bed with the TV remote in my hand.

Sixty cable television channels, and still nothing worth watching.

I tossed the remote aside, grabbed the bedside notepad and started scribbling. Before long, I had filled three pages with facts. If I were Hercule Poirot, what would they tell me? I was probably too exhausted to think straight, but one thing was clear, there were broken links in the chain. Trusting that my foggy brain would clear by morning, I turned out the light and eventually fell asleep.

The following morning, well before seven, I appeared in the lobby intending to take full advantage of their complimentary breakfast. I grabbed a cup of coffee and used it to reserve one of the small tables for two nearest the lobby, then went off to forage at the breakfast bar. I prepared a do-it-yourself waffle and smothered it with several strips of bacon and some cut-up fruit instead of whatever was in the little tub masquerading as maple syrup. Thus fortified, I sat down, ate, and got to work.

Consulting the business card he had given me, I placed a call to David Reingold's cell.

He picked up right away.

'I hope I didn't wake you,' I apologized.

'No, no. I've been stuck on the beltway staring at the Mormon Temple for the past twenty minutes. You?'

'I'm up in Syracuse, tracking down Elizabeth Stefano's family.'

'Yeah?' he said.

'You want to know what's astonishing, Mr Reingold? All of them tell me they've never been contacted by the police. Doesn't that seem odd to you?'

Instead of answering, Reingold grunted.

'*You* haven't contacted them either. Is everything being swept under the rug, like Trish feared when she entrusted me with her flash drive?'

'Relax, Mrs Ives. Ever since you left my office, I've been working on the story and believe me, something very much is going on.' A horn honked and Reingold softly swore before continuing. 'Surely you understand that when a case involves big names, as this one does, the DA keeps a tight lid on it. Needs to be airtight. Bulletproof. Same goes for me.'

'Do your sources tell you who shot Patricia Young?' I asked. 'Just yes or no.'

'No. But I can tell you that the information Mrs Young provided really greased the wheels. When the DA is ready to issue arrest warrants, the case is going to explode.'

'Warrants? There'll be more than one?'

After a moment of silence, Reingold sidestepped my question. 'You said you're in Syracuse, talking to family. Anything you'd like to share with me?'

Was there? I paused, apparently for longer than I thought.

'Mrs Ives? You still there?'

'I'm pondering your question,' I said.

'It should go without saying that I protect my sources.' Was it my imagination, or was there a hint of eagerness in his voice?

'I'm still thinking,' I said as I considered what remained of my breakfast – two soggy squares of cantaloupe I had no intention of eating.

'This traffic is going nowhere fast, so apparently I have all the time in the world,' he said, gently prodding.

I shoved my plate aside, a decision made. 'OK. The person you'll need to talk to is Mary Goodrich, a high school friend of Elizabeth Stefano's. I'll get back to Mary in a minute. I also spoke to two other family members. Their shock at learning that Liz is still alive was genuine, I think. They seem fragile to me, so I'd give them a little space until they get used to the idea that Liz has risen from the dead.'

I shared Mary's contact information with Reingold and asked him not to get in touch with her until I'd had the chance to give her a head's up. Then I brought him up to date as succinctly as possible. 'This is what I've pieced together so far. When they were fourteen, Mary and Liz ran off to New York City together. Mary confirms what Trish told me about living at the Y and working in a deli. But what Trish didn't get a chance to tell me was that she and Mary were recruited by a woman to hand out hors d'oeuvres at a party hosted by Calvin Bishop at his townhouse on Clinton Street in Brooklyn. I checked Zillow and the house hasn't changed hands since 1991 when Bishop bought it, so I presume he still owns the place.'

Reingold snorted. 'In addition to a ranch in Wyoming, a townhouse in Old Town Alexandria and an island in the Bahamas so close to the one owned by Johnny Depp that they can probably toast one another across their infinity pools.'

'Must be nice,' I muttered cattily. 'Anyway,' I rattled on, 'before long, Mary's father drags his daughter home. A couple of months after that, Liz Stefano shows up back in Syracuse, great with child. Fifteen. Years. Old. She's not saying who the baby's father is. Eventually, Liz ditches the kid and hightails it back to New York, leaving her mother to raise her little girl. Nobody seems clear about what happened after that. Liz might have been working for a caterer, or as an au pair, or for a talent agency. She either was, or was not, attending school. But what we *do* know is that four years later she's fled New York City for Syracuse carrying the documents that are represented by the images you have on that flash drive. She leaves the documents with Mary, telling her it's an insurance policy. And the next thing everybody knows, she's killed herself by jumping off a bridge.'

I paused to draw breath before moving on. 'Now, I have only a general idea of what's on that flash drive, and I'm not asking for any special favors. I don't consider myself your confidential informant when it comes to that flash drive. It belonged to Trish, not to me. I was just the delivery girl. But I'm wondering if you could check the documents for some names and get back to me.'

'Shoot,' Reingold said, sounding agreeable.

'Calvin Bishop is my prime suspect, of course. He was running the Lynx television station in New York at that time. Mary remembers the caterer who recruited them being named Siobhan' – I spelled the name out for him – 'but I don't have a last name. And then there's Nathaniel Flannigan.'

'Shit. Congressman Flannigan?'

'One and the same. Are you still stuck in traffic?'

'Inching along. Why do you ask?'

'If you were moving, I'd want you to pull over before I tell you the next bit of news.'

'I was imbedded with the troops in Afghanistan. I think I can handle it.'

'One of the women I talked to was Liz's daughter. She ran her DNA test through the matching service at GenTree. Turns out Nathaniel Flannigan is her biological father.'

Reingold whistled. 'Does Flannigan know?'

'She says not. But here's the thing. Flannigan was no pimply teen back then. I looked the guy up on Wikipedia. Flannigan was born in 1962. In 1992, when Liz got pregnant, he would have been thirty.' I let that fact hang in the air between us.

'Damn,' he said.

'So, naturally I'm sitting in an upstate New York motel drawing Jeffrey Epstein comparisons here. Does Flannigan know Bishop? Was Bishop in the habit of entertaining well-connected businessmen and politicians who like to party with underage girls? Is he still doing it?' I paused. 'Is there anything in those documents Trish provided that would support such a crazy theory?'

Reingold cleared his throat. 'That and more, Mrs Ives. Let's leave it at that.'

THIRTY-ONE

From what Mary told me, Trish's recent time in Syracuse had been short, her destinations few. She probably visited the FBI's downtown office – although that was simply a guess on my part – but nobody at the FBI would have had a reason to do her in. The most likely place to have been spotted and recognized – by a staff member, a visitor, or another patient – was while visiting her ailing father. Dicey and I weren't scheduled to meet Zack at the airport until two o'clock, so with a bit of time on my hands after talking to the reporter, I decided to drop in on Lakeview Village and poke around.

Lakeview Village, the life care community center on Onondaga Lake where Trish's father, Gregory Stefano, had spent his final years, was so posh I wondered how he could afford the fees on the salary of a retired college professor. Perhaps he'd bought into a gold-plated long-term care insurance plan.

Sprawled over twenty acres on a lushly planted hillside adjacent to beautiful Onondaga Lake Park and within walking distance of the Destiny USA mall, Lakeview's main building was designed like a turn-of-the-last-century Adirondack hotel with a porch, long and deep, running along the entire lakefront side. The 'hotel' served as the focus of a development that included an apartment building, several blocks of semi-detached town homes and a dozen or so cottages, all connected by winding lanes just wide enough for two golf carts to pass.

When I arrived, I parked in a spot reserved for visitors in front of the main building, strolled up the handicap ramp, and headed inside.

At reception, after stating my business, a young staffer asked me to sign in. With silent apologies to my father who was probably at that moment happily defying death along some hiking trail in the Guadalupe Mountains, I claimed to be shopping around for an assisted living situation for him. 'A friend recommended Lakeview. Nora Stefano? Sadly, her husband passed away recently, but she had nothing but good things to say about the care he received here.'

I paused, lowering my eyes to the floor in respectful silence.

'Ah, yes,' the receptionist said with a downturned lip. 'Mr Stefano was a lovely man. He used to teach chemistry at Ithaca College, back before he, uh, retired.' The way she said 'retired' led me to believe that it had been the dementia, not his age, that had forced retirement upon the professor. According to his obituary, he'd been only sixty-seven when he died.

'Did he have a lot of visitors, the professor?' I asked as I printed my name in the registration book, along with the time of my arrival. 'Former students and the like?'

'Not so many lately, since he, uh, you know.'

'Ah, Mrs Ives.' I turned to greet Helena Olsen, the Resident Care Manager who sailed toward me, hand outstretched. A sturdy Nordic woman in her mid-to-late forties, Ms Olsen had been summoned via intercom from a nearby office. 'We don't have any apartments available just now,' Ms Olsen told me after introductions were over, 'but I'll be happy to show you around and answer any questions you may have.'

'Oh, it's early days yet, Ms Olsen, early days. And there's always the hurdle of getting Daddy to agree to the move. He's incredibly stubborn, although I suppose I shouldn't tell you that,' I chuckled, leaned closer and added in an aside, 'You might be taking notes.'

Ms Olsen smiled stiffly, then ushered me through the lobby into a lounge where a half dozen residents were gathered in conversational groupings around a massive stone fireplace ablaze with Yule logs. 'This looks so cozy! How long is the waiting list?' I chirped.

'It's not the length that's the issue, it's that we can't predict with any degree of certainty how quickly openings may occur.'

'Naturally,' I said. 'I quite understand.' In other words, I thought, somebody would have to croak before a bed became available.

As we paused next to the tropical fish tank that served to divide the reception area from the lounge – six feet long and two-hundred-twenty-five gallons, Ms Olsen pointed out with pride, containing forty-three variety of fish personally curated by the ichthyologist at Rosamond Gifford Zoo – I scrabbled in my handbag for the brochure I'd printed out at the Hampton Inn's business center earlier that morning. 'I see from your website that in the main building, you offer one- and two-bedroom units. We're particularly interested in the one-bedroom layout,' I said, tapping the diagram of the floor plan, indicating a room that was similar to the one Dicey told me her grandfather had occupied. 'It would be worth the wait if Daddy could have a view of the lake.'

'As I mentioned, we have no openings at present, Mrs Ives, but I would be more than happy to show you one of our lake-view apartments. One of our guests is on furlough with his family for the holidays. I'm sure he wouldn't mind.'

I consulted my watch, smiled at her and said, 'I have plenty of time before I need to be at the airport. So, yes, I'd love to.'

There was nothing to be learned from seeing the room, except to say that before his mind had cruelly drifted away, necessitating a move to the secure memory care unit, Greg Stefano had been comfortably situated. He even had a pocket kitchen should the urge for a grilled cheese sandwich strike in the middle of the night. Continuing the tour, Ms Olsen escorted me briskly through the television lounge, computer lab, art room and library, past the beauty parlor and ATM, ending up just outside the dining room where uniformed wait staff bustled around making preparations for lunch.

Sensing that she had a hot prospect on the line, Ms Olsen reeled me in. 'Would you care to join us for lunch? It's Meatless Monday, but I can assure you that Chef Charles never disappoints.'

So much for my quick visit. If I ended up running late, though, I was confident a text message to Georgina would sort it out promptly. Private aviation certainly had its perks.

It had been four and a half hours since breakfast, and truthfully, I was starving. 'That's very kind of you, but I wouldn't want to intrude,' I said, just to be polite.

'Nonsense. Family members are always welcome, we just ask that they call ahead.'

'Well, I don't suppose I'll get much more than pretzels to eat on the plane,' I said to her with a smile. 'So, yes, I'll be delighted to join you.'

'Wine? Beer?' she asked, after we had taken our seats and the server had gone away with our order.

'Tempting,' I said, 'but, sadly, I have to drive.'

I had finished my zucchini ravioli – Chef Charles *was* a genius – and was digging my fork into a slice of carrot cake when a commotion in the corner of the room drew my attention. A woman was struggling to rise from her chair, one gnarled hand gripping the tabletop, the other searching blindly for her walker. Her companion, a much younger man, stood to help.

'Mother, I never said—'

When he turned around to assist with the walker, I nearly dropped my fork. I lowered my voice. 'Is that who I think it is?'

'Who?' Ms Olsen asked, looking up from her apple pie.

I bobbed my head in the direction of the bickering couple.

'Don't talk back to *me*, Sonny,' the woman snarled, jerking her arm away, refusing his assistance. 'Just wait until your father gets home!'

'That guy looks like Nathaniel Flannigan. The congressman?'

Grinning toothily – a celebrity product endorsement she didn't have to pay for! – Ms Olsen confirmed my suspicions. 'His mother can be quite the handful, as you see, but she's really an old dear at heart. The congressman comes to visit when he can, but because of his busy schedule, it's usually his wife or one of his children who draws the short straw when she's in a mood.'

The congressman and me. Here. Now. In the place where Trish had come to visit her ailing father. Paul could calculate the odds, and they must have been astronomical.

Mrs Flannigan clumped toward the door pushing the walker ahead of her, the congressman dogging her heels. I sat up straight, resisting the foolish urge to duck and cover. Flannigan didn't know me, after all. There was no way he could connect me with Elizabeth Stefano.

To my surprise, Mrs Flannigan planted her walker firmly on the carpet next to our table and fixed me with a steely-blue gaze. 'You're new here, aren't you?'

Fork halfway to my mouth, I stared.

'Lakeview, hah! My great aunt Fanny. Deathview Village is more like it.' With a backwards glance at her son that would have caused house plants to wither, she added, 'How about Abandoned Here Manor?' And then off she shuffled, muttering, 'Run away, girlie, run away. Run away while you still have the chance.'

Congressman Flannigan smiled sheepishly, shrugged a silent apology, then hustled to catch up with his mother.

I stared at his departing back. Could he have been responsible for the attempted murder of the mother of his illegitimate daughter? He wouldn't have pulled the trigger himself, of course. No doubt he had 'staff' to handle such situations.

For a fleeting second, I considered following the man, backing him into a corner and demanding answers, but if he *had* ordered the hit on Trish, that would only put my life – and Dicey's – in danger.

It was hard to reconcile the person I saw now, meekly bending over the ATM, punching keys and repeating, 'Yes Mother, no Mother, I'm sorry you feel that way, Mother' with the sardonic, sneering, smart-ass on C-Span TV, but after witnessing how surgically he dismembered the testimony of witnesses on Capitol Hill, I had no doubt that the man could be dangerous.

Nathaniel Flannigan *must* have spotted the woman he knew as Liz Stefano here at Lakeview. But how to prove it?

Dessert plate virtually licked clean, I thanked Ms Olsen profusely for lunch and the tour. After accepting a no-obligation packet for Dad should he want to apply for a spot on the future residents list, I asked for and received her permission to stroll around the grounds. Ms Olsen shook my hand and abandoned me to it.

Before heading out the double doors that led to the garden, I made a pit stop at the ladies' room, then detoured back around to the reception desk.

'Lunch was fabulous,' I told the receptionist, the same girl who had been on duty when I first came in. 'Gosh, I hope they give you time to eat.'

She consulted the oversize clock that hung on the wall directly behind her. 'Ten more minutes,' she said. 'I'm not wild about Meatless Monday, but at least I don't have to cook, you know?'

'I was asking earlier about Professor Stefano's visitors,' I reminded her. 'Do you have therapy dogs visiting here? It's sad to think of someone spending his last few months on earth kind of, well, alone.'

'We love our therapy dogs,' she said. She directed my attention to a photograph tacked up next to an oversized events calendar. It showed a pair of golden retrievers decked out in Mardi Gras attire – beads and feather boas. 'Meet Jingle and Jo. They'll be here on Saturday. But I don't know what gave you the idea the professor was alone. There was his wife, of course, regular as clockwork on Monday and Thursday mornings, and his granddaughter once a month. He always seemed to recognize them, bless his heart. And a niece popped in, too, a couple of times in the week before he passed.'

'Ah, yes,' I said. 'Was that Trish or Lizzy, do you remember?'

The receptionist shrugged, pointed at the register. 'She would have signed in.'

She didn't object, so I grabbed the register and started paging backwards. I knew when Trish had visited Syracuse, of course, so I had only to look four weeks back. 'Trish told me she'd be in Rochester on business,' I babbled. 'Thought she might drive over for a quick visit. Must have been three or four weeks ago? Middle of November?' I looked up at the receptionist and grinned. 'Trish is from San Diego. The cold weather here was killing her,' I said, glancing down at the pages again.

Trish had visited twice, on Friday and Saturday, November the eighth and ninth. Both times she'd used her 'maiden name', Patricia Tucker.

Starting with Friday, I scanned the page from top to bottom for any other names I recognized, then moved on to Saturday.

I caught my breath. On Saturday, while 'Patricia Tucker' was visiting her dear 'Uncle Greg', the elder Mrs Flannigan had been entertaining her daughter-in-law, Siobhan Flannigan.

THIRTY-TWO

Light rain was falling, but Georgina had texted *No Big Deal* since the temperature was hovering in the mid-fifties. With my windshield wipers on intermittent, I made it back to Signature Flight Support south of the Syracuse airport with more than thirty minutes to spare.

Again, I parked in a visitors' spot, leaving Kyle to return the Mustang to Hertz, as he promised. I pictured him peeling down Tuskegee Road in a rooster tail of flying slush the minute the wheels of Zach's plane lifted off the runway.

I collected my belongings from the trunk, thinking about the care center register. According to his congressional bio, Nathaniel Flannigan had married Siobhan Hennessy in 1994. Not a common name, Siobhan. Unless it was the wildest coincidence since both John Adams and Thomas Jefferson died within hours of one another on the fourth of July, Nathaniel Flannigan had married the Siobhan who worked for Calvin Bishop, the same woman who recruited Trish. It had to have been she who recognized Trish while visiting the care center, not her husband.

I found Georgina waiting in the lounge, watching *Days of Our Lives* from the comfort of an upholstered armchair. Gas logs flickered in a corner fireplace. 'If you need to use the restroom, there's time,' she said, turning her attention away from the screen. 'They play Mozart in there.'

'Of course they do,' I said. Talking to my sister about the music playing in restrooms injected a bit of normalcy into what had otherwise been a surreal day. 'So, what's going on?' I asked, pointing to the TV where the long-running soap opera was playing out on the screen.

'Frankly, I'm totally lost. Steve is now Stefano, Kayla is with Justin, and Will is in prison for killing Adrienne. Right now they're in Rome, where Eli and Lonnie are trying to talk J.J. out of executing Christian and avenging Haley's death.'

'You're making that up,' I teased. 'So, how was your weekend?'

Georgina flushed. 'Heavenly. Zack is a wonderful lover.'

'Tee Em Eye,' I laughed, making a time-out sign with my hands.

Georgina aimed the remote and silenced the TV. 'Where's Dicey?'

'She texted when she crossed the intersection of I-81 and 90, so she's right behind me.'

As we spoke, Dicey breezed in. She wore the same red parka as the first time I met her with a tasseled knit cap mashed down over her curls. Her cheeks were flushed from the cold. 'Thought I'd never get here,' she said. 'My God, a fireplace!' she exclaimed, making a beeline for it. 'This idiot kept riding my tail, so I had to slow down and let him pass.'

That brought me up short. According to Mary, Trish had worried they were being followed. 'What kind of idiot?' I asked, trying to keep my voice calm. 'Did you see what he looked like?'

Dicey shrugged. 'Not really. Just some dude in a ball cap driving a beater. He passed me and got off at exit twenty-six.'

'Where'd you park, Dicey?'

She jerked her head. 'In the parking lot by Logistics, on the other side of the chain link fence. Why? Isn't it safe?'

'It's cool,' Kyle cut in, having overheard our conversation from his chair behind the desk. 'We've got security lights and cameras out there.'

At least Dicey's safely with us, I thought, as I introduced her to my sister.

'Happy to meet you,' Georgina said. 'Please. Call me Gina.'

So the transformation is complete. Thanks to Mr Zachary Curtis, my sister was now Gina. As long as she didn't start dotting the 'i' with a heart like we did in junior high school, I figured I could live with Gina, but it would take some getting used to.

'There's coffee if you want any,' Georgina told Dicey, just as Zack popped in. He handed some paperwork over to Kyle. We introduced Zack to his last-minute passenger, he doffed an imaginary cap, then said, 'Ready to go, ladies?' Without waiting for an answer, he grabbed my bag, slung Dicey's backpack over his shoulder and headed out. 'Let's get this show on the road.'

While Zack circled the plane doing his customary pre-flight safety check, Dicey and I stood on the tarmac observing as a mechanic stuffed our bags into the belly of the plane. In a minute or two, he'd produce a stool and give us the OK – and a handup – to climb aboard.

Georgina had just strapped herself into the co-pilot's seat and closed the door, when a siren began to wail.

Whee-oooh, whee-oooh, whee-oooh!

I covered my ears and shouted, 'What's that all about?'

Shading his eyes with his hand, the mechanic stared across the airfield in the direction of the main terminal. 'Some sort of security breach,' he shouted back.

Zack froze, one hand on a propeller. I'd turned instinctively to him for guidance, so the concern written on his face wasn't reassuring.

'Holy shit!' the mechanic cried.

Zack surged forward. 'What the hell does he think he's doing?' A maroon car, seemingly out of control, was barreling diagonally across the airstrip, heading directly toward Zach's Piper Aztec.

My heart did a somersault. With a mother's instinct, I grabbed Dicey by the hand.

'Run!' Zack shouted. 'Get into the hangar!'

I didn't need to be told twice. Dicey and I sprinted away, trying to keep the plane between us and the fast approaching car until we got safely inside the hangar.

Pop-Ping!

A bullet tore into the aluminum siding not ten feet away. Dicey and I ducked behind the bulk of a stationary pushback tractor.

Pop-Ping!

'Zack!' Georgina's voice rang out, shrill and distinct even over the siren. Oh my God! Had my sister been hurt?

Crouching low, Dicey dared to peek around the enormous wheel of the pushback tractor. 'Goddamn! That's the car that was following me!'

'Keep your head down!' I hissed, flattening her against the floor, partially covering her with my body. With my nose squashed against the cold concrete, I could smell years of accumulated oil and gasoline, mixed with my own fear. Breast cancer couldn't kill me, but I was going to die on a cold concrete floor in Syracuse Flipping New York, for sure. Paul would never forgive me.

I flinched as two more shots thudded dully into the tractor.

'Why would anybody want to shoot me?' Dicey cried, her voice ragged and breathless. I could feel her body shaking beneath mine. 'It's my mom who collected all that evidence, not me!'

'Shhhh, shhhh,' I whispered in Dicey's ear. 'Don't you understand, Dicey? You *are* the evidence.'

Another shot rang out, then suddenly everything went quiet. Even the siren had ceased to wail. I held my breath, straining to hear, fearing the sound of approaching footsteps, at the same time dreading what we might see if we were to step out from our hiding place.

'Hannah, where are you?' A familiar voice echoed around the vast interior of the hangar. 'Dicey! Are you OK?'

I poked out a cautious head, like a prairie dog checking for coyotes. Zack was striding toward our hiding place, holding a gun.

'No!' I screamed, ducking back down. 'He's got a gun!'

'I'm not—' Zack shouted.

'It's OK, it's OK,' another voice cut in, sounding like Kyle. 'Zack shot the guy.'

When I worked up the courage to peek, Zack was tucking the pistol he had been carrying into a holster at the small of his back. He displayed his empty hands.

'Who was it?' I asked, my voice quavering.

'Just a kid,' Zack told me as I crept out of our hiding space.

I extended a hand and helped Dicey to her feet. 'Is he . . .?'

'Don't worry, he'll live. I shot him in the leg.'

'Georgina?' I asked, my voice quavering.

'She's fine, too,' Zack assured me.

'Well, fuck this!' Dicey said, shaking her arm free from my grasp. Before I could stop her, she chugged off in the direction of our assailant who was sprawled on the tarmac near the tail of the airplane. A first aid kit lay open on the ground. The mechanic knelt between it and the injured man, applying a tourniquet to a wound in the young man's calf.

'Dicey, come back!' I yelled.

'He's not dead,' she called over her shoulder. 'I'm going to give the son of a bitch a piece of my mind!'

I stumbled after her, relieved when I emerged from the hangar to see Georgina's worried face peering out the window, observing what was going on from the safety of the cockpit.

'Where's Kyle?' I asked Zack.

'He's calling for an ambulance,' Zack told me.

When I caught up with Dicey, she loomed like an avenging angel over the prostrate form of a young man who I took to be in his mid-to-late twenties. The ball cap she'd mentioned earlier sat soaking up to its NY logo in a nearby puddle, leaving his blond hair free to flutter in the brisk wind.

'Wait a minute! I know this guy!' Dicey said. If looks could kill, the guy would have been dead twice over. 'I recognize him from his Facebook page. He's one of my half-brothers.' She stepped closer, prodding him in the side with the toe of her boot. 'You're William, aren't you? Billy. Congressman Flannigan's son.'

Billy, if it was indeed Billy Flannigan, simply moaned.

'What the hell kind of game are you playing?' Dicey's boot crept closer to Billy's outflung hand. When he didn't respond, she positioned her boot over his fingers and inched the toe slowly down.

'You were going to ruin everything!' Billy whined.

'What was that?' Dicey said, her voice calm and steady. 'Speak up, I couldn't hear you.'

'Everything was fine until you showed up!' he shouted.

'What do you mean, dirt bag?' Dicey spit. For someone who spent hours with her head buried in ancient Greek texts, she certainly had an impressive command of Anglo-Saxon vocabulary. 'How could I ruin anything for you, you worthless piece of shit! I've never even met you!'

'Not just you. *All* of you!' he whimpered.

'Ah . . .' Dicey said. 'You must be referring to the battalion of bastards that your father sired? How did you find out about that?'

Was it my imagination, or was she pressing harder on Billy's fingers? If so, nobody, least of all me, made any move to tell her to stop. Dicey had the situation well under control. Besides, I wanted to know what Billy had to say.

'I showed Mom my DNA links on GenTree,' Billy whined. 'You'd think she'd be pissed off at Dad, but, no, Mom blamed the sluts!' Billy jerked his hand away, raising the arm it was attached to as a shield, as if expecting Dicey to knock him silly. 'Slut is her word, not mine!'

'Listen to him,' Dicey said, her voice oozing disgust. 'Whining like a baby. What did you think, huh? We're all going to show up on Capitol Hill, march into your father's office and demand to be included in his will?' She laughed. 'As if.'

'No, no, you don't understand! Nobody's supposed to know, but Dad's on the shortlist. They're vetting him for vice president. If any of this hits the papers . . .' His head lolled and he moaned.

Paul and I followed politics fairly closely, but this was news to me. It wasn't unheard of for a president to switch running mates in a bid for another term – Roosevelt did it in 1944, tapping Truman over Wallace – but it was unusual in modern times. Still, who knew what was going on behind the scenes in a revolving-door adminis- tration as dysfunctional as the current one.

As I stood there, agape, Dicey laughed out loud and said what we all must have been thinking. 'You're out of your fucking mind if you think the vice president is going to step aside and clear the way for anyone, least of all a pissant congressman from New York state, to take his place. God, that's the funniest thing I've heard in years.

'Were you planning to kill us, then?' she snarled. 'And how about *my* mother? Did you shoot her, too?'

'Not me! Mother!'

'Oh, I see,' Dicey scoffed. 'Blame everything on your mother.'

'She knows who to call,' Billy whimpered.

'Sounds like a confession to me,' Dicey said. Her eyes flicked from Billy on the ground up to me. 'This guy definitely didn't graduate from Harvard like it says on his Facebook profile. If he did, someone else must have taken his exams. I ought to—'

Whatever Dicey was about to say was interrupted by a squeal of tires announcing the arrival of a white and gray sedan bearing the distinctive red logo of the airport's security firm. The driver slammed on the brakes, stopping just short of the battered Cadillac Deville William Flannigan had been driving. A uniformed officer emerged, tugging his quilted vest over his belt. He swaggered over to the plane. Incredibly, the man was grinning. 'Hey, Curtis,' he said, addressing Zack.

'Murphy,' Zack said.

Of course they know each other, I thought, overcoming my initial surprise. When you repo planes, you must be acquainted with police and security personnel at every airport in the country.

At the officer's appearance, Dicey casually wandered over to stand by me.

'What we got here, then? A repo gone bad?' Murphy inquired, sounding amused.

Zack chuckled. 'Nah. It's my plane. What's the story?' he asked, bobbing his head in the direction of William Flannigan's abandoned vehicle, driver's door yawning open, its engine still running.

'Crazy sonofabitch crashed through the fence over by air cargo,' Murphy said. 'Trying to steal your plane?'

'Something like that,' Zack replied.

I opened my mouth, intending to blurt out everything I knew about the criminal Flannigan family, but Zack caught my eye. His mouth was set in a firm, straight line, the shake of his head barely noticeable. He knows something I don't know. He's telling me to shut up.

I passed Zack's message on to Dicey with a silent squeeze of her hand.

Murphy glanced from Dicey to me, cocked his thumb at Zack. 'Nobody messes with this guy, ladies. There was this flight school guy? Drunk as a skunk. When Zack tried to repo his Cherokee, he attacked Zack with a two-by-four.'

Zack grinned good-naturedly. 'That's why I carry the gun.'

'I think that's the other guy's gun,' I said, pointing helpfully at a gun-shaped object lying under the fuselage of Zack's Piper Aztec. The security guard bent double and duck-walked under the plane, grunting with every step. He scooped up the gun by the trigger using a pen, carried it over to his patrol car and climbed in.

'Was that a Glock?' I whispered to Zack when Murphy's back was turned.

Zack touched my arm. 'Looks like it.'

'Do you think it's the same—?'

'Zack?' Georgina had opened the cockpit door. She'd swiveled in the seat, her legs dangling. 'I need some help here, please.'

Zack raised a finger and said to me, 'Hold that thought.'

As Georgina slid out of the co-pilot's chair, Zack caught her with both hands around her waist, set her feet gently on the ground. My poor sister looked like a raccoon – her eyeliner had smudged and mascara streaked her cheeks, but Zack didn't seem to mind. They had a brief conversation. He brushed the hair away from her forehead and kissed the spot. A quiet word in her ear, then he led her by the hand over to us.

'Dicey, will you go with Georgina to the ladies' room? Help her freshen up?'

Dicey looked puzzled, but agreed.

When I was alone with Zack, he said, 'I need to explain.'

'Darn right,' I snapped. 'This guy comes after us with a gun, apparently on orders from his mother who happens to be married to a US congressman, and you want me to sit on it?'

'You need to hold off for a couple of days, at least until—'

'Why? Do you know something I don't?' I pointed over to the sorry mound that was Billy Flannigan, now wrapped like a taco in an aluminum emergency blanket. 'You just heard him confess. He fingered his mother. He says she ordered the hit on Trish.'

'The investigation into Calvin Bishop has been going on for months, Hannah. Because of the powerful people involved, it has to be conducted in utmost secrecy.' He bobbed his head toward the patrol car. 'The cops are on their way. Murphy's probably talking with them now. If you blow the whistle on the Flannigans, particularly to the locals, it'll tip off Calvin Bishop and the whole operation could fall apart. He could take off to a jurisdiction where they don't have extradition and they may never get him back. Best to keep Flannigan busy worrying about why his youngest son was trying to hijack a private plane. Aircraft piracy is a serious federal offense. Shooting up a hanger, not so much.'

A cold knot of fear tightened in my stomach as the realization struck me. 'How do you know all this?' I stepped back. 'Are you a Fed? Are you only dating my sister to keep an eye on me after what happened to Trish?'

Zack seized me by both arms, shook me gently. 'No! Listen to me, Hannah!'

Frozen in place by the intensity of his eyes, I listened.

'I love your sister. Shit, I'm going to marry her if she'll have me.'

I still wasn't buying it. I glared at him through slitted eyes. 'Then explain to me how you know so much about Calvin Bishop.'

'Thanksgiving dinner. Remember?'

'Oh, yeah,' I said, feeling my cheeks grow hot as the memory flooded back. 'I kinda let it all hang out, didn't I? Maybe it was the wine.'

'Or a sugar high from the pie,' Zack said gently. 'Anyway, I heard what you said about Trish and a possible connection to the higher-ups at Lynx, and I decided to make a few phone calls. Both my contacts at the Bureau suggested in pretty strong language that I back off, which told me almost everything I needed to know.'

'And so?'

'And so, I talked to his pilots.'

I nearly fainted with relief. Of course he did. 'But—'

'No buts.'

'So, how long do we have to wait?'

'My guess? Tomorrow or the next day. His pilots are standing down.'

'That looks cozy,' I heard Georgina say.

I backed away from Zack, flashing my sister an uneasy smile. 'You know me, Georgina. About to go off half-cocked. Zack's trying to talk some sense into me.'

'The cops will be here shortly, ladies. Listen. This is what we need to do.'

Not long after the ambulance carted Billy Flannigan away, accompanied by one of the city cops assigned to the airport, we regrouped in the lounge where we spoke on the record to the police officer in charge.

Zack was our pilot. We were his customers. The name Flannigan didn't come up.

Eventually, Zack stood. 'Look,' he said, addressing Murphy. 'This gal's got a mother in a shock trauma center down in Baltimore who needs to see her.'

'Sure, go ahead,' Murphy said. 'We'll clean up here. If we need anything, we'll be in touch.'

'Thanks, man,' Zack said. 'I won't forget this.'

THIRTY-THREE

Flying low over Baltimore after dark is a magical thing. Rush hour traffic turned the streets into undulating ribbons of red and white. One bright ribbon encircled Mount Vernon Place where the monument to George Washington stood tall, bathed in a peculiar lavender light. Minutes beyond, at the end of Charles Street, the Inner Harbor teemed with light and life, the glass pyramid of the National Aquarium's rainforest lit from within, sparkling like a crown jewel.

Even though our departure had been delayed by almost two hours, we touched down on the lighted runway just after six, leaving plenty of time to drive Dicey to the hospital before visiting hours ended.

Peter had added Dicey's name to the visitors' list at Shock Trauma, but was reluctant to intrude on the mother-daughter reunion. 'There'll be time enough for me later on,' he'd said when I telephoned earlier in the day to bring him up to date. 'Call me tomorrow, OK?' he said. I could hear the nervousness in his voice. 'We'll keep it low-key. Over coffee or something.'

When Dicey and I reached the nurse's station adjoining Trish's room, Dicey, surprisingly, held back. 'You go in first,' she urged.

I shot her an enquiring look.

'I'm all pins and needles,' she explained, grasping the strap on her backpack like a lifeline. 'What will I say?'

I wrapped an arm around her shoulder, drew her close and whispered in her ear. 'Tell her what's in your heart. You'll be fine.'

I left Dicey in the hallway, backed up against the wall just outside her mother's door, staring at her shoes.

When I tiptoed in, I was relieved to find the ventilator gone. Although Peter had said his wife had been weaned off the machine, the difference it made surprised me. Its very size, and the noise it made – *shhhh paah, shhhh paah* – had dominated the room, dwarfing the patient to which it was attached.

To assist with her breathing Trish now wore a tracheotomy tube, attached to her like a necklace with Velcro. The nurse had propped her patient up in bed, and her head was turned slightly away from the door. The television was on, the audio emanating from a controller tied to the side rail of her hospital bed. She seemed to be watching *Jeopardy*.

Potpourri for 800, Alex.

The name of this NFL team from California is a type of horse.

Colts? Broncos? I racked my brain. I'd flunk that category.

'Trish?' I said instead.

Trish turned her head and, when she recognized me, smiled. I couldn't believe the improvement in the relatively short time I'd been away. Not only had the ventilator disappeared, but the bandage that had swathed her head like an Egyptian mummy cloth had noticeably shrunk. Both her eyes were now visible, and the black and blue coloration of her left forehead and cheek had faded from blackish-blue to greenish-yellow.

I leaned over the bed, hands resting on the rail. 'You're looking so much better.' I caressed her scalp, feeling the soft, brown stubble under my fingertips. 'And your hair is growing back from where they shaved it for surgery.' I grinned. 'I don't think God intended for you to be blond.'

Trish grunted, as if clearing her throat, but her eyes smiled.

Because of the trach, I knew she couldn't talk. Normally, air passes over your vocal chords, Peter had explained, but the tracheotomy tube bypasses all that. The speech therapist had started working with her, but learning to speak required breath control and Trish wasn't there yet.

'Don't try to talk,' I told my friend. 'Just listen. There's somebody here who has been waiting a long time to see you.'

Trish's eyebrow twitched.

I felt Dicey approach from behind, so I stepped aside. For a moment, nothing changed, and then suddenly, the air in the room seemed to bristle with static electricity.

'Hello, you,' Dicey said, stepping forward to take my place. 'It's been a long time.'

A high-pitched whine escaped from Trish's throat. Her eyes overflowed, tears coursed down her cheeks.

'It's all OK,' Dicey said, reaching for her mother's hand. 'I'm here. Everybody's safe. Nobody's in danger any more.'

Trish's chest heaved with the effort to speak.

Dicey laid her fingers gently against her mother's cheek, wiping tears away with her thumb. 'Shhhh, shhhh,' she soothed.

I snatched a tissue out of a box on the bedside table and handed it to Dicey who used it to dry her mother's face. 'I don't know what to call you,' she said after a little time had passed. 'Liz? Trish?'

Trish's free hand fluttered up to the trach at her neck. She pressed two fingers against the opening, took a deep breath and pushed air out forcefully over her lips. 'Muuuuh.' Clearly unsatisfied with the effort, Trish closed her eyes, grabbed another breath, and with the strain showing on her face, rasped, 'Mom.'

Dicey burst into tears.

Feeling like a fifth wheel, I snatched a tissue out of the box for myself and slipped out of the room.

When I looked in again to collect Dicey for the drive back to Annapolis, the bed rail had been lowered and Dicey was asleep, her head resting on her mother's breast and in the circle of her arms.

The following morning, I crawled out of bed just after dawn, awakened not by the sun, but by the pinging of my iPhone.

Paul was already up, drinking coffee alone at the kitchen table. 'Dicey?' he asked when I appeared before him, slightly disheveled and rubbing sleep out of my eyes.

'Still asleep,' I said. 'I'll be surprised if we see her before noon. It was an exhausting day.'

Paul rose from his chair and folded me into his arms. 'I'm glad it's over,' he said, his breath warm against my forehead.

'Not quite over,' I said, lifting the hand that held my cell phone. 'I have a text from David Reingold.'

Paul squinted at the screen and read Reingold's message aloud. 'Hold tight. It's happening.'

'Turn on the TV,' I said, heading straight for the Keurig machine, 'I'm right behind you.'

When I joined my husband on the sofa two minutes later, Paul was aiming the remote at the TV, surfing through the channels. 'It's a mystery to me how they can all be running ads at the same time,' he grumped.

I grabbed his arm. 'Stop! That's CNN.'

We sat through an ad assuring us that we'd be in good hands, insurance-wise, with Allstate, then news anchor John Herman came on to report that a volcano had erupted off the coast of New Zealand, killing five. The story that followed informed us that the Russians were being banned from the Olympics for four years because of doping.

'Imagine my surprise,' Paul said, aiming the remote. 'Let's switch to Lynx.'

'Wait! If this *is* about Calvin Bishop, do you think Lynx is going to carry the story? Other than to say it's a hoax?'

'A team representing Russia cannot participate,' Herman was winding up the Russia story, 'but if there is a mechanism put in place, then they can apply to participate on a neutral basis, just not as representatives of Russia.

'Now, this just in,' he continued. 'Early this morning, FBI agents raided the Brooklyn townhouse of Lynx Media Corporation executive, Calvin J Bishop, using a crowbar to break through the front door of one of the most luxurious private homes in the upscale Clinton Hill neighborhood.'

I poked Paul in the ribs with my elbow. 'That's it! That's the house! I recognize it from Zillow!'

'According to agents familiar with the case,' Herman said, 'this was a well-coordinated effort, with simultaneous raids at the media tycoon's ranch near Whitefish, Montana and at his Alexandria townhouse. FBI authorities later descended upon the private island owned by Mr Bishop in the Bahamas.'

The Brooklyn townhouse with a U-Haul vehicle parked on the sidewalk morphed into an aerial shot, probably taken by drone, of a lush green island set in a turquoise sea.

'A local snorkeling guide unwittingly led a group of tourists right into the dragnet,' a reporter dressed in a Hawaiian shirt was saying.

The camera panned to a bronzed dude in swim trunks wearing

his snorkel gear perched like an antler on top of his head. 'They arrived in Border Patrol boats,' the dude spoke into the camera, 'wearing uniforms with big yellow letters on them. They were crawling all over the island. It was nuts.'

'Bishop,' the CNN reporter continued, 'whose friends have included ex-presidents, foreign heads of state, royalty and numerous A-List celebrities, was arrested late last night at an airport outside New York City after his private jet touched down from the Bahamas. A task force of federal agents and NY City police officers met the plane at Westchester County Airport and took Bishop into custody. He is being held at the Metropolitan Correctional Center, a federal jail near the Manhattan courthouse where he is due to appear on Friday.

'According to officials who spoke to CNN on the condition of anonymity because they were not authorized to discuss the pending case, agents at the Brooklyn location found a vast trove of hand-labeled compact discs containing hundreds, perhaps thousands, of sexually suggestive photographs of fully-or-partially-nude females, some appearing as young as thirteen. Sex toys and computers were also seized in the raid.'

'Disgusting,' I said, thinking of my granddaughter. Paul squeezed my hand.

'Bishop is charged in a fifteen-page federal indictment with sex trafficking and sex trafficking conspiracy. It is alleged that some trafficking victims were just fourteen years old.

'According to a court filing that just came into my hands,' Herman continued, 'the government is requesting that Bishop not be released prior to trial since he is an extraordinary flight risk, considering his exorbitant wealth, his ownership of and access to private aircraft capable of international travel, and his significant international ties.

'This was a covert operation taking many months, a government spokesman told CNN news. Court documents related to the case had been kept under seal, but now that the indictment has been unsealed, prosecutors hope many more individuals, either victims or witnesses, will come forward.

'We called the number given for Mr Bishop's home. A man who identified himself as Harry abruptly hung up on this reporter without commenting. Mr Bishop's lawyer did not respond to messages seeking comment. Stay tuned to CNN for more as this story develops.'

While Dicey remained blissfully asleep in the guest room recently occupied by her stepfather, I texted David Reingold: *Well done. Call me about Syracuse.*

An hour later, Reingold returned my call. 'I filed my story. It'll go live in about an hour.'

Meanwhile, I filled him in on my adventures in Syracuse, stopping from time to time to answer his questions. 'Those papers Trish gave you,' I said after I finished. 'I don't know what was in them, but you do. Is Trish in trouble?'

'My bet?' Reingold said. 'Most likely she cut a deal with the FBI long before turning them over. Most significantly, it was the information Mrs Young provided that gave the government the reasonable cause they needed to obtain the search warrants that resulted in these raids. If it hadn't been for her . . .' His voice trailed off. 'Well, if it hadn't been for your friend, Trish, Cal Bishop would still be using his considerable wealth and power to abuse young women.'

'Will she need to testify?' I asked, wondering as the words tumbled out of my mouth if Trish would ever be *able* to testify.

'I doubt it,' Reingold said. 'The government has plenty of witnesses now – victims of more recent vintage than Mrs Young. But it's always a good idea to consult an attorney.'

'Thanks, Mr Reingold. I'm looking forward to reading your story.'

'No, it's I who need to thank you. And when Mrs Young is well enough, I plan to thank her in person, too.

'In the meantime,' he continued, 'I urge you to download a copy of the indictment.' He gave me the URL and I jotted it down. 'I'm only guessing, of course, but I think *Unindicted Co-conspirator-1* and *Individual-1* have a lot to worry about.'

'Bedtime reading?' I suggested.

'Go get the popcorn, Hannah. The show is about to begin.'

THIRTY-FOUR

I n the days that followed, life returned to what passed for normal in the Ives household. I shopped for groceries, prepared meals, ran car pool for my grandsons' soccer games, and – inspired by Hobie – volunteered as a cat socializer at the local SPCA.

Dicey flew back to Ithaca, on American Airlines this time, where she hoped to wrap up work on her dissertation, although she emailed there was 'always something that needed fixing'. With the help of hospital staff, she and her mother were FaceTiming via iPhone twice a week.

I paid a visit to Detective Irene Fogarty in Millersville. I warned her over the telephone that I was bringing 'twenty-seven eight-by-ten glossy photographs with circles and arrows and a paragraph on the back of each one' but, not old enough to be an Arlo Guthrie fan, she didn't get the joke. So I left her a detailed report on everything I'd found out in Syracuse. Bringing the Flannigans to justice for the attempted murder of Trish was her job now, and not mine.

Early in the week before Christmas, Trish was transferred to the University of Maryland's Rehabilitation Hospital off Windsor Mill Road in northwest Baltimore. I allowed enough time for her to get settled in, then drove up for a visit. I'd called ahead, so the hospital staff knew I was coming.

At the information desk, I traded in my driver's license for a swipe badge that would give me access to the Traumatic Brain Injury Unit where Trish was being treated. I found Trish sitting in a wheelchair, a thermal blanket draped over her legs. Her feet were propped up on the footrests and clad in a pair of fleecy, psychedelic socks so ridiculous they made me grin.

'It's a warm day,' the nurse said. 'Why don't you take her for a walk in the Healing Garden?'

I didn't consider forty degrees particularly warm, but I knew from a previous visit that the Healing Garden, adjacent to the cafeteria on the terrace level, was sheltered between buildings and the sun was shining, so I thought OK, why not give it a try.

'How's that sound, Trish?' I asked.

Trish smiled at me and nodded.

'She's making excellent progress with the SLP,' the nurse told me as she opened the door to the wardrobe and reached in. Trish had yet to regain control over the right side of her body; her right arm flopped uselessly as the nurse helped her into a sweater.

'What's an SLP?' I asked.

The nurse smiled, adjusted Trish's legs, then tucked the blanket more securely into the space between Trish's thighs and the arms of the wheelchair. 'Our Speech Language Pathologist has been helping Trish learn to talk. See that little red gizmo in her trach?'

I did.

'It's a Passy-Muir speaking valve. Eventually Trish will learn how to put it in and take it out herself, but right now, we do it for her.' The nurse leaned over her patient. 'It sure beats having to close off the trach with your fingers, doesn't it, sweetheart?'

Trish spoke in short, experimental bursts. 'Hannah.' *Deep breath.* 'Hi.'

After over a month of silence, hearing my friend speak again seemed like a miracle.

'A bit raspy, but you sure sound like the Trish I know.'

'Dicey? Peter?' she croaked. *Deep breath.* 'Did they . . .?'

'Get along?' I said, guessing her question.

She smiled and nodded.

'Famously,' I told her. 'What else to expect when you put a St John's College professor together with a PhD in classical Greek?'

Trish barked, but I knew she was laughing.

'Last time we had them over, they were discussing Plato's allegory of the cave and its influence on movies like *The Matrix* and *The Truman Show.*' I grabbed the handles on the wheelchair and started pushing it toward the door. 'You know *Rebel Without a Cause*, that fifties' movie starring James Dean and Natalie Wood?'

Trish's head bobbed.

I leaned close to her ear and said, 'Well, your daughter claims that it's no coincidence that the Sal Mineo character is named John *Plato* Crawford.' I snorted. 'Way too deep for me.'

As I wheeled Trish out of the room, the nurse said, 'Don't tire her out now!'

I rolled Trish down the hallway, onto an elevator and out into the Healing Garden. We strolled under a trellis and along a winding stone path before parking ourselves near a pool where bronze herons stood watch, knee deep in lily pads.

'Are you warm enough?'

She nodded.

This was the first time Trish and I had been alone. I'd decided not to stress her with questions, but as difficult as it might be for her, she clearly wanted to talk.

'What happen?' – *Deep breath* – 'With Nat?'

Trish knew all about Calvin Bishop's arrest – Peter told me she'd been following the story closely on television – but she shared the apprehension we all felt about the Flannigans remaining at large.

I described my recent meeting with Detective Fogarty. 'It's all unraveling for the congressman,' I said. 'His wife will almost certainly be indicted for conspiring with Bishop to entice minors to engage in illegal sex acts. His youngest son could get up to twenty years for the attempt to hijack Zack's plane.'

She raised an eyebrow. 'Hijack?'

'That's Zack's story and he's sticking to it,' I said with a grin. 'And you remember the DA's hope that other victims, like you, will come forward? Well, they have. You aren't the only minor victim who Flannigan raped.'

'I thought . . . was love,' Trish breathed.

'You were fifteen, Trish. A vulnerable bundle of angry, raging hormones. Nicholas Flannigan was twice your age.'

'High school,' Trish said.

I wasn't sure where she was going with that, so I said, 'Right. Mary told me they sent you to school.'

Trish nodded. 'Stuyvesant.'

Ah. I knew Stuy by reputation – one of New York's famous magnet schools. Thirty-five-hundred students, give or take, almost all of them college-bound.

'I recruited . . . girls to work . . . parties.' She winced. The confession clearly pained her.

'They lured you in, groomed you, abused you, Trish. *You* were the victim.' After a moment, I asked, 'Was Siobhan running the show?'

Trish nodded. 'She seemed . . . sophisticated. I wanted . . . like her.'

'What happened to Susie?' I asked. 'Mary Goodrich told me you were worried about a girl named Susie.'

'Year older. She aged . . . out. Disappeared.'

Aged out. I felt a chill that had nothing to do with the sun ducking behind a passing cloud. 'Do you think Siobhan *killed* Susie?'

Trish shrugged. 'Jealous. Big fight.'

She drooped in the chair, wagged her head slowly. I wasn't sure who had been jealous of whom, but I decided not to press it. Although I was confident Trish would never be charged with a crime, I wondered if she would ever get over the guilt.

Trish pointed at her forehead. 'Me?'

'Siobhan must have seen you while visiting her mother-in-law at Lakeview,' I explained. 'According to her son, Billy, she hired someone . . .'

'Ahhh.' The sound leaked out of her, like air out of a balloon.

'I've tired you out. Should we go back?'

'No,' she rasped. She flapped her good hand in the direction of a wooden footbridge.

'Let's walk a little farther, then,' I said, as I released the brake on the wheelchair.

When I parked again, it was next to a bench that overlooked the Chinese herb garden. We sat without talking as a pair of starlings settled a dispute over an abandoned French fry.

Trish was the first to break the silence. 'Almost jumped . . . Long time . . . looking down.'

I knew she was back in Syracuse on a hot August afternoon, standing on a bridge, staring into the water swirling below.

Before I could say anything, she said, 'Wimped out . . . Took Greyhound.'

For some reason, this made me laugh. I reached out, grabbed her hand and held on tight. 'I'm so glad you caught that bus.

'Dicey tells me she's bringing Nora down for a visit in January,' I said, trying to sound upbeat about the upcoming mother-daughter reunion.

A half-smile brightened Trish's face. 'Could be . . . interesting.'

It wasn't until we were back in Trish's hospital room that she spoke again. 'Don't know how . . . Thank you,' she said, each word delivered slowly, with obvious effort. The garden outing had clearly exhausted her.

'Peter already did,' I said breezily.

Instead of wasting precious breath, Trish wrinkled her brow.

'You know that gas range I've been lusting after? The Wolf?'

She nodded.

'Yesterday, Peter showed up with his crew and installed one in our kitchen. Stainless steel with red knobs. I think I'm in love.'

I dug my iPhone out of my handbag, tapped the photo app and showed her a picture of the newly installed stove. 'We had to sacrifice the trash compactor to make it fit, but the darn thing never worked properly anyway so I was happy to see it go.'

I tucked the phone away, and said, 'OK, friend. When are you coming for dinner?'

She managed a wan smile. Her eyes scanned the room, taking in all the paraphernalia that was allowing her to function. She shrugged.

'Let's do it soon.' I stooped to kiss her cheek. 'I owe you an Italian dinner, you know. This time, I'll make the tiramisu.'

June -- 2021